DREAMS OF ANUBIS
by Maria Isabel Pita

Dreams of Anubis

maria isabel pita

an erotic romance

Dreams of Anubis

First Magic Carpet Inc. edition September 2003

Published in 2003

Manufactured in th United States of America
Published by Magic Carpet Books

Magic Carpet Books
PO Box 473
New Milford, CT 06776

Library of Congress Cataloging in Publication Date

Dreams of Anubis by Maria Isabel Pita
ISBN 0-9726339-3-6

cover design: stella by design contact: stellabydesign@aol.com

To Stinger, now and always

PROLOGUE

My life-long friend, Caroline Jordan, was working in Cairo, Egypt. She had found what I considered the dream job—photographing mastabas in Saqqara for an Egyptologist who was writing a book on the Old Kingdom burial ground. Yet I was the one who had loved ancient Egypt since I was a little girl.

At approximately five-years-old, I'd accompanied my mother to a public library, where I'd wandered through the maze of bookshelves pulling volumes out at random. I remember one particularly dark and heavy tome was too much for me, and falling from my grasp it landed open at my feet. I know now that I was looking at a black-and-white photograph of an Egyptian bas-relief, but at the time all I could do was feel. I eagerly ran to find my mother, dragged her by the hand back to the book lying on the floor, and pointing down at it cried, 'Home!'

During the long plane rides from Boston to Cairo, I passed the time lost in colorful daydreams, and by the time we landed,

I felt stiff as a butterfly born in a jar. It had taken me fifteen hours and twenty-two years to finally make it to Egypt. I was so excited that the throbbing, teeming chaos of the airport didn't surprise me; it seemed natural, like an extension of my racing pulse.

It took me another small eternity to get through Customs, but at last my blue passport was imprinted with a circular red hieroglyph, and stepping through the gate I spotted my friend almost at once. Her long pale arm was swaying like a branch over a darkly heaving sea of native heads.

'Carol!' I cried.

'Mary, over here!'

'Carol!' I threaded my way to her through the tapestry of races crowding the airport. There seemed to be people from all over the world there, which was not surprising since it was the middle of winter and the height of the tourist season.

'You look great!' I cried over the roar of voices as we quickly hugged each other. 'But how can you manage to still be as pale as a ghost in Egypt?'

'We'll talk in the car,' she said, relieving me of one of my carry-on bags, the smaller and lighter one.

Following her, I paused to stare up in awe at the two stone colossi who sat smiling peacefully over the teeming masses at their feet as if looking serenely into the past. 'Carol, where's the baggage claim?' I asked anxiously.

'Right over there.' She indicated a wall where native men clad in the traditional galabiyya were lifting suitcases out of a dark hole and quite literally tossing the luggage back into a waiting crowd.

'Oh, my God,' I exclaimed, 'that one's mine!' just as a black suitcase hit the floor with an ominous thud, and burst open like a giant seed. Immediately a crowd of Egyptian men descended upon the colorful petals of my clothing and undergarments, passionately caressing everything back into place, and clearly enjoying the task. Then one of these men sat on top of my suitcase to force it closed. Carol purposefully grabbed the handle, and he leapt to his feet, grinning at me.

'Don't worry, Mary,' she said, 'my maid will wash and iron everything for you in the morning.' She gestured to a more sober looking native to help carry the suitcase out for us.

'Your maid,' I repeated numbly.

Her chauffeur was waiting for us outside in a big blue Chevrolet that easily became king of the road. Once again I was sealed away in an air-conditioned technological cocoon and the land I had dreamed of seeing all my life remained as unreal as a film playing on the window screens. The broad avenue we followed away from the airport might have been anywhere in the world if not for the colossal statue of Ramses II that loomed over us at an intersection. Then we turned right and suddenly there was an explosion of life. Our American boat now shared the road with a tumultuous sea of pedestrians and assorted vehicles. We appeared to be passing through a marketplace, where black clouds of flies hovering over food stalls matched the robes of the women strolling by. Some of them balanced large, heavy urns on their heads while their hips swayed with a slow, timeless rhythm offering a mysterious counterpoint to the chaos of life around them. Usually it was not so much a matter of driving as of squeezing between things, and the trickling flow of traffic wasn't helped by donkeys pulling heavily loaded carts while flicking centuries away with their tails as casually as flies.

'And I thought rush hour in Boston was bad,' I remarked.

'We'll be out of it soon,' Carol assured me placidly, sitting in the backseat beside me. 'You cut your hair, Mary.' She finally noticed. 'It looks nice, very Old Kingdom.'

Her apartment was located in a foreign residential area of Cairo free of any noisy street life, and took up the entire ninth floor of a white building surrounded by palm trees.

'Well, it sure beats your attic in Newton,' I grumbled.

'Well, normally us lowly archeologists can't afford such a nice place, but Simon has a friend in U.S. A.I. D. who's away for a year, and he was nice enough to let me borrow it.'

'You're not an archeologist,' I snapped. 'Oh, God, I need a shower...'

'I'm afraid you'll be a little disappointed with the water pressure, Mary. I recommend a bath.'

'That'll be wonderful. Thank you. Who's Simon?' I asked belatedly; my mental synapses were functioning on emergency power.

'My boss.'

'Oh.' I glanced beyond the unimaginatively furnished modern living room into the more traditional and even more boring dining room. 'Wine?' I asked hopefully.

Carol avoided my eyes. 'I tried to buy things you would like, Mary, but I couldn't afford what the Commissary charges for wine.'

'Oh, well,' I said bravely, and would have shrugged if my shoulders hadn't felt so heavy.

'You poor thing, come on, it took me a whole week to recover from the jetlag. Here, I put some towels out for you.' She showed me where everything was in the spacious bathroom—the soap, the shampoo and conditioner, the body lotions and scented powders—like a golden-haired angel giving me a quick tour of paradise. 'I spend more time in here than in any other room. The air is so dry outside it's heaven soaking in a bath at night. How would you like a dirty martini? Hard liquor is a lot cheaper at the Commissary, and you can set your glass right here where

I usually put my tea cup.'

Thirty minutes later, I could not have felt much better if my fairy godmother had tapped me on the shoulder with the wand of my olive-tipped crystal stirrer. Sipping the ice-cold vodka from an inverted glass pyramid, I ranked the martini as one of civilization's greatest achievements while contemplating the wonderful days to come. I gazed down at my breasts, which I'm proud to say are completely natural. I've never done anything to them except watch them grow and shape themselves into the tender buds crowning my torso now. More than one man has commented on what perfect handfuls they are, just big enough to cup and weigh and get a good luscious grip on. When I was younger I had wondered if my aureoles and nipples were a bit too big, a little too exuberantly fertile in relation to the rest of my gently swelling mounds. That was until men praised them with moaning, hungry attention; delighting in the generous rosy nipples, as they'd gently catch them between their teeth.

I set the fragile tulip of my martini glass carefully down on the rim of the tub and paid full attention to my breasts swelling like twin half moons out of the sky-blue water. Instead of the traditional boring bubbles, I had chosen mineral rocks from one of the many jars available to me. Carol's bathrooms always made me think of an alchemist's laboratory. In my friend's mind, every benign substance on earth should be translatable into the pleasure it gives her skin at the end of the day when she ritually soaks all her cares away in a hot and fragrant bath. Usually I prefer showers, but I was on vacation now, relaxing and deliberately letting myself become aroused by the sight of my naked body.

I sank a little deeper into the water's hot embrace, grateful for the pillow cushioning my shoulders and the back of my neck as I stretched my long legs out in the tub's delightfully accommodating dimensions. The curves of my figure were only slightly distorted by the clear blue liquid washing over them and imbuing my skin with a sapphire's glistening radiance, except that my body was infinitely more precious. It was true I had made a gift of it to more than a few men, but none of them had been worthy of me in the end, and I had taken myself back without feeling I had lost anything except a little time. I think that for a while I was actually in love with every man I fucked. Yet it was really only lust, sexual infatuation, physical obsession, whatever you wanted to call it. It wasn't love, true love, in which I still fervently believed despite so many profound disappointments.

I settled more comfortably against the pillow watching both my hands lightly caressing the insides of my thighs, and smiled to myself hearing again a chorus of men's voices in my head all saying, 'You have great legs, Mary'. Whenever I looked in the mirror now, I didn't just see what my own critical eyes told me, I saw the way men had touched and kissed and caressed my body with their hands, lips, tongues, and erect cocks. Remembering how passionately they had possessed me, how rock-hard they had become just holding me, telling me how beautiful I was better than any mirror ever could.

I was teasing myself, letting a sweet ache kindle in my pussy for something more than the gentle lapping of hot water as my hands kept slowly stroking my thighs around it. It was a luscious torment working my sex up to the moment when I would touch it, gently and tentatively at first, before a deepening excitement inevitably made me start boldly stroking myself. I didn't like to use dildos when I masturbated. My vagina was offended by the cold, lifeless feel of plastic, a pathetic substitute for the warm, thrusting energy of a real live penis. I preferred enjoying the soft fullness of my labial lips as my fingertips gently parted them, and then relishing the slick tightness of my pussy as I gently penetrated myself. I used two, sometimes three fingers knowing this divinely silky sensation was what a man's erection experienced sliding in and out of me.

My vulva was frustratingly stimulated and sensitized by the mineral-rich currents lapping against it, and I finally took mercy on it by slipping my right hand between my legs. I caught my breath from the shock of pleasure it gave me just to touch the heart of my labia, that wonderfully sensitive spot just over the entrance to the dark hungry hole in my flesh. The puckered lips of my sex were in full, sensitive bloom, and I realized my mental and emotional excitement at being in Egypt, the land of all my most sensual fantasies, had mysteriously aroused my body, too. I was exquisitely open to anything in every sense, and when I grazed my clitoral hood with the tip of my forefinger, I gasped when I felt how firm my skin's magical button was. All it would take was the relentless pressure of my rhythmically moving fingertips to send me over the edge.

I closed my eyes, and more swiftly than I believed possible, it was as if my soul began magically slipping out of the confines of my skin, escaping my skeleton's cage on a climax's invisible wings. As I came, in my mind's eye I saw a colorful falcon soaring against a vivid blue sky above the phallic trunks of palm trees, between which I glimpsed a distant pyramid rising up out of the desert's hot flesh, glowing a molten gold, my own clitoris burning and dissolving into the most divine sensation possible...

'My God,' I breathed, opening my eyes, and for a timeless moment I wasn't sure where I was. My gaze first landed on a rare plant, belonging in a tropical garden around a pool tiled in lapis-lazuli blue...but I realized a few disappointed heartbeats later that I was actually inside a bathroom.

'Wow,' I whispered, awed by the powerful orgasm I had just given myself. No doubt my body's jetlagged exhaustion had contributed to making the pleasure almost blindingly intense, but I had seen something as I came, an image as sharp and detailed as a photograph flashing in my brain as though squeezed out of my deepest memory by the muscles contracting within me. My orgasm had come with a vision much more distinctly real than the fantasies I excited myself with when I masturbated. I couldn't explain it, but I had always suspected my sensuality and my imagination were intimately related, and my body was finally in the embrace of a sacred atmosphere, sitting in a bath in an ancient land I had daydreamed about ever since I could remember.

I sighed happily and reached for my martini. I sipped it appreciatively, draining my glass down to the last drop while wonderfully romantic possibilities lapped in and out of my mind as pleasantly as the sky-blue water around my body... I was in Egypt!

CHAPTER ONE

The next morning I could have cared less that I was in Egypt. My head felt as heavy as a stone from the pyramid, and Carol's quiet knock was easy to ignore.

'Get up, Mary,' she urged through the door, 'we have to leave soon.'

'Okay,' I groaned, 'but please just let my lie in one of the mastabas and sleep all day.'

'Would you prefer coffee or tea?'

'Coffee!'

A short while later, I felt a bit better, but not much.

'You'll be fine,' Carol assured me.

'Really? I thought it took you a week to recover.'

'Oh, it did, but you're stronger than I am.' She meant less sensitive. 'Anyway, you can take it easy today. Simon wants us to finish the mastaba we're working in, then I'll be free to show you the sights. Here.' She handed me a large thermos. 'Now, let's go,

Hamud's waiting for us downstairs.'

* * * *

Hamud, Carol's chauffeur, was still in the same short-sleeved blue shirt and brown polyester pants he had been wearing yesterday when he picked us up at the airport, and I met the woman who laundered them on the way down the stairs. His wife was the maid, and Carol explained to her by way of a mixture of English, Arabic and sign language that all my clothes required washing and ironing. The woman's broad smile smoothed a few wrinkles from her leathery skin, and she nodded with such fervor I was sure she had not understood a word.

We had to walk around a sleeping family – a father and a mother and two young children—to get to the car. They were lying beneath a group of palm trees on the decorative island in front of the building and looked quite peaceful in the cool morning with their arms wrapped protectively around each other.

The crisp air helped clear my head, and I actually felt a stab of excitement as Hamud opened the back door for us with a good-natured grin.

Once again, we drove through a tumultuous sea of life, and then, at last, I got my first look at the Nile. Hamud floored the accelerator and we flew south along the east bank, the silver water on our right flowing north towards the Delta and the Mediterranean.

I felt as though we were driving back into the past. Apart from a few isolated housing complexes Carol informed me were U.S. A.I.D. projects and that resembled dried-out honeycombs, there were nothing but green and brown fields on our left where robed figures bent towards the earth in the eternal dance of sowing and reaping...time seemed to slow down...and to press against my heart like the head of an invisible lover lying contentedly against me after centuries of lovemaking…

I was jolted out of my reverie when Hamud abruptly turned right onto a narrow bridge.

'You'll be able to see the Step Pyramid soon,' Carol informed me, breaking our dreamy silence.

We entered a forest of date palms. The ancient Egyptians made wine from dates, and it was so easy for me to picture tanned young men in scanty white loincloths climbing up the slender trunks. Then we drove through a miserable little village where Hamud was forced to slow down as a small herd of naked children surrounded the car.

'Baksheesh!' they shrieked. 'Baksheesh!'

I did not have any Egyptian money on me yet, and passing this way every morning, Carol had hardened herself to the scene. Her waist-length blonde hair firmly braided, she looked straight ahead, and not a muscle in her aristocratic face twitched when I heard what distinctly sounded like curses hurled after us along with equally harmless pebbles.

I could not help myself; a lecture began forming in my mind like a storm cloud. 'The Old Kingdom Nomarch of this province would have been horrified by these living conditions!' Hamud jumped as my indignant voice thundered through the car's contented silence. 'Thousands of years ago those children would have had a much better life.'

Carol glanced at me with an abstracted little smile, and I could not tell if she was listening to me or lost in a daydream. I knew my friend had long ago learned to tune me out when she wanted to.

I didn't care. 'A Nomarch was personally responsible for every individual in his domain just like a father,' I went on fervently. 'Each of his subjects was as much a part of him as his own vital organs. Everyone played a different role in sustaining the living body of the province, and their well-being was a reflection of the Nomarch's own physical and spiritual health…'

'There it is,' Carol announced, sounding relieved.

Nearly invisible on the trembling haze of the horizon, Zoser's Step Pyramid was distinguishable from the flesh-colored desert only by its geometric purity. I stared at it in awe, and watched in fascination as the sand inexorably crept up around the palm trees. It wasn't long before the desert took over completely and we found ourselves at the foot of a rocky cliff studded with signs.

I gripped Hamud's bony shoulder. 'Stop, please.' I stepped out into the beautiful morning and just stood there for a full minute savoring the fact that I was really here at last. An arrow indicated that the mastaba of Ptah-Hotep, author of the famous maxims, lay straight ahead to the west, while the eternal home of the handsome nobleman, Ti, was to be found to the north. I was so excited these great men were still here in a mysterious sense that my exhaustion evaporated. I got back into the car. 'Let's go,' I said eagerly.

His dark eyes shining at me through the rearview mirror, Hamud rewarded my reverence for his country's history by burning rubber up the winding slope, throwing Carol and me into each other's arms, a sight that brought the teeth out in his grin. He must have driven this way a thousand times before, because I swear he did not look at the road once. We crunched to a stop in a flat open space where two tourist buses lay abandoned in the soft morning sunshine in front of an amazingly modern-looking wall.

'Shukron, Hamud,' I said breathlessly, enunciating my first Arabic word in order to thank him.

'Sa-eeda,' Carol added briskly. 'Ba-dayn.'

'What did you just say to him?' I asked curiously.

'"Good-bye" and "later".'

'Well, that's specific.'

'It's specific enough for Egypt, believe me.'

Still grinning lasciviously at his success in getting Carol and me to hold on to each other in response to his prowess behind the wheel, Hamud drove off and my friend and I approached the wall. Its dark golden stone was made vividly three-dimensional by a pattern of recesses and projections that could easily have placed it in the twenty-first century. I was wearing white shorts and a short-sleeved white shirt in order to reflect the sun and expose as much of my pale skin to its tanning rays as was decent.

'Isn't it beautiful, Mary?' She finally showed some real emotion. 'I can understand why Victorian architects came to Egypt for inspiration and to get away from that awful cluttered style that was so popular back then. Only the first twelve feet up is the original wall,' she added in a clipped, academic tone. 'The rest was restored.' She had always been good at recording information, and I assumed this little speech had been edited from a longer one delivered by her employer.

Behind the enclosure wall that stretched for miles around the burial ground but only a fragment of which remains, Zoser's pyramid rose step by crumbling step into the cloudless sky.

'What mastaba are you working in now, Carol?' I asked, my excitement building.

'Oh just a small one, but it's lovely. I like it better than some of the big famous ones, maybe because it belonged to a princess.'

We passed through the opening in the wall and found ourselves in a shadowy antechamber where the stone ceiling had been carved to simulate bunches of logs roped together. But it was the false doors to the left and right of the entrance that I found truly haunting. Carved to look as if they had just begun to open, they were symbolic entrances to another dimension as impossible for the mortal mind to conceive of as it is for the body to step into solid rock. Directly ahead of us stretched a long pillared hall.

'Simon says it's ridiculous to think the Egyptians used engaged columns because they didn't know free-standing columns could withstand vertical stress,' Carol informed me. 'He says there are so many innovations in Saqqara there's no reason they couldn't have used freestanding columns if they'd really wanted to.'

'Whatever,' I replied. I had no idea what she was talking about and nor did she, which for the first time made me wonder what Simon looked like. That he had managed to impress these abstract facts on my friend's visually oriented brain was significant. Carol was a photographer and a painter; her perception and experience of the world lay entirely within the framework of images. I was the verbal, philosophical one. Physically, we were opposites as well. I have shoulder-length black hair and honey-brown eyes while Carol resembles a living doll with her waist-length blonde mane and traditional big baby-blue's.

Sunlight streamed down between the columns in hazy rays that struck me as wordless sentences my heart could almost mysteriously understand. I had done a lot of reading on the plane in between daydreaming, so I knew the columns were carved to look like bunches of reeds tied together, and that the distance between them gradually narrows as the colonnade progresses west, creating an impression of great distance. We moved silently as ghosts across the sand towards a door of pure white light at the end, but when we passed through it we found ourselves in another hot and empty section of desert, not in the magically fertile fields of the next world.

* * * *

How Carol found the particular mastaba she was working in is beyond me. She must have charted her way by counting sand dunes as I wandered behind her, enthralled by the desert's featureless haze and the lovely violet color shimmering above the horizon like a veil separating this harsh world from a softer, more flowing dimension not yet broken up into space and time, shape and sound. The silence was so intense I could almost hear it—a subliminal hollow, haunting sound like the wind blowing through the shell of my skull. The lifeless emptiness pressed against my senses in a strangely arousing way, and as I paused to fully experience it, in that instant Carol disappeared. I staggered across the deep sand in the direction I had last seen her, and was relieved to catch sight of her just below me as I crested a hill, that was steeper than I had thought. Distances and appearances were obviously deceptive in the desert, where there were no landmarks to judge them by. We passed the sights of several ongoing excavations—deep pits in the sand it would have been disturbingly easy to fall into. None of the doggedly patient archeologists responsible for them were in evidence, but clearly Saqqara had not yet yielded up all its treasures.

Infinitely glad to be free of my administrative position in a Beacon Hill law firm for nearly a month, I once again found myself regretting I had not studied Egyptology as I had dreamed of doing when I was a little girl. Walls covered with ancient hieroglyphs were profoundly more interesting than modern legal forms.

Up and down we went over increasingly rocky dunes, during which time we both paused to take several long sips from our thermoses. I had never experienced such dry air before, yet despite the sun's relentlessly penetrating rays, the temperature was ideal.

'We're almost there,' Carol announced as we reached the summit of another steep incline.

I ran my fingers through my hair. Thanks to the desert's natural blow dryer, it was incredibly soft and straight. Carol skipped gracefully down the hill, but preoccupied as I was with the paradoxical cosmetic benefits of a deadly environment, I tripped near the top and gathered so much momentum on the way down that I could not stop myself from running straight into a man's arms.

Seemingly unsurprised by my abrupt and passionate embrace, he detached me from him gently and smiled. 'Hello,' he said, and I might have been looking straight through his skull at the sky his eyes were so intensely blue.

'Hello!' I gasped, letting go of him as I regained my balance. 'I'm so sorry!'

'It was my pleasure. Have you come to help with the work?'

'No, I'm on vacation.'

His smile disappeared. 'Then I suggest you stay out of the way.'

'Um, Simon,' Carol said hesitantly, 'this is Mary, you know, my friend from Boston. I told you she was coming, remember?'

Now I knew exactly why she had learned so much about ancient Egypt.

'Oh, yes, nice to meet you, Mary,' Simon said, staring into my eyes as if they were dark pools into which he tossed the coins of these polite words, while making a silent wish. Then he turned away and disappeared into a rock outcropping that I realized must be a mastaba.

Carol stared after him. 'He likes you, Mary. I knew he would.'

'Likes me? He thinks I'm a stupid little tourist! I should have offered to help.'

'Don't worry about it,' she said, and followed her employer into the tomb.

Anxious not to interfere with their work, I paused in the pleasantly cool little corridor at the entrance to the mastaba. Smiling figures the size of my fingers moved in procession towards the burial chamber in row upon row of bas-reliefs still glowing with life after centuries. Much of the original paint remained, especially the red-brown tone of flesh and the ghostly white of dresses and loincloths.

Losing myself in vivid scenes of daily life, I was especially captivated by a boat depicted over a row of tiny pyramids—a stylized rendering of the river's surface—beneath which a variety of fish were carved in exquisitely realistic detail. My eyes ensnared by the scenes bursting with life around me, I set the thermos down and let my purse slip from my shoulder onto the sand. Whatever more literal-minded Egyptologists think, I could not believe these bas-reliefs were merely simple representations of daily activities, and they could not possibly be the ancient Egyptians' crudely literal conception of paradise either, for some of life's more pleasurable activities were obviously missing.

I stood there staring at one of the walls trying to find words for my own theory. I focused on a perfectly proportioned young man carrying the entire hind leg of a cow in his arms, part of the delectable fare being offered to the deceased. It was as if the whole world was being laid before her piece by piece, a process during which she asserted her sensual connection with nature as well as her spirit's mastery over it. The giant baskets of fruit being carried towards the burial chamber might be meant to represent her emotions, the fish in the river her thoughts...

Looking away from a cat clutching a duck in its jaws, I suddenly found myself studying a pair of very fine, life-size brown legs. I suffered the impression that one of the young men carved on the wall had been released from his stone spell and made real before me as my eyes traveled slowly up to his bare chest, and lingered there appreciatively before moving up to his smile.

'Hi,' he said, revealing a bright crescent of teeth.

'Hi,' I echoed, peering at him closely. I was able to tell now that he was wearing ragged shorts, not a loincloth.

He offered me his hand. 'You must be Carol's friend, Mary. I'm Steve.'

I was very pleased by his firm grip. 'Nice to meet you, Steve.'

He glanced at the bas-reliefs I had been studying. 'Beautiful, aren't they?'

'Totally beautiful,' I agreed fervently.

'When did you arrive? Have you been to the Cairo Museum yet?'

'No, I just flew in yesterday afternoon.'

'You're going to love Egypt, Mary. Well, excuse me.' He slipped past me on his way out of the tomb.

For a wonderful moment I had mistaken his shining skin for a spiritual aura, but I realized now it was merely a thick coat of sunscreen. Wondering if it was Playgirl Magazine who was financing this expedition, I followed the procession of bas-reliefs deeper into the mastaba.

* * * *

Carol's photographic equipment resembled a lunar module just landed on the otherworldly sand of the silent tomb. Silver light-stands reared their black hooded heads around the camera that was focused on one small section of wall.

Staying away from the sensitive equipment, I examined the bas-reliefs on the opposite wall while Simon and Carol took an astronomically long time setting up just one shot. I must admit,

I found it difficult to concentrate on the tomb paintings with such an exquisite three-dimensional representation of the male form occupying the same space with me, and not a very large space at that. If I had known Egyptologists could look like Simon and Steve, nothing would have stopped me from getting my degree. I kept casting surreptitious glances over my shoulder at my friend and her employer. He was dressed just like the traditional Great White Hunter, in khaki shorts and a matching short-sleeved button-down shirt, an adventurous style somewhat marred by clean white socks and very cushy-looking sneakers. He was bent over the camera, which gave me a very good view of his...let's just say trekking through the desert every day hadn't hurt his physique, which was already very nice to begin with. He was tight and tan everywhere, and either he had bought stock in Coppertone or he had been blessed with a magical gene that enabled his fair skin to turn golden instead of red beneath the sun, a stunning contrast to his Nordic-blond hair and blue eyes.

I wondered how Carol was able to concentrate on her work, yet I wasn't surprised she hadn't told me how attractive her boss was. I loved her dearly, but ever since grade school she had done her best to keep me away from any boy she was interested in. I wondered what had prompted her to tell me that Simon liked me. Was she jealous of sharing his attention? I would definitely have to have a talk with her when we got back to the apartment, because if she wanted Simon to do more than sign her paycheck, then I would somehow have to control how attracted I was to him. I don't normally run straight into the arms of a man I've never met (although of course I hadn't meant to). The fact that he was an Egyptologist as well as stunningly handsome added up to the very annoying fact that I could not concentrate on bas-reliefs I had waited all my life to see.

We were in one of the very early mastabas, and it had clearly belonged to a woman. As she was brought the world piece-by-piece, she looked incredibly peaceful, happy and assured of her immortality. The clean, form-fitting lines of her ankle-length dress and her casually pulled back hair also struck me as strangely contemporary, as if I were looking at a princess of the twenty-second or twenty-third century rather than at a girl who lived thousands of years ago. Her image was considerably larger than those of the people bringing her offerings, yet I could barely make her out on the pale stone wall in her tight white dress. She was holding a lotus flower up to her smiling face, inhaling its fragrance—a metaphor for the soul's ability to bloom inside one body and then another and another, each one decaying like a seed in the eternal rhythm of flowering.

'Amazing,' Simon suddenly murmured in my ear, 'I thought only horses fell asleep on their feet.'

The princess's smile seemed to deepen as I kept my eyes fixed on her face. 'I wasn't asleep,' I replied serenely.

'You know, if you put your hair up in a ponytail like that, you would look like her, Mary.' He sounded perfectly serious.

I smiled, pleased he was testing me like this. 'I would very much like to believe there is an eternal energy inside me which clothes itself in different forms,' I stated matter-of-factly, still looking at the princess. 'However, I didn't come to Egypt to shop for my soul's old dresses. I don't think I was Cleopatra or a high priestess of Isis in a past life, or anything like that.' I turned my head and looked him straight in the eye. 'If that's what you're thinking.'

A smile flickered across his thin mouth like energy traveling down a wire. 'I stand corrected, Mary,' he apologized in his soft, even voice.

There was a series of lightning-like flashes as Carol finally took the same picture ten times.

The strobe-like flashes were reflected by the nerve-endings deep in my belly as Simon's hand reached up and lightly held my arm, ostensibly to steady me during the brief technological storm. But he was staring deep into my eyes again in a way that made my emotions feel like hieroglyphs he could read and appreciate.

'Simon, I'm ready to set up the next shot,' Carol declared plaintively.

'Mm,' he said, continuing to hold my eyes for a few steady moments that had the opposite effect on my pulse. Then he turned back to his work with a light, almost apologetic squeeze of my shoulder.

Hurrying out of the mastaba, I nearly collided with the walking bas-relief, Steve, on his way back in.

'Off to see some more tombs?' he asked cheerfully.

'Yep.'

'Well, I recommend you start with the one behind and to the right of this one. It's gorgeous.'

'Thanks, I'll do that.'

The princess's mastaba was indeed part of a small group—the first townhouses were tombs. Still suffering from jetlag, I really didn't have the energy to do them justice today, so I decided to take a nap in one of them for a while. I followed painted processions into an empty burial chamber, and settled down in a nice cool corner. Praying no tourists would disturb my rest, I beat my purse into a relatively comfortable pillow and spread myself across the soft, cool sand. The only part of me that wasn't tired were my lips, which curved upwards as my eyes closed...

'Meow?'

'Go away,' I mumble, 'can't you see I'm resting?'

'Purrrrrrrrr...'

My smile deepening, I open my eyes, and giggle in surprised delight as a cat's cold little nose touches the tip of mine in greeting. 'E'Ahmose, my love...' I sit up and take the big feline in my arms. 'There, are you happy now, baby?'

'Purrr...purrr...purrr...'

'You knew I wasn't asleep anyway because you're the wisest and most beautiful of cats, aren't you?' I set him down on the floor at my feet, admiring the way his supple body pours out of my arms like molten gold. 'Now go catch some mice, and if you're a good boy and keep the kitchens perfectly clean, I promise I'll take you fowling soon, perhaps on the next full moon.'

He listens intently as I speak, sitting perfectly still as though posing for a statue, then casually lowers his handsome head to lick one of his angular shoulders before turning away in the direction of the eastern garden, and the path that will take him to the kitchens.

It is true I had not been asleep, although I had been dreaming. My heart feels perched on the vines of my veins like a bird on the verge of taking wing; whenever I see him, my heart seems to flutter joyfully right into his hands. I cannot possibly rest when I know he is coming, when I know that any moment now I will see his tall figure approaching along the western path, more alive and more beautiful than anything else growing in my garden. There is no comparing the parts of his body to other parts of nature; a perfect man such as my Priest of Anubis is the most beautiful thing in the world, the form of Ptah-Hotep himself, shaper of all creation. I feel as though I am embracing the god when I am with my lover. When I sink to my knees before him, it is Min's very phallus I worship as I give thanks for the divine sensations he fills me with when I bathe his shaft with my tongue and polish it with my lips, while cradling his heavy ball-sack, filled with the white gold of his seed, reverently in my hands.

As I get up off the couch, I admire my almond-colored toenails—ten silvery half moons I have often seen rising over the desert slopes of his bare shoulders when he lifts my legs up against his chest to thrust as deeply as possible into my warm and yielding flesh. In those moments we are Nut and her consort Geb in reverse, with the feminine sky lying below the masculine earth, the weight of his rock-hard muscles pressing me down into the soft pillows making it hard for me to breathe, and yet nothing on earth feels better than his body beating against mine, his cool balls slapping against my wet heat—the sound of the river lapping against the shore as the juices of my pleasure rise into full flood around him.

I pace the floor with restless excitement as colorful fish dart beneath me between blossoming lotuses and thick green papyrus plants. I like the feel of the painted tiles against my bare feet, but they do nothing to cool the intoxicating expectation flowing through my blood like warm spiced wine as I await the arrival of E-Ahmose, High priest of Anubis, leader of the Winged Sandals—and my lover, now and forever. I raise a polished gold mirror in the shape of the lunar disc before my face from which Hathor's cow ears sprout at the base, happy to know the Nile will flood countless more times before my skin dries out and my reflection fails to please me. My golden-brown irises shine like sunlit honey framed by my coal-darkened eyes, and my smiling lips are those of a woman in full bloom. It seems I am always smiling since I met my beloved E'Ahmose, Born of the Moon.

As though invoked by my thoughts, he appears silhouetted against a sky the deep red color of my lips, as if all the goddesses deem his powerful silhouette worthy of their combined sensual kiss.

I set the mirror down carefully, afraid of dropping it, for the sight of him always makes me feel strangely weak. Then I realize that both E'Ahmose's are approaching my bedroom—my cat returning with a dead gift in his jaws for me, and my lover with a living gift hidden in his moon-white loincloth, a gift that will rise to heavenly dimensions the instant I sink to my knees to worship it.

'Oh E'Ahmose!' I say fervently, at once addressing the man striding down the garden path who cannot yet hear me, and my devoted feline who has just laid an inert mouse at my feet. 'Thank you, my sweet little boy, but you must take that away at once. My lord approaches, and it would be very rude to greet him with something dead.'

As though he understands perfectly, E'Ahmose the cat retrieves his prize and dashes out of the room again into the eastern garden, just as my Priest of Anubis steps inside from the west.

I approach him slowly, so he can appreciate the sight of my naked body, which is how he likes me to wait for him. I dismissed my servant when she came around earlier to light the lamps, so I cannot see the face of the man silhouetted against the burning twilight, but I know him as I have never known another. He is the lord of my heart, for it is our love for each other that makes my heart light as the feather that will be weighed against Maat, goddess of truth, after my death. It is our love for each other that is the very nature of eternity, for if we cannot always be together I have no desire to live forever.

'Nefermun,' he says my name quietly, coming to meet me in the center of the room.

I raise my face to his for the caress of his greeting, closing my eyes to better absorb the warmth of his skin as for a blessed instant his palm hovers just above my features before lightly caressing my cheek down to the side of my neck, where his hand comes to rest.

'E'Ahmose,' I whisper, planting my hands on his bare chest in order to feel him, and to brace myself as our lips meet. When I was a little girl, I asked my father if statues had tongues hidden behind their stone lips. He replied, 'One day you will find out' and now I know that every smile holds the secret of what it is like to kiss someone you love. It is like being a child again running around and playing, but infinitely better, because below our energetically wrestling tongues are two adult bodies straining against each other aching to merge and become one. 'Oh E'Ahmose!' I say his precious name again breathlessly. 'It's not possible, and yet it's true that I love you even more today than I did yesterday.'

'Sweet Nefermun, it's not possible and yet it's true,' he unhooks the jackal-headed broach holding his loincloth closed, 'that I am even harder for you this evening than I was last night.'

We both laugh quietly together as he lets the stiff white linen fall to the floor at our feet so that we stand naked together in the newborn night. The western sky is no longer visible between the leaves of the date palms; darkness has fallen and the first jewels of Nut's black dress shine above the trees as I sink to my knees before him. His erect penis is so magnificent it mysteriously takes my breath away before I even fill my mouth with its demanding dimensions. Even though it looks just as rigid, this is no cold stone phallus rising out of a statue but a living cock that is at once firm and tender against the welcoming caress of my tongue. Letting it slip all the way out of my mouth again, I kiss its crown, and am rewarded with a glimmer of semen reminding me of the stars in the sky and the mysterious fact that his pleasure is everything to me.

'Oh Nefermun, I have no need to build a tomb,' he grips the base of his erection with one hand, 'for I wish to be buried inside your mouth forever.' He guides himself slowly between my devoted lips.

I moan with joy and also from the effort it costs me to help him fulfill his deepest desire. Yet every night my throat opens up around him more easily. I experience a thrill of pride each time my lips kiss his groin as I swallow him whole. I squeeze my eyes closed to better relax the muscles of my neck as he holds himself inside me for a few excitingly arduous moments. Then, very slowly, he slips out of the loving seal of my lips, and grasping my arms, pulls me swiftly back up to my feet.

I turn away towards the couch blessed by Hathor where we always make love.

He stops me. 'No,' he commands, 'right here.' He reaches down and clutches the backs of my thighs.

'My lord!' I gasp as he lifts me up off the floor, forcing my arms to cling to him, my legs tight around his hips.

'I want you to pleasure yourself, Nefermun. I want you to use me as you would the god Himself. Do not be afraid. I want all your servants to hear you scream with pleasure, for you are my one true love, now and forever!'

He thrusts this declaration into me with such force there can be absolutely no doubt inside me that he means every word, and the pleasure I experience as he rams the indelible proof of his love into my body is almost unbearable. I cling to him, holding on to him for all I am worth, as he moves my hips swiftly up and down over his erection, relentlessly probing my innermost flesh, over and over again. He strokes his full length into my tight depths, savoring the dewy kiss of my labial lips, lifting me almost all the way off him before stabbing into me again.

'Oh, yes, my lord, yes!' I cry shamelessly, and then moan, 'E'Ahmose?' because for some reason he is trying to pull away from me and I don't want him to stop, I never want him to stop…

'Mary, wake up, you're dreaming.'

The climax inexorably building between my thighs was about

to carry me away when I opened my eyes, and suddenly the intense pleasure ebbed, leaving me stranded on dry sand inside a lifeless mastaba.

'Are you awake now?' Simon asked warily.

My heart sank as I looked into the clear daylight of Simon's eyes abruptly replacing the sight of a star-filled night and another man. 'Oh…' I quickly slipped my arms from around the Egyptologist's neck. 'I'm sorry.' I sat back awkwardly.

'That must have been some nightmare,' he said, remaining crouched before me on the floor of the mastaba. 'You were gasping and moaning, and when I tried to wake you up, you wouldn't let go of me for anything.'

'It wasn't a nightmare,' I murmured, brushing sand off my legs.

'Oh, no?' His right eyebrow arched like the top of a question mark as a curious dimple appeared in his cheek below it. 'What was it, then?'

I beat my purse back into shape. 'Just a dream.' I was too dazed to understand why all I was feeling was an intense disappointment.

He rose and offered me his hand so I could brace myself on it as I got up. He seemed to realize I was feeling strangely weak and needed his help.

'You have a bad case of jetlag, Mary.'

I shrugged.

'Are you hungry?'

'Yes,' I said even though I still wasn't feeling anything except a disappointment so profound all my thoughts and feelings were sucked into an emotional black hole such as I had never known.

'Then let's go grab some lunch.'

CHAPTER TWO

Carol, Simon and I had lunch in a large open-air tent in the middle of the desert, sharing the shade beneath the white canopy with busloads of tourists. We ate the surprisingly tasty gourmet hummus, lettuce and cucumber sandwiches Simon produced from his battered backpack, and drank the local soda, which tasted like polluted water with a truckload of sugar dumped into it. It did nothing to assuage my thirst, but I drank it anyway. Carol, however, wisely ordered boiling water and added her own herbal tea bag. The living bas-relief, Steve, was not present, having vanished on yet another errand.

I didn't care that Carol was probably sick and tired of hearing about Saqqara; I shamelessly pumped Simon for his knowledge, and he obviously didn't mind.

'Saqqara is an Arabic term which comes from the Egyptian Sokar,' he was saying.

'The one who fashioned man,' I threw in eagerly. The vivid

dream I had had while napping in a mastaba was beginning to fade, and I wasn't really making an effort to hold on to it. I couldn't deal with the pain of something that had been so intensely wonderful not being real.

'Sokar is the hawk-headed version of the god Ptah,' he went on as though I hadn't spoken, 'reflecting one of the chief triads of the capital of Memphis, Ptah, Sokar and Nefertum. The Necropolis was a true city of the dead. What is known as Saqqara today is just the area containing Zoser's funerary complex, but originally it stretched over thirty miles all along the western bank.'

I sighed, 'I love the Old Kingdom!'

'Saqqara is full of tombs and funerary structures from all periods of Egypt's history,' he pointed out. 'There are even some early Christian remains here.'

'But that's awful!' I exclaimed, my jetlag taking the form of inflated sentimentality. 'If people in later dynasties took over older tombs, what was the point then? Didn't they just expect someone to do that to them in a few hundred years?'

'Saqqara was built in the third dynasty,' Simon continued, once again ignoring my outburst. 'It's the oldest stone complex in the world besides the pyramids at Giza.' He glanced at Carol—a sober person condemned to sit at a table with two ancient Egyptian addicts.

'Go on,' she said indulgently, 'Mary's really into this.' She attempted to smile, but it was more like her lips curdled in her creamy complexion.

I gathered my courage and told Simon how I felt about the offerings so meticulously depicted in mastabas—that they stood for aspects of the natural world the deceased was expressing his, or her, union with, and his, or her, power over at the same time. I couldn't tell whether his eyes narrowed as I spoke because he thought I was being a flake or because the sun was bothering him.

'I agree, Mary, that what is represented in the early tombs, especially those of the king, are symbolic stages of transformation,' he answered carefully. 'Just like a caterpillar dies to its former state inside the cocoon and emerges as a winged creature of light, so did the king rise from his tomb. The Egyptians made extensive use of this kind of symbolism. You're right,' he admitted finally, 'the scenes of daily life in the mastabas we're documenting are in fact scenes of transformation. But brought up as we are with a rationalist view of the world, it's difficult to know exactly what each scene symbolizes.' He gazed out at the desert. 'It's a fascinating challenge.'

'Uh-huh.' I propped my chin in my hands and gazed at him happily. 'That's exactly how I feel.'

'The tombs of the kings are completely spiritual.' He continued staring past me as he spoke. 'They describe, in metaphorical form, the processes experienced by the disembodied soul in its journey to resurrection. Represented are all the different stages of transformation.'

There was nothing even I could think to say after that, but there was no need, for Simon continued.

'A temple or a pyramid imposes its meaning on us through complex factors,' he leaned over the table towards me, 'which are ultimately reducible to numbers and mathematics.' His long fingers played with the wrapping from his straw, which in my eyes was transformed from a meaningless strip of paper into a snake's mystically shed skin as I remembered the way those same fingers had wrapped around my arm in the tomb. 'You see,' he went on earnestly, his thoughts seeming to brace themselves on my wide-eyed fascination, 'we can't help but respond to the harmonies and proportions controlling their mass. With sculptures and friezes it's different, yet even these were carefully planned according to harmonic and geometric laws, and this is essentially what we respond to when we look at ancient Egyptian art. Yet the symbolic meaning, the actual motivating force behind the work, is lost to us. We're essentially dealing with an alien culture whose symbols correspond to nothing we know. Artists are all that remain now of this way of perceiving the world.' He glanced at Carol again.

'Oh I don't really know what I'm doing,' she stated with admirable humility and annoying vagueness.

'So, do you think the great Imhotep was a real man, Simon?' I was far from finished with him yet. 'Or is he just a legendary creation made up of different figures from the Old Kingdom?'

He stared sharply into my eyes. 'Why do you ask, Mary?'

'Um...' His penetrating stare nearly made me forget my question. 'Why not?'

He sat back. 'The legendary Imhotep,' he began in a detached, lecture-like tone completely different from the one in which he had been speaking only a moment ago, 'prototype of man as creative genius. His titles included that of Sage, Architect, High Priest, Astronomer and Doctor. He was deified by the Egyptians and two-thousand years later usurped by the Greeks for their own prototype healer, Asclepius, founder of medicine.'

'But that doesn't answer my question,' I reminded him, intrigued by his reaction.

He smoothed his hair away from his forehead so forcefully the dark-blonde strands shone like molten gold poured over the stone of his skull. 'The nineteen twenty-four excavation put flesh on the legend,' he declared, almost sounding angry. 'A pedestal of a statue of Zoser was found, and on it Imhotep is mentioned with all his titles, Chancellor of the King of Lower Egypt, Administrator of the Great Palace, Hereditary Lord, the High Priest of Heliopolis,

Imhotep the Builder, the Sculptor and the maker of stone vases.'

I laughed. 'Well, I guess that last title gives it away then, Imhotep was a real man.'

He pushed his chair away from the table and stood up. 'Back to work,' he said. 'I'd like to get as much done this afternoon as possible, Carol, so you and your friend can spend the next few days together sightseeing.'

My stomach a sloshing bog of cheap cola, I nevertheless rose with alacrity. 'I'd like to help if I may, Simon.'

'That's okay, Mary, you go ahead and take another nap. I can recommend an even cozier little mastaba, and I have a blanket in the car I'd be happy to lend you.'

'Thanks, but I'm wide awake now...although I had the most incredibly vivid dream this morning.'

'I know. It was so vivid you nearly dragged me into it. That's what you get for sleeping in an Egyptian tomb.'

Without thinking I declared, 'I'd like to spend a whole night in one!'

'I might be able to arrange that.'

The way he looked at me threatened to dissolve my insides, and made me self-consciously aware of my panties clinging to my wet sex. We were walking side-by-side, but now I paused, letting him go on ahead while I waited for Carol to catch up with me.

'See?!' she whispered ambiguously, and I slipped into the backseat of the Egyptologist's beat-up little white car while she took her usual place up front.

Simon glanced back at me. 'I was serious when I said I could arrange your spending a night in a tomb, Mary.'

'You're allowed to do that?' I made a supreme effort to sound only mildly interested.

'A little baksheesh goes a long way here in Egypt,' he stated bluntly.

'I imagine. Um...so what is Steve doing now?' I quickly changed the subject in an effort to control my pulse. 'He's been running around all morning.'

'He's just mapping the area,' Simon said dismissively. 'How would you two ladies like to see the Sound and Light Show at the pyramids tonight?'

'We'd love too,' I declared without consulting Carol.

'Good. I'll pick you both up at six.'

* * * *

I spent most of the rest of the afternoon sleeping deep inside the same mastaba hoping to return to the intensely vivid dream I had had, but only nonsensical images paraded through my subconscious that left me feeling strangely groggy mentally even as the rest of me felt physically refreshed. It was a bit disturbing how natural it felt to wake up in a tomb, and I smiled dreamily up at the faded bas-reliefs embracing me, until discomfort made me realize the clasp on my purse was creating a seal-like imprint in my cheek.

I found Carol alone in the princess's mastaba packing up her gear. There was no sign of Simon or Steve, and I was relieved. I was sure I didn't look my best at the moment, and my brain wasn't functioning at full capacity. I imagined if the princess in whose mastaba I was standing was abruptly resurrected in the twenty-first century that she would feel very much as I did in those moments—profoundly at home and yet strangely lost and unable to think straight. I could see everything so clearly, every little carving on the wall, every little smiling figure. What seemed unreal to me and was already fading from my memory was my job and my life (or lack thereof) back in Boston. The dream I had had in the mastaba that morning felt infinitely more real. Apparently, I was suffering from a case of jetlag so severe it bordered on the mystical.

'Did you enjoy your nap?' Carol asked me, and then added before my mental synapses had a chance to communicate with my vocal chords, 'Simon's already left.'

'I gathered as much,' I replied. 'Can we go now, too?'

'As soon as I'm finished packing up my stuff.'

Hamud was parked out in front of the entrance waiting for us.

'Carol, please tell him not to drive like a maniac, my head's already spinning.'

'Why don't you tell him?'

'Because I don't know how to say, "don't drive like a maniac" in Arabic.'

'Neither do I.'

My friend and me were clearly not getting along at the moment and I didn't need to be able to think straight to know why.

Hamud carefully helped Carol store her gear in the trunk, and then she and I both slipped into the backseat, slumping against the exquisitely comfortable leather. During the long drive we were as silent as two recently exhumed and beautifully preserved mummies. I was grateful Hamud didn't speak much English and that my Arabic was next to non-existent, which meant I didn't feel compelled to make polite conversation with him.

Once back in her spacious apartment, Carol said generously, 'You can have the bathroom first.'

'Oh no, that's okay, you go first,' I offered just as magnanimously. 'And please take your time; don't rush on my account, I know how much you love your long meditative soaks.'

'Okay, thanks.'

I wanted to ask her exactly how she felt about Simon, but I couldn't get the words out. The question seemed too blunt, and I suppose part of me was afraid of the answer. If she had her heart set on him, then I would simply have to remember I was returning to the United States in a few weeks and forget about him, even though already he felt like the ideal man for me.

Hamud's wife had indeed washed and ironed the entire contents of my suitcase, which was empty now and tucked away in a corner of the guestroom. My dresses and blouses were hanging in the closet and my shirts, shorts and socks were all neatly folded in the dresser drawers. Hamud's hard-working spouse had also unpacked all my make-up and jewelry, which was laid out on top of the dresser as neatly as a museum exhibit. I did not doubt curiosity had prompted her to do a bit more than her job required, and I certainly didn't mind. In fact, her interest in me made me feel curiously rich as I stared at my reflection in the mirror. Millions of women the world over can afford inexpensive cosmetics and gems made of colored paste, but beauty is an asset that cannot be earned; it's something you're born with. And yet, I thought, staring intently into my eyes, maybe I did earn it, in a past life...

I had not been lying when I told Simon I did not believe I was actually a reincarnated Egyptian princess, although enough men, and even women, had remarked I looked like Cleopatra enough times to encourage such a delusion on my part. Yet ever since I had that experience in the library as a little girl, I flirted with the idea of past lives, specifically a past life, or lives, in ancient Egypt. I had felt an instant, inexplicable affinity with that black-and-white bas-relief the moment I laid eyes on it. At the tender age of five, I was in no intellectual position to flirt with the concept of past existences; my emotional reaction was hauntingly real and rationally inexplicable. I must have come across the names

E'Ahmose and Nefermun in some book once and they had surfaced in my dream. E'Ahmose, Born of the Moon, High Priest of Anubis...my subconscious had been amazingly specific; I had never had such a vivid, detailed dream in my life. Even now I could hardly bare to think about it because the sadness I had experienced when I woke was still there like a thorn in my heart—a thorn I could do nothing about except ignore.

I changed the subject in my head by wondering what Simon's personal beliefs were. I was at once nervous and excited that we were having dinner with him tonight after the Sound and Light Show, to which he had so kindly offered to accompany us. I was nervous because I was much too attracted to him, especially considering how little time I had to get to know him, and because he was strictly off-limits if Carol was interested in him. It wasn't just a matter of friendship ethics, for she had three months head-start and would be staying in Cairo...but I was wasting time with these catty thoughts, and I had a very important task before me—deciding what to wear on my first real night in Egypt.

* * * *

The spectacle at the pyramids would have been a serious disappointment if Simon had not been there. I was elegantly and daringly clad in a form-fitting, long-sleeved violet dress with a scoop neck that only fell to mid-thigh, and black knee-high boots. Around my neck I was wearing a genuine scarab beetle amulet on a gold chain that I considered my good luck charm, and all my essentials were tucked into a small black designer purse shaped like a crescent moon. The night was more than cold enough to encourage my appreciation of the archaeologist's warm body sitting next to mine. He had diplomatically placed himself between Carol and me on one of the foldout chairs behind the Mina House hotel in the makeshift auditorium full of a reverently hushed international crowd. The sun had set while Hamud drove us to the lobby of the hotel at the foot of the pyramids where Simon was waiting for us. Now, finally, a wave of darkness descended over the audience and a phosphorescent tide of red, yellow and green lights flooded the Sphinx's enigmatic smile. Behind it, the Great Pyramid soared straight up into the darkness of space, the spotlights trained on it barely able to grasp its full mass. Its dimensions filled my heart to bursting, but not just with the sentimental pleasure of at last achieving my life-long dream of experiencing the Great Pyramid in person. The feeling that possessed me was much fuller and deeper. Staring at the only remaining wonders of the ancient world, I was filled with a wonderful sense of hope and certainty. It was as though I was beholding incontrovertible physical evidence that there is indeed a divine dimension to human existence. The two more 'modest' pyramids rose one after the other behind it as the lights shone over them. Originally, all three structures had been covered by a layer of limestone that would have made them shine as brightly as lighthouses in a sea of sand.

The Sound and Light Show at Giza still managed to be an impressive spectacle despite unimaginative translations of ancient texts recited over loud speakers. There is enough speculation concerning the construction of the pyramids for me to feel that no one really knows exactly how the Egyptian's managed to build them, and I fully intended to ask Simon what he thought about it. I also wanted to query him about the Egyptologist John Anthony West's theory that the Sphinx is much older than previously believed; that the erosion marks on its body were made by water rather than sand, which would link its mysterious smile with the legends of Atlantis.

I was intensely aware of Simon's warm presence beside me the whole time, especially when he shifted in his seat and his shoulder brushed mine, and at some point during the show, I found the courage to glance at him. I expected to see his slightly bored profile, but instead I caught him gazing down at me. He immediately looked away, but it was too late; I had seen a speculative look in his eyes that made me feel faint with happiness. Soon after what I already considered a landmark moment in my personal history, the audio shut off with a disenchanting crackle and a blessedly non-psychedelic light flooded the open space behind the Mina House. Wearing high-heeled boots forced me to concentrate on my footing as we slowly followed the rest of the crowd back into the hotel, and helped bring me down to earth a little, enough for me to remember the increasingly distressing fact that I would only be in Egypt a few weeks. And I still had to have that little, but extremely major, talk with Carol about her beautiful boss. Back at the apartment, we had both been too busy getting ready for our evening out, and in the car we were both reluctant to talk about anything significant since we didn't really know just how much English Hamud understood. However, the fact that my friend's glorious blonde hair was still neatly restrained in a braid worthy of a nineteenth century schoolteacher was a good sign, because whenever Carol was interested in a man she let her hair down.

Despite the ghastly Egyptian cola, I had enjoyed our lunch in the open-air tent more than I relished our dinner in the four-star hotel dining room. Once again, I could have been anywhere in the world, and I found myself wishing the management had opted for an ancient Egyptian banquet hall décor. However, there was something to be said for not sharing Simon's attention with a bunch of naked dancing girls, and it was impossible to picture Carol in a black wig dripping with perfume as the scented wax cone on top of her head gradually melted.

Simon recommended some local specialties to me, including a dip made of ground eggplant and spices. He politely asked me questions about my life in Boston, and volunteered a little information about himself in the process. I was not at my most eloquent, half hypnotized as I was by the symmetry of his features beneath a tan that looked very much like a layer of gold applied by the finest artisan. His eyes were the stunning final touch, especially when the candlelight hit them as he looked intently at me while I answered one of his questions. But what truly made his regard so devastating was the mind behind it—an Egyptologist's mind, a mind obsessed with ancient Egypt just like mine. As I picked daintily at chunks of lamb swimming in a delicious yogurt-cucumber sauce, I reminded myself to occasionally look at Carol and break my trance-like contemplation of her employer. Fortunately, he had no problem carrying the conversation while I chewed and admired his broad shoulders. I was infinitely pleased if not surprised that he wasn't married, as most women would find it difficult to set up housekeeping in tombs. I learned he had been in Egypt for nearly a year now, the lucky recipient of a major grant, but I couldn't quite tell if those were faint wrinkles around his eyes or squint lines.

'Excuse me a moment,' he said, and left the table, ostensibly in search of the men's room.

I looked at Carol.

'Yes,' she sighed, 'I know.'

'God,' I took another long, bracing sip of white wine, 'how can you stand it?'

'I couldn't stand it,' she agreed, sipping her herbal tea, 'so I just got it over with.'

I almost choked on a piece of pita bread.

'Look, we would only have wasted a bunch of time and energy wondering what it would have been like, so we just got it over with.'

I asked slowly, 'You got what over with?'

'We slept together, okay? Now we can work together without any tension and just be friends.'

'Right.' I felt irrationally betrayed.

'Look, Mary, don't be upset, we're not each other's type. It just had to happen, it was inevitable, but you're much more-'

'Are you all right, Mary?' Simon slipped back into his seat intently studying my face again.

'Oh I'm fine, thank you.'

'You look like you might be coming down with a touch of pharaoh's revenge,' he observed.

'Oh it's worse than that,' Carol said breezily.

'I'm fine,' I repeated firmly.

'Well, I'm glad to hear it,' Simon said. 'We wouldn't want you wasting any time in bed.'

* * * *

The Khan el-Khalili Bazaar—the dark and timeless bowels of the city of Cairo—proved to be a labyrinth of lamp-lit alleys littered with merchandise overflowing from a myriad of tiny shops.

Simon had kindly exchanged some of my American money at the hotel for Egyptian currency, and there was a precious moment when his fingers brushed mine as he handed me the colorful bills. We had both drunk wine with dinner, our coordination wasn't at its best, so I tried not to make too much of it. Ever since Carol's revelation, I was trying to remain detached from this man, who was suspiciously too much like a dream come true for me.

Strolling leisurely through the bazaar's exotic maze, we passed dozens of jewelry shops selling reproductions of ancient Egyptian pieces that probably looked good to the average tourist but did not fool me. The faces of the gods and goddesses forming the center of elaborate pectoral pendants wore sour expressions nothing like the profoundly peaceful smiles found on ancient originals. The personalities of the modern artisans were revealed in the often-harsh casts of the deities' features and their discontented frowns, which completely failed to capture the profoundly positive ancient Egyptian spirit. All my life I had gotten into countless arguments with people who insisted people in the time of the pharaohs were morbid because they were obsessed with death, and I had tried my best (usually not very patiently) to make them understand the Egyptians were obsessed with life and all its pleasures, and therefore had no desire to give it up.

Carol stopped to inspect a cart loaded with bundles of dried herbs and what looked like every kind of incense known to man. Simon had apparently talked himself out at dinner, because he walked silently between us looking a bit bored. After all, he must have been to the bazaar dozens of times already. Or perhaps he was distracted by his thoughts; there was a slightly preoccupied air about him. His shoulder brushed mine as he turned away from the aromatic cart, obviously realizing it was going to be a while before Carol finished inspecting it, and the contact triggered something inside me.

'You know, people make the mistake of thinking the Egyptians drew the human figure the way they did because they didn't know how to do it right,' I said, pursuing my thoughts out loud. 'But I read a fascinating book once that said they drew the body the way they did in order to capture the essence of each feature and present an essentially whole picture of the human being. I mean…I mean they drew the shoulders facing forward beneath a profile in which the eye was also fully visible while the torso was turned sideways, because that way we see the person in his entirety all at once. Their use of perspective attempted to conquer the limits of time and space. Do you know what I mean?'

He opened his mouth to speak just as Carol thrust a stick of incense beneath his nose to get his opinion on it, and he ended up responding to both our queries by sneezing.

'Bless you!' my friend and I cried in chorus.

'Thank you.' He sniffed. 'Mm, that's...interesting, Carol.' He said, and then facing me with his body, he turned his profile on me. 'It's a damned uncomfortable perspective if you ask me.' His one eye winked.

Considering the distraction, I forgave him this irreverent response to my enlightened observation.

Carol waved the same stick of incense in my face. 'Doesn't it smell delicious, Mary?'

I took a step back. 'Jesus, that's one potent stick.'

'Damn right it is,' Simon murmured, brushing past me. 'Come on, Carol.' He pulled her away from the cart by her braid. 'You don't need any more incense. When my friend returns to his apartment, I'm going to have a hell of a time trying to explain what you've been doing in there.'

I trailed behind them, gazing admiringly at Simon's broad shoulders, narrow waist and long legs. In his white shirt and shorts he was as tall as an ancient Egyptian nobleman in white linen, an effect marred only by his blond hair. He and Carol turned into a shop that sold what appeared to be footrests—large red cushions embroidered with eighteenth dynasty dancing girls in gilded thread—while I chose to remain out in the cool alleyway. A strip of sky showed between the awnings, but the golden glow of the lamps strung between them washed out the stars. I should have known better than to just stand there all by myself, however; a crowd of merchants immediately surrounded me. As each one gestured passionately for me to follow him to his cart, I attempted to escape by diving between the choppy waves of their dark robes. I waited for Simon to rescue me, but there was no sign of him.

'No...la, shukron,' I said. 'No, la...la la!' I sounded as if I was about to break out into song as I fervently repeated the Arabic word for 'no'. The tide of merchants ebbed away reluctantly, and I quickly entered the shop of footstools in search of Carol and her boss. The small space was empty except for the owner, who swooped towards me like a vulture in his black robe. I turned and hurried back out into the alley. At a loss as to where my companions could have gone, I glanced into the dark space between two shops just in time to see two luminous heads coming together and the tendons in Simon's arms standing out like serpents as he pressed my friend's slender body hard against his.

Without thinking, I ran from the sight.

My hurt indignation carved its way through groups of tourists and eager vendors who did their best to intercept me, and how hard my heart was beating told me it was at least a full minute before I finally stopped to catch my breath. I went for long jogs in Boston three days a week, but never after dinner and wine through dark, lamp-lit alleys wearing high-heeled boots. I had always possessed a flare for the dramatic, and in the back of my mind I hoped Simon had observed me run off and would follow me. Obviously, I had seen too many romantic movies, because naturally he wasn't following me; he had been too busy kissing Carol to even notice me. Once again I was in the eye of a storm of shopkeepers, one of whom abruptly grabbed my arm and began forcibly leading me somewhere.

I clutched my purse close to my body and tried to remember

more of the Arabic words Carol had taught me. 'Ana mish...eis,' I said breathlessly. 'I don't want any,' I translated for my own benefit. 'Ana mish eis,' I repeated, to no effect. My captor shoved me up a short flight of steps, reached past me to open the door, and gave me another encouraging shove. I turned around to give this unbelievably fascist merchant a piece of my mind, but he was gone and had closed the trailer door behind me.

I turned around again. I was standing in a tiny perfume shop. Cushioned seats ran along both walls in front of a glass display case full of colorful little vials that made me think of miniature genie bottles. The exotic trailer was empty, and I turned back towards the door with the intention of opening it.

'Good evening, my lady,' a cultured male voice said from behind me.

I whirled around again. 'I don't want any,' I cried. 'Mafish!' I was developing a nice little vocabulary, for all the good it did me. Then the robed figure behind the counter flung off his hood and I found myself at a loss for words in any language.

'I believe you have it backwards, love.' His deep voice was lightened by a sophisticated English accent. He slipped out from behind the counter and approached me. 'You have something I want.'

'I do?' I asked hopefully.

He took my flushed and confused face in his large hands. 'Yes,' he said quietly, 'I suspect you do.' There was a deeply serious expression in his slate gray-green eyes as he caressed both my cheeks with his thumbs very much like a sculptor assessing the quality of my bone structure, and I suffered the impression he was mysteriously determining my worth. I opened my mouth with the idea of saying something, but was distracted by the pale crescent of a scar just below his own mouth that gave him a dangerous aura.

Part of me knew I should be worried to suddenly find myself completely alone in a pungent trailer with a total stranger boasting a scar on his face. Yet it was beginning to feel wonderfully natural to run into strikingly handsome men in Egypt, so I simply accepted what was happening. He had the most remarkable eyes, and it wasn't just because his pupils were rimmed in gold...there was something very familiar about the way they looked at me...

'My lady,' he whispered fervently, and suddenly kissed me softly on the lips.

It was not just a paralyzing blend of shock and pleasure (or was it that the pleasure was shocking?) that kept me from pulling away, I simply couldn't; I had absolutely no desire to pull away from him. On the contrary, I was magnetically drawn to this total stranger. While we spoke, I had been standing as close to him as I possibly could, trying to fight an irrational but almost irresistible desire to fall into his arms. It was an intense relief when he kissed me, as though I had been waiting forever for his lips to press against mine like this again.

He pulled back to observe my reaction, and a gratified smile I might have found humiliating had I been thinking straight, turned his firm mouth up at the corners. Caressing the sleek black hair on both sides of my face, he kept my head reverently in his hands, making me feel precious as an ancient bust he had just unearthed. 'What do you know about it?' he whispered.

'Know about what?' I whispered back. He was dressed like a native Egyptian in a traditional white galabiyya. At first I had thought his black hair was cut short, but now I realized it was actually long and pulled back in a ponytail. I wondered if he had tired of the long winters back home in England and come to sunny Egypt to run a cozy little perfume shop, but I dismissed the possibility at once because there was absolutely nothing retired looking about this man. He wanted something, and I found myself hoping I had it to give.

'Don't you remember?' He looked searchingly down into my eyes.

'Remember what?' I asked even though it sounded silly, because if I remembered I wouldn't need to ask what I had forgotten.

'Your dreams.'

'Yes, actually, I do.' I didn't even think to wonder why a complete stranger was asking me about my dreams in the heart of the Khan el-Khalili bazaar since for some reason it felt perfectly natural. 'I had a particularly vivid dream today, as a matter of fact, when I was taking a nap inside a mastaba.'

He glanced at the door to the trailer. 'We don't have much time,' he warned quietly, and then suddenly laughed as though what he had said was extremely funny.

The naked joy in his smile struck me as a bright light reaching into the darkest corners of my mind, illuminating something I had always known but had only just realized. 'There's no such thing as time,' I declared happily because it was the only way I could translate the wonderful feeling suddenly possessing me into words.

'Most people don't realize that.'

'Well, I'm not most people.'

'No,' he agreed fervently, reaching for my hand, 'you're not.' He led me over to the counter.

For a highly confused and disappointed moment I thought he was going to try and sell me some perfume, and that our encounter had only been some kind of mercantile foreplay found only in Egypt, so I was both relieved and surprised when he grabbed me by the waist and lifted me up onto the glass surface. My short dress hiked shamelessly up my thighs, nearly exposing the black lace bikini panties my dinner with a sexy Egyptologist has inspired me to wear beneath it.

'I love these boots,' he told me, sinking to one knee before me like an old-fashioned cobbler cradling the backs of my high-heels in his hands as though admiring his work.

'Thank you…hey, what are you doing?' I leaned back against the counter even as I made an effort to keep my thighs modestly pressed together, but it was impossible simply because I didn't really want to. It wasn't his hands gripping my boots that were spreading my legs as much as my own shameless yet irresistible desire to open myself to this man.

'Just having a little taste, love, don't be afraid.' He urged, caressing the smooth black leather up to my knees and gently shoving them even further apart. 'Tell me your name.'

'Mary!' I gasped, desperately trying to control my pussy's sudden wanton hunger in the face of my usual modest behavior and in his face, the proximity of which was making my sex so hot and wet, my panty was clinging to my labial lips in a dangerously tantalizing way; teasing me with the wicked knowledge that what I really wanted was to feel his strikingly handsome features between them.

'Mary…' He savored my name on his tongue before glancing up at my face. 'May I?'

I didn't respond, riveted by his intensely earnest expression and by how much I wanted to feel it between my legs.

'Time is a man-made concept, and as a result,' he indicated the door behind him with a slight tilt of his head, 'we don't have much of it now. All I ask, Mary, is a taste of what's to come.'

I inclined my head in wordless ascent.

He reached up beneath what there was of my dress and gripped the edges of my panties, holding my eyes the whole time in a way that was both reassuring and hypnotic.

I lifted my hips off the cool glass and let him slide the skimpy lace garment over my knees, down my boots, and off. He kept bracing me on his stare as he exposed my pussy, not letting me look away shyly, forcing me to face what was happening in a way that excited me even more. It had been a long time since I'd been so intensely turned on that I couldn't control myself.

'Oh my God,' I breathed, scarcely able to believe the sight of a complete stranger's face framed by my bare thighs as he draped them over his strong shoulders. But it was truly happening, and I sighed, 'Oh yes!' watching the lips on his face touch the lips of my sex, which were much wetter and fuller as I was so aroused by this wickedly daring encounter. I couldn't believe I was letting a man whose name I didn't even know lick my pussy. A man who could conceivably be dangerous was eating me out with a violent skill that even as it frightened my mind, it also literally thrilled me to the core of my being.

I leaned back against the counter to brace myself, and watching his head working between my legs, I began longing to take hold of it and caress the sleek dark hair that I could now see fell all the way down his back.

'Who are you?' I gasped, not really expecting or wanting an answer because his mouth and his tongue were doing something much more important than talking. The need my brain felt to hear his name was nowhere near as important as the pleasure his absolute wordless attention was giving me. And even though it made no sense, somehow everything about him felt more familiar than all my other lovers combined. Was it him, or was he so perfect because I didn't know anything about him and it was actually only my own fantasies that were wreaking such divine havoc on me? No, it was definitely him because oral sex had never felt so unbelievably good to me no matter what I was daydreaming about at the time.

'Mm!' he moaned, and the deep vibration of his satisfaction against my vulva contributed another layer to the ecstasy of his tongue diving in and out of my hot hole. I had never experienced such a hard, thrusting tongue and it was starting to drive me wild with the desire to ride it. I edged my hips forward on the counter in a breathless effort to impale myself on his tongue's thick, rigid energy, crying out softly as its gloriously agile hardness penetrated me as deeply as possible, and then licked my vulva soothingly, as though apologizing for not being a penis by treating me to sensations distinct from the pleasures a cock could offer. And when his firm lips caught my aching clit between them, I forgot my delicious frustration and succumbed to a sweet, sharp, almost unbearable pleasure as he toyed with my swollen seed, alternating between flicking the tip of his tongue against it and slowly circling it.

'Oh my God,' I repeated helplessly, because it didn't seem possible that a man I didn't know at all knew exactly how to please me. He seemed magically in touch with the current of my delight. It was as if he had sensed it ebb slightly when he sucked directly on my clitoris and knew that indirect pressure and stimulation were what would direct the rush of exquisite feelings inside me into the irresistible undertow of an orgasm. Of all the things I couldn't believe about this encounter, the most unbelievable was the fact that I felt myself coming. My pussy seemed to be dissolving in his mouth, the whirlpool of a climax forming around his spiraling tongue threatening to suck my awareness of everything into the tumultuous depths of uncontrollable vaginal spasms as I came.

'Oh yes!' I cried breathlessly. 'Yes...yes...oh my God...' I closed my eyes and flung my head back as an orgasm broke between my thighs, flooding my pelvis before crashing through my blood with such power I nearly fell back across the counter as my elbows buckled. Even after the searing ecstasy dimmed, my sex kept throbbing contentedly, and I could hardly stand it as he continued lapping up my juices, the deep, gratified sounds rising from his throat only adding to my blissful torment.

'Smooth as alabaster,' he said approvingly, running the tip of a finger down between the full bloom of my labial lips glistening with the sticky sap of my climax, 'and soft as a flower.' His mouth shiningly anointed with my body's delicate musty scent, he smiled up at me. 'I like it that you shave, Mary.' My thighs were still resting on his shoulders; I couldn't seem to move, I was feeling so beautifully relaxed. 'I want you to always keep yourself smooth for me like this.'

I had to bite my lip to keep from asking, 'Does that mean I'm going to see you again?' A nameless stranger had just eaten me alive, yet my only concern was that he would vanish forever as suddenly and mysteriously as he had appeared. 'All right,' I said instead.

'Did you like that?'

'Are you kidding?' I replied an instant before I realized he was teasing me.

He laughed quietly as he gently brushed my legs off his shoulders and stood up, my black lace panties in his hand. 'I'm going to keep these,' he told me, lifting them to his face and inhaling the unique fragrance of my pussy still clinging to them thanks to how excited he had gotten me before he slipped them off. 'To remind me of you until we meet again, Mary.'

'Aren't you going to tell me your name?' I asked finally, sitting up straight and attempting to smooth my dress down over my thighs, which were still subliminally quivering.

'You know my name, Mary.' He glanced behind him at the trailer door again.

'No I don't, you never told me.'

He gave me a long, sober look. 'Yes, you do,' he insisted quietly, 'you just don't realize it yet.'

'But...'

There was suddenly the sound of a commotion outside.

He stashed my panties in his robe, and slipping a strong arm around my waist lifted me off the counter so that my boots barely touched the floor as he held me against him. I could scarcely breathe he was holding me so tightly, and I wondered if (I hoped) he would kiss me again, but all he did was stare deep into my eyes while stroking my hair away from my face. 'Remember your dreams, Mary,' he urged quietly, and suddenly I was standing alone on trembling legs inside a trailer full of exotic glass perfume vials in the middle of Cairo trying to wrap my brain around the exhilarating pleasure I had just experienced, the aftermath of which was still making my whole body feel deliciously weak.

The trailer door burst open.

'Jesus, Mary, there you are! Why the hell did you run off like that?' Simon demanded. 'We've been looking everywhere for you.'

I wasn't surprised he had found me sooner than later; a trail of grinning merchants had undoubtedly pointed the way for him. I glanced over my shoulder at the softly swaying curtains behind which my mysterious British sheik had vanished, feeling bereft. 'I thought you and Carol wanted to be alone,' I replied sulkily.

'Was someone in here with you?' he asked accusingly.

I didn't reply, but I have always had a very expressive face.

Brushing past me abruptly, he too slipped behind the glass counter, and vanished between the curtains.

I held my breath, wanting very much to learn the identify of the stranger whose sensually eloquent lips and tongue had made such a beautiful impression on my pussy. I did not, however, want him and Simon in the same room; an explosive combination that I feared would destroy my chances with the Egyptologist if he realized what had just, literally, gone down between me and the handsome Brit. So when Carol's boss returned a moment later, alone, I was at once disappointed and relieved. I let out my breath in a long, languid sigh, strangely glad my mysterious friend had made good his escape.

Simon came to stand before me, and gripping both my arms stared searchingly down into my eyes. 'Who was here with you, Mary?' he demanded to know.

'I have no idea,' I replied, gratified to be able to protect the robed stranger even while telling the absolute truth.

'Was he an Egyptian?'

'No, actually, he sounded British.'

Simon's grip on my arms tightened almost painfully. 'What did he say to you?'

'Why do you want to know?'

'Just answer my question, Mary.'

'He said I had something he wanted...' I couldn't speak for a moment, breathlessly remembering how his tongue had swirled around the glowing jewel of my clitoris. 'Then he asked me how much I knew about it. And for some reason, he called me "my lady".' I glanced pointedly at his hands clutching my arms to indicate this was no way to treat a lady, and he let go of me self-consciously. 'And he also asked me if I remembered my dreams. I have no idea why, but he was extremely...pleasant.' My sex lips were still tingling from how extremely pleasant he had been to them.

'Did he say anything else?'

'Yes, just before he left he told me to remember my dreams,' I confessed.

'Mary!' Carol exclaimed, appearing in the doorway of the trailer with what looked like a small crowd of native men in gleeful pursuit, their combined curiosity lapping like an intangible wave against the trailer. 'What's the matter with you?' she gasped, catching her breath. 'Why did you run off like that?'

I didn't answer. I was too busy enjoying both the consternated and possessive way I fancied Simon was looking at me, and being deliciously haunted by the stranger's kisses, both on my mouth and the lips of my pussy, both of which had opened for him willingly.

'Let's get the hell out of here,' Simon said.

CHAPTER THREE

I opened my eyes. The blinds in the guestroom were closed, but the golden light framing each one told me the sun had been up for a while now. Freed of her photographic duties for a few days, Carol was sleeping in (and would remain entombed all morning unless I forcibly exhumed her) whereas only the lingering exhaustion of crossing half a dozen time zones had enabled me to rest so deeply for so long. Simon's blond head immediately rose into my mind as I sat up, flooded with excitement, just as the handsome Englishman's compelling eyes pulled like moons on my blood.

Remembering the mysterious sheik I had encountered in the bazaar the night before, I fell back against the pillows again, overwhelmed by the shamelessly wicked memory. My body came fully awake remembering the unexpected gift of ecstasy his lips and tongue had so generously given me, but my brain was still trying to shift into working gear. As I lay there in the comfortable guest bed, I got absolutely nowhere trying to understand what in the world was going on. Where had he come from? How had he known I was in that trailer? Then I remembered the man I had believed to be a rudely determined shopkeeper practically shoving me into the perfume shop, and wondered whether or not it was possible my British sheik had had me brought to him. Yet none of it made any sense, none of it except the incredible sensation his lips had made against mine when he kissed me, and the indescribably wonderful sensation his mouth had made when his dark head was buried between my legs.

I had run away from the sight of Simon and Carol embracing in a dark alley, ending up in that sweet-smelling little trailer by accident. Or had I? The stranger had said I knew who he was, but there was no way on earth I would have forgotten him if we had met before. Maybe—and this thought caused me to squirm against the soft mattress in distress—this had been his poetic way of not telling me his name since he never planned on seeing me again, my juicy pussy only an idle passing treat for him. Yet he had asked me for a taste of what was to come, and told me to always keep myself shaved for him, all of which seemed to promise I would see him again. I fervently hoped I would, but it still did not explain why he had asked me about my dreams and urged me to remember them.

Finally, I gave up trying to make sense of the encounter and decided it was time to exchange memories and daydreams for reality, which meant getting out of bed. I walked over to the window and opened the blinds. As I had suspected, it was a bit too late for an outing to the Cairo Museum, which is lit strictly by sunlight. By the time Carol and I made it there, it would be mid afternoon and the place would be closing at sunset. The Cairo Museum required at least one whole day to appreciate. I intended to spend hours wandering its crowded halls, and because the display rooms are illuminated only by daylight, it is necessary to get an early start. I also wasn't quite ready for the pyramids yet as I already had two wonders of the world on my mind this morning—a mysterious dark-haired Englishman and a blond American Egyptologist.

I turned away from the window and the blue sky beyond it, and noticed an envelope lying on the table beneath it. For some reason, I stood staring at it for almost a full minute. It was so worn around the edges and darkened by almost sinister-looking stains it looked as though it had been around the world ten times at least. I wondered if it perhaps belonged to Carol's maid (an old love letter from Hamud she carried with her everywhere?) as I picked it up gingerly between a thumb and forefinger. There was nothing written on either side. The envelope had never been mailed, or even addressed to anyone, but I could tell there was something inside it. I raised the loose tattered flap and withdrew a single photograph.

* * * *

'But I can't read hieroglyphs,' Carol mumbled in protest to my request, rubbing her sleep-swollen eyes with the back of her hands in a way that made me think of a cat taking a very thorough bath. Her hair fell straight as gilded tent flaps around her face between which her eyes peered out at me resentfully, for I had committed the grievous sin of awakening her.

'Oh come on,' I insisted. 'You must have developed some feel for hieroglyphs. After all, they're lovely little pictures, right up your alley, and you've been photographing them for over three months now.' I got up off the edge of her bed and ruthlessly pulled up the blinds.

She wailed like an affronted vampire as she covered her face with both hands.

I sat down beside her again. 'Wake up, Carol, and take it one character at a time, please. What does this feather stand for?' I pointed at the photograph. 'We know we're looking at a name because the hieroglyphs are enclosed in a cartouche. You do know what a cartouche is?'

'Of course I know what a cartouche is.' She uncovered one eye and studied the picture with a sullen frown. 'I think that's an I,' she said finally, 'and that's an M...I need to make some tea...'

I held her down. 'Not until you decipher this for me.'

'Mary, I can't,' she protested desperately. 'Why don't you...?' she yawned cavernously. 'Why don't you ask Simon what it says?'

'Because, don't you get it, Carol? Something strange is going on. I think Simon might be up to something he hasn't told you about.'

'What?'

I wondered myself what I meant; I had not been fully conscious of my suspicion until I voiced it out loud. 'Carol, think. Are you sure you didn't take this picture for him and just forgot about it?'

Her facial muscles got their first exercise of the day in a look of indignation. 'I remember every photograph I take, Mary.'

'So, where did this one come from then? It wasn't in the guestroom yesterday morning, which means your maid must have put the envelope on the table when she was going through my stuff. And I didn't notice it until this morning because yesterday I was too busy getting ready to go to the Sound and Light Show with Simon. And I was too, um, distracted when we got back from the bazaar last night and went straight to bed.'

'Well it's definitely not one of my photographs.' She snatched the print from me and scowled at it. 'It's not even in focus.'

'That's true, but who cares? Just tell me whose name is in the cartouche, please.'

'Mary, I told you, I can't read hieroglyphs, I really can't.' She handed me back the photo and slipped out of bed.

'Carol, I have to tell you something,' I said, and told her about my encounter with the British sheik in the perfume shop, for the moment omitting the fact that he had kissed me and then gone down on me, very skillfully. 'He didn't admit it, but I have a feeling Simon knows who the man is and what he meant when he said I had something he wanted...I think your boss is up to something,' I concluded with a flash of intuition. I wasn't sure if the idea upset or intrigued me, but in either case it made Simon seem even sexier than he already was, and made my illicit encounter with a mysterious stranger feel even more excitingly dangerous.

Carol opened a drawer and quickly slipped into a pair of cut-off denim shorts, and then selected a T-shirt to go with them that even the Salvation Army would have shunned. 'You trust some stranger you met for a minute in the bazaar more than the respectable Egyptologist I've been working with for months?'

'Don't forget, Carol, Simon is a stranger to me, too. I've only known him for a day.'

'Well I know him very well, and he would never—what exactly are you accusing him of anyway?'

I suddenly recalled the snake-like tendons in Simon's arms as he pressed her slender body against his in the dark alley. 'Nothing,' I snapped. 'Forget it.' I hurried back to my bedroom, taking the photograph with me. I set it back down on the table where I had found it and began making the bed. Or rather, I started throwing pillows around in frustration.

Carol appeared in the hall and watched me from the safety of the doorway. 'Mary, what's wrong with you?'

'Nothing. I'm happy for you, really.'

'You don't need to make the bed. What are you happy about?'

'I saw you and Simon in the alley,' I admitted finally, and abandoning the bed pretended to search for something I vitally needed in the dresser.

'Oh that.' She flung her hair behind her back. 'I told you, Mary, we're just friends, but he still thought I might be a little upset if he...anyway, I told him I wasn't jealous and we hugged, that's all.'

I stared at her over my shoulder in the mirror. 'He thought you might be upset if he what?' My reflection held its breath.

'Oh stop acting so insecure.' She turned away in disgust. 'You know perfectly well he likes you.'

* * * *

My body adequately fortified by a cup of coffee with cream and sugar, two pieces of whole grain toast with butter, and two eggs over-easy, my spirits were soaring dangerously as Carol and I lay facedown on the plush carpet in her living room. We were once again examining the photograph that had inexplicably materialized in the guestroom.

'Are you sure the first two letters are an I and an M?' I queried, finding it hard now to concentrate on the blurry cartouche as I kept seeing the way Simon's eyes had looked when he entered the perfume shop, blue and hard as lapis-lazuli...

'No, but I'm pretty sure they are.' Holding the photograph in one hand, resting her chin in the other, her knees bent and her ankles crossed, Carol resembled a living hieroglyph herself. 'And this little maze-like box here...that's an H sound, I think.'

'I, M, H...Imhotep? There are four more letters, so it very well could say Imhotep, especially if the photo was taken in Saqqara...Carol, this could say Imhotep! Weren't you listening to our conversation at lunch yesterday? Didn't you notice the way Simon reacted when I asked him about Imhotep?'

'Not really. Don't you find him just a little boring the way he goes on and on? But I guess you're interested in what he's saying. I've learned to tune him out.'

I snatched the photograph out of her hand and sat up, staring at it intently. It was a close-up of a stone fragment containing the bas-relief of a cartouche, yet there was nothing else in the picture except rubble, and even though I studied it carefully, I could not tell if what I was seeing were small pebbles or large rocks, which made it impossible to determine the cartouche's size. There was no doubt, however, that the exquisitely carved hieroglyphs dated from the Old Kingdom. The last two characters in the cartouche were a half circle and a rectangle standing on one end. 'Carol,' I whispered, 'if this really says Imhotep, do you know what it could mean?'

'What?' She almost sounded bored.

'Don't you see?' I glanced around the living room, a chill traveling down my spine. 'This cartouche could mark the entrance to Imhotep's tomb, the tomb every Egyptologist dreams of finding.'

'Mary, there was absolutely nothing in your room before you got here,' she informed me abruptly. 'I know because I cleaned it myself.'

Her domestic thoroughness had always inspired me with a reluctant awe. 'And when you clean, Carol, you clean.'

'That's right. I even polished the insides of the dresser drawers for you.'

'Wow.' I would have to remember to appreciate this later when I was dressing. 'Thanks.'

'In other words,' she went on, quickly following the trail of her thoughts lest they get away from her, as they often did, 'unless Azi brought the photo with her-'

'Azi?'

'Hamud's wife. Unless she brought the photo with her and left it in your room for some completely inexplicable reason, the envelope must have been in your suitcase and she found it there when she was taking all your clothes out to wash and iron them.'

'In my suitcase,' I repeated blankly. 'How could it have been in my suitcase? It's not my envelope.'

'The airport, Mary! Somebody must have dropped the envelope in the airport and one of the men who helped put your stuff back in your suitcase when it burst open thought it was yours. It's just some stupid tourist's picture.'

This was a highly disappointing, if logical, conclusion and I could not suppress the feeling that there was something wrong with her reasoning. 'Or someone deliberately put the envelope in my suitcase,' I suggested, for this train of thought was decidedly much more entertaining, and also more in keeping with the mysterious sheik's remark in the perfume shop, that I had something he wanted. 'Carol, that beautiful Englishman was dressed like a native,' I went on excitedly. 'It could be he was one of the men in the airport who...no.' I shook my head, dismissing the idea at once.

'Why not?' she asked eagerly, her interest in the conversation resurrecting.

'Because, he's too tall and his shoulders are too broad and none of the native men around my suitcase in the airport were that well-built.'

'Oh...was he really that attractive?'

'Yes,' I sighed, 'he was striking! He had long black hair pulled back in a ponytail, and his eyes were so intense, I mean, the way he looked at me, and there was this gold rim around his pupils—I've never seen eyes like his. His irises were the most unique color, somewhere between gray and dark-green...and he kissed me.'

'He what?'

'Oh, it was just a polite little peck on the lips.'

I looked away, knowing it was only a matter of time before I told her everything, but I was resisting the temptation a little longer. I had never done anything so daring before—I had never been so impulsively wicked—and I was not in the mood for a lecture on the dangers inherent in such wanton behavior. I also didn't want any bad vibes ruining the strangely pure memory of a handsome stranger orally worshipping me in the dark heart of an ancient bazaar. Because the truth was I couldn't remember a man ever making me feel so beautiful and so precious.

'Mary,' Carol's big round eyes evoked pictures of the earth taken from outer space, 'do you realize you could easily have gotten raped running off like that by yourself?'

'Raped?' I repeated incredulously, and then laughed nervously, a little unsettled that the possibility had not even occurred to me. 'He only kissed me,' I lied, looking down at the photograph again without seeing it. 'I let him kiss me…'

'You let a complete stranger kiss you? Was it exciting?' she asked in one breath.

'I can't stop thinking about him,' I admitted. 'I also wish I knew what he meant when he said that I have something he wants. He asked me how much I knew about it. Do you think it could have something to do with this photograph?'

'Mary, we have no idea who this man is. He could be dangerous.'

I smiled wistfully. 'Yes…'

'This is serious,' she insisted sternly. 'If you see him again-'

'He went down on me.'

Her pupils dilated into black holes as she stared at my face, and at the soft, reminiscent smile I made no artificial effort to suppress. 'Excuse me?' she said tightly.

I rephrased it. 'He licked my pussy,' I said, enjoying her shock and deliberately stoking it.

'He licked your pussy,' she repeated.

'Yes, and he made me come. I never knew oral sex could be so devastatingly effective. I mean, I've come that way before, but never so fast and so...intensely, there's no other word for it.'

My friend let out a Banshee-like shriek and flung herself at me. 'Are you crazy?' She grabbed me by the shoulders and made a literal effort to shake some sense into me. 'You let a strange man you just met go down on you?'

'Yes!' I laughed, gratified by her dramatic reaction.

She fell back across the carpet clutching her chest as if shot in the heart, and then abruptly sat up again in a parody of resurrection. 'Tell me everything,' she commanded. 'Right now! I can't believe you didn't tell me this last night when we got home.' She seemed more offended by the fact that I had failed to confide in her than by my sinful behavior.

'I'm sorry, but I was exhausted.'

'He made you come?'

'And then some!'

'I don't believe you,' she concluded abruptly. 'You're making this up. What's his name?'

'I don't know, he didn't tell me. When I asked him, he said I knew who he was, and when I said I didn't, he insisted I did and that I just didn't remember yet. And just before he left, he urged me to remember my dreams.'

'Why would a complete stranger talk about your dreams and go down on you?' she asked more calmly.

'I have no idea, but it felt so natural at the time, so right. I can't describe it. I know it doesn't really make any sense in retrospect, but somehow it made sense at the time, and he made me feel so good, Carol, so beautiful and sensual…' my voice trailed away.

'You weren't afraid?' she asked quietly, a strangely reverent tone in her own voice now.

'I don't think so, maybe for a second, but only because I thought I should be afraid, but not because I actually was. He lifted me up onto the glass counter and knelt before me…he was so beautiful, Carol, his face and the way he looked at me. He said he just wanted a taste of what was to come, so…so I let him pull off my panties.'

'Oh, my God.' She closed her eyes as if she couldn't bear to face what I was saying, either that or she was trying to picture it.

'I know that objectively it seems like an incredibly dangerous thing I did, having a sexual encounter with a total stranger in the middle of a strange city at night,' I admitted, 'but obviously nothing bad happened, on the contrary, it was so strangely beautiful that if I don't see him again—' I couldn't even conceive of the thought.

'Oh, my God,' she repeated, opening her eyes. 'You're already falling in love with him and you don't even know his name. Mary, you're not thinking straight.' She sounded genuinely concerned now. 'You know absolutely nothing about him except that he likes to go down on girls he just met.'

'No,' I said firmly, 'he went down on me because—because there was something special between us, I could feel it!'

'Oh, Mary.' She rolled her eyes.

'You weren't there, Carol,' I insisted angrily. 'You didn't even see him, much less feel what I did.'

'You're falling in love with him because he gave you a really great orgasm and because you know nothing about him so he's the perfect fantasy, but you were really lucky, Mary, he could easily have turned out to be—'

The phone rang, blessedly interrupting her moral tirade as we both gasped and leapt to our feet, then giggled self-consciously at our melodramatic reaction.

Carol's 'Hello?' as she picked up the receiver was slightly suspicious, but then I saw her body relax. 'Oh, hi,' she purred, and her husky voice told me there was a man on the other end of the line. 'Well, I don't know,' she said, glancing over at me, 'I'll ask her. Mary, Simon wants to know if we'd like to camp out in a tomb tonight.'

By way of reply, I covered my heart with both hands and stared at her with the wide, beseeching eyes of a painted sarcophagus.

'Yes, she says that would be lovely.'

* * * *

Once again Hamud dropped us off at Saqqara, but this time he only took us as far as that glorious rock-face studded with signs pointing in the direction of different mastabas. From there, Carol and I set off on foot in the direction of the nobleman Ti's eternal resting place, although to the Egyptians this term would have been anathema; the idea of resting for all eternity would have scared them to death. It was more as if we were making our way to Ti's eternal party house, although that is also an erroneous way to describe the ancient Egyptian belief in an afterlife since they were not merely superficial hedonists. These were the nature of my thoughts as I walked a few steps behind my friend. Packing for our night in a tomb had been lots of fun. We were both hunched beneath backpacks stuffed to bursting with absolute essentials such as toilet paper; sweaters and sweatpants (because the temperature drops dramatically in the desert after sunset); a first aid kit just in case one of us got bitten (by what I did not care to ask); make-up, since I couldn't very well have the girls on the tomb walls looking better than I did; and so on.

It was four o'clock in the afternoon when we started across the featureless sand in what I sincerely hoped was truly the direction of Ti's mastaba.

It wasn't long before all I could see through the dark windows of my sunglasses was a featureless brightness in every direction, and the unearthly silence began pressing against my heart like another burden. It was extremely surreal to come upon two headless robed statues dating from the Greco-Roman period that suddenly rose up against the sky as if from the depths of my own subconscious. Whatever monument they had once adorned had long since vanished or been buried beneath the sand, and the silence was so absolute I felt as though I were moving through a dream landscape rather than through objective space. It was as if the desert horizon formed the borders of my mind, which made the bleached white statues seem a haunting part of my own imagination-filled skull.

'Carol,' I said, and was startled by the way my voice filled the world, 'I have to rest for a second. I'm thirsty again.' I blamed lingering jetlag for my testiness, but I knew it was only an excuse; I was feeling tense for a myriad of other reasons, not the least of which was how exciting nearly every second of my stay in Egypt had been so far. That was not the problem, certainly, the problem was that I would have to go home soon, back to boring days at work that all flowed monotonously into each other like the desert's featureless haze.

Carol didn't seem to hear because she trudged on, her long legs making swift progress across the deep sand.

I hurried to catch up with her, stumbled, and fell in curious slow motion. The fall was like one in a dream in that it seemed to go on forever, and then abruptly I found myself on my hands and knees facing slightly to the right of Carol's relentless course. At first I thought what I was seeing had to be a mirage created by the projector-like glare of the sun on its slow way down and by my eyelids blinking swiftly to get sand out of my eyes. I stared, and stared, waiting for the vision to vanish, but it refused to do so. Brushing sand off my knees, elbows and hands, I stood up and approached it curiously.

'Carol,' I cried, 'wait up, there's something…oh, my God!' I dumped my backpack behind me and fell to my knees again.

Carol strode impatiently towards me. 'Mary, what are you doing? I thought you were in good shape. You can't keep resting or we'll never…oh, my God!' She shed her own backpack and knelt beside me. 'Oh my God,' she repeated, 'it's Steve!'

'We have to do something,' I declared brilliantly.

'But what if he's hurt?' She made to touch him, then snatched her hand back. 'If we move him we could make him worse.'

'Obviously he's hurt,' I snapped. 'He's not out here sunbathing.'

Steve lay on his stomach with his arms bent around his dark head, one of his cheeks resting against the sand, a soft smile deepening the one corner of his mouth I could see. Like yesterday, all he was wearing were cut-off shorts, socks and sneakers. 'Maybe he collapsed from sunstroke,' I suggested, admiring his long tanned back.

'Oh no, he's used to the sun.'

'Hmm…let's try to give him some water. Maybe he's dehydrated.'

'No, he's used to-'

'He can't be that used to it or he wouldn't be lying out here unconscious!'

He was wearing lotion all over his body, and the sun glittered off the sand stuck to the oil in a way that made his skin shine like gold mixed with bronze. He was so perfectly still he might have been a fallen statue, and suddenly fear lapped like cold water against my heart. 'He is breathing, isn't he, Carol?'

She rested the back of her hand beneath his nose as we both held our own breath. 'Yes,' she sighed, and for a few seconds we were both too relieved to do anything. Then my friend somehow managed to free herself from the spell his helpless beauty had wrought upon our strained systems. Beginning at his ankles, she began caressing him slowly. 'I don't think anything's broken,' she diagnosed uncertainly.

Tearing my eyes away from his slender, but strong and muscular, thighs, I fished the thermos out of my backpack and quickly filled the cap. I noticed my hands were shaking slightly as I baptized the smiling mouth with a thin stream of the blessedly cold water. But he did not react as in the movies, by immediately stirring to life and appreciatively licking his lips. He did not react at all.

'We've got to get him out of the sun,' Carol stated urgently.

'Right,' I agreed. 'But how? He's too heavy for us to carry.'

'We'll just have to drag him.'

'Drag him?'

'Can you come up with a better idea, Mary?'

'Go for help?'

'We're almost at Ti's mastaba. If we can get him there and out of the sun, then one of us can stay with him while the other one goes for help. I'll go. You won't be able to find Simon.'

'Okay, let's do it.'

We slipped our backpacks on again, and then very gently turned Steve over onto his back.

'You take his feet,' Carol instructed, 'and I'll grab him under the arms. Maybe that way we can lift him a little.'

We could not lift him. After only a few feet, we abandoned

the idea and simply dragged him. Standing at his head, Carol took one of his hands, I grasped the other one, and together we pulled him along behind us like a living sleigh. I hated straining his muscles like that, and the way his head fell back terrified me that we would break his neck, but at least only his legs, and his very nice tight backside, came into contact with the hot sand.

I'm really not sure how we made it all the way to the tomb. It seems the body does indeed produce extra amounts of adrenaline in an emergency. 'He's an idiot for not wearing a shirt in this climate,' I gasped. 'What was he thinking?'

'We're almost there,' Carol assured me for the tenth time.

'Almost where? There isn't anything for…oh!' I was suddenly looking straight down into a courtyard.

'Look out,' she warned belatedly.

'Falling in would be the easiest way to get him down there,' I observed. The alternative was a long, narrow flight of steps on the other side of a gaping hole in the sand.

'I'll get the boab guarding the tomb to carry him down.' Literally dropping Steve, she ran around the pit and down the steps into the courtyard. I watched her disappear into the mastaba, and waited with Steve, hot and breathless for all the wrong reasons.

A moment later, Carol raced across the courtyard again and back up the steps, followed more slowly by a native man on whose dark face lazy suspicion battled with greed as he anticipated the large tip this special service would entail. He asked no questions, however. He simply bent over, draped Steve over one of his skinny shoulders, the strength of which surprised me, and carefully descended the stairs with him.

Walking at the rear of this strange procession, I was reminded of the ones depicted on mastaba walls. If I had been an Old Kingdom princess, I would definitely have liked for my loving relatives to offer me young men like Steve in addition to cows' legs and baskets of fish.

It was wonderful stepping out of the sun into the cool and shadowy mastaba, and I shed my backpack with a heart-felt groan in the chamber at the end of a long corridor. Then I suffered a pleasant shock when I saw the handsome face staring out at me through a small rectangular opening in the back wall.

Ti's smile was so enigmatically alive, it took my brain a second to register it was only a statue I was seeing. He stood within a small sealed chamber behind the wall known as a serdab, gazing out from another dimension at all the loved ones who desired to commune with his Ba, the human-headed bird symbolizing his soul.

'Stay with him while I go get help,' Carol said briskly. 'And see if you can't get him to wake up and drink some water. But don't let him drink too much or he'll go into shock.' She ran back down the corridor and the native man hurried after her with the unmistakable gleam of baksheesh in his eyes. He had spread Steve out in the center of the chamber, and it was my impression he would have dropped him like a sack if Carol and I had not been watching him like hawks.

Once again, I sank to my knees beside the young Egyptologist's inert body. I gazed down at his smooth, hairless chest, perhaps a little longer than was necessary, and then moved my gaze down to the sunken valley of his stomach wondering how I should go about trying to rouse him. Should I slap him? Should I shake him gently by the shoulders? Yet if being dragged across hot sand had not revived him, I doubted any more subtle methods would work.

Trying not to enjoy myself too much, I straddled him and tentatively slapped one of his cheeks. His head fell to one side, but that was the only reaction I got from him...I think. It was probably only my imagination that his body grew a little firmer beneath me, meaning the bulge in his shorts swelled and stiffened slightly against my own soft crotch. Tempted to tentatively rub myself against him and test my theory, I quickly got up, feeling guilty. I could not make it a habit to give in to every sinful temptation that came my way.

I pulled my thermos out of my backpack, and crouching beside Steve, again poured a little water over his cheek, then a little more over his chest, slowly caressing it into his warm and oily skin. I continued my delicate libations, kneeling beside him like Isis trying to revive Osiris, after she had traveled the lengths of the earth gathering together the pieces of his body the evil Set had scattered to make it impossible for Isis to resurrect her beloved consort. She had found all the pieces except for one. I glanced down at Steve's shorts. Whatever was wrong with him, at least a crocodile hadn't eaten that vital piece of his anatomy.

I relaxed into a cross-legged position and looked up at a section of the bas-reliefs carved around me. I could tell right away this particular scene depicted the nobleman Ti and his wife. Behind them stretched fields of wild game and cattle, and a table before them was laid out with a delectable assortment of food and drink.

Rising, I approached their smiling figures. Because I was in his tomb, Ti was twice the size of his wife. He was seated on a chair while she knelt at his feet, her arms wrapped around one of his legs even as her face and torso looked away from his body, ostensibly in the direction of his immortality. I desperately longed to feel that way about a man, yet so far it had remained only a romantic dream. None of the men I dated had even remotely inspired such love and devotion in me.

A soft moan penetrated the stillness of the chamber.

I quickly knelt beside Steve again, and held my breath as his head turned slowly from side to side. I glimpsed the gleam of his irises as he nearly reached the surface of consciousness, but then I sensed him sink back into the comfortable peace of oblivion again. I sighed in frustration and sat back on my heels. The room I was trapped in with a young man who resembled a statue of Ti escaped from his serdab, felt oppressively timeless. His pulse and mine were the only measure of time's passage, and already I felt as though I had been alone with him for hours even though it had only been minutes.

Steve was so motionless I had to reassure myself again he was breathing by resting a finger just above his upper lip and feeling his warm exhalations bathe my skin. And as I did, I suffered the haunting impression that all the other brown male chests depicted around me were also rising and falling, so slowly their movement was nearly invisible.

Suddenly the procession of little reddish-brown figures circling the chamber struck me as a reflection of my own blood cells flowing through my body, the mastaba's separate chambers symbolizing my different vital organs. However, in this particular mastaba there was only one other room besides the one in which I was now, plus the serdab, from which Ti continued regarding me so enigmatically. If I remembered correctly, the space Steve and I were in was the sacrificial chapel. Strikingly realistic effigies of Ti once stared through three rectangular slits in the western wall, now only one statue remains, a replica of the original in the Cairo museum, the shining black stones used for his eyes giving it a marvelously life-like stare.

I glanced down at the bare chest I was kneeling beside, and then back up at Ti's firm brown torso depicted all around me. Steve's head was turned away, and his black hair could easily have belonged to an ancient Egyptian nobleman's. I looked over at the serdab and Ti's secretly smiling face, then back down at Steve's neck and broad shoulders. If I took off his shorts, I could easily make myself believe it was Ti's body lying before me and that the eyes of his Ba statue were challenging the priestess of Isis inside me to revive him, to bring him back to life with the mysterious powers of my female sexuality.

Abandoning myself to the fantasy, in the back of my mind justifying my actions with the thought that they might actually help rouse Steve from his dangerous stupor as nothing else had, I planted my hands on his warm chest and slowly caressed his pecs. They were almost as hard as a statue's, but his skin was tender, alive, inviting my nails to scratch it lightly and leave ghostly trails that gradually faded away. I found myself straddling him again, less carefully and hesitantly this time, encouraged by the haunting way Ti's smile seemed to deepen as my pulse accelerated. I ran my hands down to his firm belly, which was also vulnerably soft, appreciating the low-cut shorts that enabled me to penetrate the vulnerable little space of his navel with my fingertip and make a crescent-like imprint around it with my nail as I pressed it gently but firmly into his skin.

He did not make a sound or move a muscle in response to my gently vicious probe, and yet I realized he did, in a way, as I became even more stimulatingly aware of the bulge in his crotch between my legs. I bit my lip, hesitating for an instant before obeying Ti's smiling command to rub my pussy against his growing hard-on, for in my imagination Ti's virile ancient soul was magically possessing the inert body of the young man lying below me. I immediately felt frustrated by all the layers of cloth separating my hungry hole from the stiff fullness I distinctly felt pressing against my vulva now and insinuating itself between my labial lips through our shorts. I moaned, allowing all my weight to sink down against the buried erection that I was bringing fully to life without his even knowing it, and leaning forward slightly to brace myself against his chest, I began rubbing myself against it selfishly.

'Oh yes,' I whispered, because the top button on his shorts was in just the right place to give my clit an excitingly hard kiss every time I moved my hips up and down against him, and my panties provided a teasingly effective friction that told me I could come like this if I wanted to.

I was sorely tempted to take myself all the way. It would be so easy with Ti's metaphysical voyeurism caressing my imagination, combined with the memory of the handsome Englishman's tongue flicking with devastating skill against my clitoris. I was already swelling with the promise of an orgasm taking divine root between my thighs. Whatever the conscious Steve might think about it, his body was obviously enjoying what I was doing with him, and I wondered if my intimate caress was causing the synapses in his brain to flash a sexy dream on the screen of his closed eyelids.

It certainly couldn't hurt to stimulate him like this. And after thinking all day about what had happened the night before in the bazaar, I was more than ready for the momentary reprieve and relief of a climax.

I rode the timelessly handsome young man beneath me with concentrated abandon, working myself to a pitch by alternately gazing down at his black hair and broad shoulders, then over at Ti's supernaturally sexy smile, merging them in my fantasy until for a few stunning instants they actually seemed to become one in my body.

The intensity of my pleasure was reflected by my breathless silence as I came, the divine throes of my vaginal muscles contracting as ecstasy expanded within me. I was sure Steve would turn his head and look up at me, that the subliminal vibrations of my orgasm had been powerful enough to penetrate his psyche. But nothing happened except that his penis remained frustratingly stiff against my hot wet pussy.

Telling myself I had done all I could for him, I waited until my legs could comfortably support me again before I got up to resume my examination of the exquisite bas-reliefs.

I noticed that quite a few scenes involved the capture and taming of wild animals, which according to John Anthony West, one of the more inspired Egyptologists, symbolized the human spirit imposing a sense of order and meaning over the chaotic impulses of nature and the flesh. Continuing on in this vain, Ti's banquet table could be seen as being rich with the emotions he had learned to master, his soul a field sown with the belief in a divine harvest of life's experiences. In this light, the artwork around me was effectively a complex equation for immortality.

I went and stood directly in front of the serdab. 'What were you really like?' I asked Ti's smiling face, my voice reverently quiet. 'Were you as naïve and idealistic as a child, or were you strong and wise like the man I've always dreamed of?' Perhaps like the man in the bazaar last night, I thought, before I forced myself to stop thinking about him. 'Yet I feel as though you're still waiting for something, as if the eternity you believed in depends on what becomes of humanity itself. Maybe an afterlife doesn't just happen any more than life does. Maybe we have to build it ourselves with the energy of our desire.'

'I don't have any damned energy left to desire anything,' Ti's lips magically spoke without moving, his voice hoarse from the centuries that it had remained buried in his throat, 'except a drink of water, please.'

* * * *

'Steve, that's enough,' I protested gently. 'It's bad for you to overdo it. Just sip it.'

He paid me not the slightest heed; the thermos gradually rose until it was almost perpendicular with the ceiling as he guzzled the water.

'You should know better than to walk around in the desert without a shirt on,' I scolded him, my compassion for him all but dried up.

He finally set my cooler down, and collapsed back across the sand again.

'Steve?' I asked, concerned. His eyes were closed, but his smile told me he was awake, and aware of my hands gripping his shoulders. 'What happened to you?'

His uncanny resemblance to Ti vanished when his eyes opened again. His irises were the vivid green of spring leaves, a delicate color not found in Egypt's tougher foliage. 'Nothing happened to me,' was his infuriating reply.

'Excuse me, nothing? I suppose that's why we found you lying unconscious in the middle of the desert.'

He shrugged, and then winced in pain. 'How did I get here?' He sounded only mildly curious.

'Carol and I dragged you here, and it wasn't easy.'

'Carol?' He raised his head for a moment and looked around. 'Where is she?'

'She went to get help, naturally.'

'Help?' His shoulder-length hair formed a black halo across the white sand. 'What for?' With the typical stubbornness of his sex, he was pretending nothing was wrong with him, but I could sense his exhaustion as his eyes closed again.

'Steve, you could have died out there,' I said soberly. 'What happened to you?'

'Don't worry about it, Mary, I'm all right now.'

'Yes, but if we hadn't found you, you wouldn't be all right, not at all. Could your misfortune possibly have something to do with Imhotep's tomb?'

His eyes flew open. 'What?'

I smiled. 'Well, for some reason, Steve, I'm in possession of a photograph that—'

'You have it?' He sat up abruptly, and my surprise enabled him to push me back across the sand and straddle me just as I had him.

The pleasant shock, as well as the considerable weight of his hard muscles, took my breath away.

He grabbed both my wrists, and pinned them down over my head as he leaned over me. 'Where did you get it, Mary?' he asked quietly, his hair raining sand down into my face.

'Ouch!' I squeezed my eyes shut reluctantly, because his broad shoulders were quite an inspiring view.

'Tell me, Mary,' he whispered coaxingly in my ear.

'I didn't get it anywhere, it just appeared in my room at Carol's place.'

'Please tell me you haven't shown it to anyone, Mary.'

'I haven't shown it to anyone,' I said obediently, 'except Carol, of course.'

Apparently his relief was so great that he kissed me. 'Where is it now?' he asked, his lips moving against mine. 'Tell me...' He thrust his tongue between my lips as if he could wrestle the answer out of me.

'Mary!' Carol shrieked.

Steve rolled off me as suddenly as if the sound of her voice was a gunshot mortally wounding him.

'I see she managed to revive him,' Simon commented dryly.

He strode into the chamber and yanked me to my feet, not very gently.

'Baksheesh!' The mastaba's native guard had returned with them. 'Baksheesh!' he demanded from the doorway.

Carol turned to settle our account with him as Steve got carefully to his feet. 'Mary has the photograph,' he informed Simon.

'I know, Carol told me.'

'I—'

Simon cut her off. 'What happened to you, Steve?'

Wincing in pain, Ti's look-alike bent over and gingerly caressed the backs of his sunburned calves. 'I ran into some friends,' he replied absently, increasingly engrossed in his skin's budding misery. He was beginning to realize just what his body had been through while his consciousness was on sabbatical. 'I guess it upset them that I didn't have much to say.'

'I didn't—' Carol tried a second time to make a vital point, but this time she was interrupted by a man staggering into the sacrificial chamber looking as though he had just crossed the entire Sahara on foot.

'Where's the patient?' the newcomer gasped, removing his safari hat to caress his bald scalp as if to make sure it's egg-like surface hadn't cracked from the strain.

I assumed he was a doctor, even though of all the people in the mastaba he was the only one who looked in need of medical attention. I stepped up to Carol. 'You didn't what?' I whispered.

'I didn't tell Simon about the photograph,' she whispered back.

'Then he knew I had it?'

'Where's the patient?' the little bald man asked again, a bit hysterically. He was beginning to suspect his arduous race across the sand had been for nothing.

'I'm here,' Steve groaned. 'My lovely saviors burned the skin off my legs.'

With a gratified 'Humph!' the doctor hurried over to inspect him.

'Well, so much for our cozy night in a tomb,' I declared.

'Lost your nerve already?' Simon taunted.

'No, but someone just tried to kill—'

'Quiet, Mary.' He glanced at the doctor. The man was conferring with Carol, who had efficiently pulled out her little first aid kit to assist him. Standing perfectly still between them, Steve truly resembled a statue wearing a relieved smile on his lips as the doctor began applying a soothing balm to his back like the artist's finishing coat of paint.

Simon abruptly grabbed my arm and pulled me out into the corridor. 'Don't be silly, Mary, no one tried to kill Steve.' He led me into the smaller chamber.

'But—'

'No buts.'

'But how did you know about the photograph, and that I had it?'

'Where is it now?' In typical male fashion, he parried my question with one of his own. However, I was expected to provide an answer even though he had not.

'It's back at the apartment,' I lied impulsively; it was actually in my backpack.

'Good,' he said firmly, 'keep it there.'

'Does the cartouche in the picture mark the entrance to Imhotep's tomb?' I whispered eagerly.

'Yes, I believe it does,' he admitted, frowning at the wall behind me. 'That's the problem.'

'My God, you discovered Imhotep's tomb?!'

He put a hand over my mouth. 'Would you kindly lower your voice, Mary?'

'Sorry,' I mumbled against his palm. His skin was slightly rough and salty, and I didn't think I had ever tasted anything quite so delicious. Then there was the added spice of his face so close to mine, and his penetrating stare stirring up all sorts of feelings inside me.

He uncovered my mouth, and gripped both my arms the way he had in the perfume shop. 'Getting around like a little butterfly, aren't you?' he accused, and pulled me roughly against him.

I was lost in his crushing embrace and in the joy of his tongue suddenly leading mine around and around in a breathless dance.

'Ahem?'

I had no idea how long the doctor had been standing in the doorway watching us, but with my blood singing, his flushed little frame made me think of the dwarf-god, Bes, whom the ancient Egyptians had associated with music and childbirth.

'I believe my work is done here,' he said.

I was forced to rediscover gravity when Simon released me abruptly. 'We're sorry to have troubled you, sir.' He pulled a wad of colorful bills out of his back pocket that made me think of dried flower petals.

'Oh I couldn't possibly…' Bes eyed the money greedily.

'I insist.' Simon shoved the paper garishly decorated with Sphinx heads and pyramids into the doctor's hand. 'Just don't mention this little incident to anyone, please. The local authorities can be so trying, you know.'

'Oh but of course.' Bes smiled. 'Mention what?'

CHAPTER FOUR

I never would have thought I could be so happy and comfortable in a tomb. We were sitting against a wall of Ti's courtyard gazing meditatively at the fire burning in its center, and the Chardonnay we were drinking that was soaking deliciously into my tired muscles made staring up at the sky feel like looking up at a divine vineyard. I could not believe how many stars there were, all of them glistening like juicy grapes making our sun and earth just one vintage in a multitude of intoxicatingly beautiful and exciting worlds. Carol and I had brought the basic necessities, but Simon provided a small world of luxuries.

Shortly after the doctor departed, three native men (one of whom looked distinctly familiar when he grinned at me) paid a visit to the mastaba like the Three Kings stripped of all their finery, and among the wonderful gifts they unwrapped for us were several bottles of wine accompanied by canned delicacies such as smoked oysters and chicken liver Pâté.

When I was feeling so good that I was nearly incapable of speech, Simon began answering the questions I did not have the energy to ask him out loud. He seemed able to read my mind, however, and I hung on his every word because it kept me from falling asleep. We were sharing a blanket, and the side of me resting against him felt wonderfully warm while the other half of me shivered in the rapidly dropping temperature. I could hear Carol talking quietly with Steve on Simon's other side, his profile looming large as a colossi's from my cozy position beneath his arm, and I hoped she was feeling as good as I was.

'I've had my man, Halaf, watching you ever since you got here, Mary,' Simon informed me, 'and it's a good thing too, or I wouldn't have found you so quickly at the bazaar when you ran away, foolish girl.'

I was trying not think about the man I had met as a result of my foolishness, not to mention the pleasure my impulsive act had resulted in. 'Halaf…he was just here, wasn't he, the tall one of the three who delivered this wonderful wine and everything else? I thought he looked familiar. After he helped put everything back in my suitcase at the airport he sat on top of it grinning like a maniac.'

Simon chuckled. 'Yes, that was him.'

With my free hand, I lifted the paper cup to my lips. To my chagrin, I discovered it was empty again.

'Need a refill?' He reached for the bottle, careful not to disturb the exquisite cuddle we had achieved as he did so.

'Thank you,' I said as he filled my cup nearly to overflowing.

'My pleasure, Mary.'

'So…' It was an effort to speak, but I wanted to take advantage of his confidential mood. 'So you had Halaf slip the photograph into my suitcase. Why?'

'Because I needed a good place to hide it.'

'Halaf deliberately threw my suitcase half way across the airport so it would burst open?' I was too tired to feel indignant. I did not question why Simon had chosen me as the photo's recipient since at the moment I was not opposed to him choosing me for anything he desired.

'I'm sorry Mary, but my stuff, and Steve's too, would inevitably have been searched by interested parties once the rumor got out.'

'So you put me in danger instead?' I asked mildly, still not able to find it in me to be angry with him thanks to the conciliatory wine flowing through my veins.

'I told you, Mary,' he said patiently, 'there's no danger.'

'But someone roughed Steve up, didn't they? They left him lying unconscious in the desert, and if Carol and I hadn't found him, he might have-'

'Don't be silly. It would take a hell of a lot more than that to kill Steve. They were merely trying to intimidate us into revealing the location of the tomb, because even if they got a hold of the rumored photograph, it wouldn't tell them anything. There's no way they can determine the mastaba's location from the picture. However, ownership of the photo is important for claiming first excavation rights, so I made sure there wasn't a negative. I borrowed Carol's Polaroid when she wasn't looking, and then Steve and I re-buried the evidence. Actually, I really don't know what possessed me to give you the photo. It was an odd inspiration. I couldn't put it in a safe deposit box, or anywhere else similarly practical, because Egyptian archaeologists watch us like vultures just waiting to move in on a kill. If even one of them got a look at that picture the Antiquities Department would be all over us like jackals. Then Carol told me about her friend who was coming to visit her from Boston, and I thought that's it, no one will suspect a stupid little tourist.'

'Excuse me?'

'I didn't know you at the time, Mary.'

His apology was very effective—another long, lingering kiss in which his tongue pointed out all sorts of fascinating new twists to an age-old activity. I had to admit, Simon Taylor was an excellent kisser. He was so good I wouldn't have been surprised to learn he had a PhD in the subject. I was tired, and relaxed by decadently good food and wine, a condition that made kissing the sexy Egyptologist who had been gracious enough to arrange a night in a tomb for me feel like the perfect pastime, even if in the back of my mind I couldn't stop thinking about another man...'But I'm staying with Carol,' I somehow remembered what we had been talking about when he let me up for air, 'and she works for you.'

'True. However, there's very tight security around her building, and in the unlikely event anyone dared to break into her apartment, they would concentrate on her possessions and not yours. Anyway, I told you, it was an odd inspiration. I'm not normally so impulsive. Some strange intuition must have told me,' his arm tightened around my shoulders, 'I would want you intimately involved in all my affairs.'

This statement turned my head towards his again for another session of mouth-to-mouth stimulation, as the wine and his heavy arm around me drowned all the frustration I had been feeling remembering my mysterious sheik from the bazaar. Part of me felt anxious wondering if I would ever see him again, while another part of me did not doubt for a second that I would.

'Who was the man in the perfume shop, Simon?' I asked as casually as I possibly could. 'He seems to know I have the photograph. He said I had something he wanted, and asked me how much I knew about it, and I got the impression last night that you knew who he was.'

'I do.'

I waited breathlessly for him to volunteer more information, but suddenly he seemed content to just sip his wine. 'Well, who is he?' I couldn't quite disguise my impatient eagerness.

'How long were you alone with him, Mary?'

I squirmed beneath his arm in frustration that he was fighting my question with another question again. 'Who was I alone with?' I countered.

'A rich bastard.'

'He's rich?' I asked in surprise, because in the twenty-four hours I had spent thinking about the strikingly attractive stranger from the bazaar I had not once speculated about his profession or financial standing. There was something about him that had seemed above all such concerns, and I couldn't explain way, but I was sure I would have continued to feel this way about him even if Simon had told me he was a beggar.

'He's obscenely rich. Does that appeal to you, Mary?'

I wasn't so tipsy that I couldn't tell the question was a test. 'I could care less,' I replied truthfully.

He rewarded me for not being a materialistic girl with another academically perfect merging of our lips that scored big with the nerve-endings in my belly as his tongue's thrusting, surging skill made me wonder what it would be like to have him kissing me at the same time that his stiff cock plunged in and out of my pussy.

I moaned and looked searchingly up into his light eyes when he finally pulled his head back.

'I'm sorry I put you in this position, Mary,' he said soberly. 'It was stupid to involve you like this. I could easily have found a much more rational hiding place for the photograph, but it was such an unexpected monumental discovery, I guess I wasn't thinking straight. And when Carol mentioned her friend who was coming to visit from the States, I don't know, I just—'

'It's all right, Simon, I don't mind,' I assured him, because if he hadn't put me in this position by slipping the photograph into my suitcase, the nameless Englishman would not have put me in the position he did on the glass counter. 'Yet how did that man who was with me in the trailer know I have the photograph?' I was glad to have another objective excuse to ask about him.

'Because that bastard has a way of knowing everything. I wouldn't be surprised if half of Cairo was on his unofficial payroll.'

I was not happy that despite my cleverly detached questioning, the only name I could still give my beautiful sheik was bastard.

'And yet the mere rumor of this discovery has the vultures circling already, Mary. Steve and I didn't breathe a word of it to anyone, not even Carol knew about it until today, and yet somehow rumors started flying around, and that bastard's the eye of the storm, I'm sure of it.'

'Would you please stop calling him a bastard.' This was no way to refer to a man so admirably skilled in the age-old art of cunnilingus. 'I'm sure he has a name, and if he's so interested in the discovery of a mastaba, then that means he's an Egyptologist, too?'

'He's not.' Simon replied shortly. 'He's just rich enough to be able to make a hobby of Egyptology, and he's only one nuisance in my life right now. Do you know what will happen when it's made public that the entrance to Imhotep's mastaba has been discovered? All hell will break loose here, that's what, and I want to finish my book on Saqqara before that happens. I won't be able to hold them back much longer, though.'

'Why can't you include Imhotep's mastaba in your book?' I suggested brilliantly. 'Wouldn't that be the crowning glory?'

'Because, Mary, proper excavation of Imhotep's eternal resting place will take nearly as long as he's been dead, and Egypt will jealously horde all the initial glory for itself. I'd be surprised if they even let Steve and I work on it that much even though we discovered it.'

'How did you discover it?' I asked excitedly. 'I can understand why you're feeling frustrated, but you must be thrilled, too, aren't you?'

'Oh yes, I'm thrilled,' he made it sound like a medical condition he had been cured of long ago by a heavy dose of reality, 'and the discovery was an accident, of course. All the really good ones are. I'll spare you the boring details.'

'I wouldn't find them boring,' I protested, but without much conviction. 'If I wasn't so sleepy,' I added more honestly.

'What, tired already?' he teased. 'I thought you might like to join me in a nocturnal exploration of Ti's burial chamber.'

'Oh, that would be lovely!' I struggled to convey my mental excitement to my legs, without success. 'But I can't seem to move…'

He chuckled. 'Lovely isn't exactly the adjective I'd use to describe it.' His arm slipped from around me as he slipped the blanket we were sharing off his shoulder and stood up. His back was to the fire as he stood facing me, and his tall silhouette might have been Ti's magical Shade reaching down for my hand.

I set my cup down, and let him pull me up towards Nut's beautiful starry womb, shedding the blanket like a shroud. 'But why didn't you even tell Steve I had the photograph?' It suddenly occurred to me to ask. Steve and Carol were also sharing a blanket, and they ignored us as we got up.

'Because, if he didn't know where it was, he couldn't tell anyone else, could he?'

'Simon, I—'

'No more questions, Mary.' He took my hand and led me past the dying fire.

'But I have to— '

'I said drop it.'

'I can't drop it, I really have to go to the bathroom.' Standing had made me fully aware of my pressing need.

'That's where we're headed,' he said, and laughed softly when I hesitated. 'Don't worry, the desert's big enough for both of us.' He switched on a flashlight as we walked past the fire across the courtyard, and then let me walk up the steps ahead of him, half hypnotizing me with the undulating pool of light he kept focused at my feet. At the top of the stairs, he gave me a playful shove, and I started off alone into the pitch-black darkness.

I had stuffed some toilet paper into one of the pockets of my shorts earlier, and I was glad for my forethought now when I judged I had wandered off far enough. I pulled my shorts and panties down and squatted as I gazed up at the heavens. My urine was hot and pungent in contrast to the cold night air, and the countless stars winking down at me were stimulating company. I had known since I was a little girl that the earth's sun is only one of a multitude of suns, and tonight I found this fact more thrilling than ever, not only because I could actually see and feel that it was true, but because I was sure I had found him at last. The man I had been waiting for all my life was here in Egypt, there was no doubt about it in my heart, and it was entirely possible I had met him last night at the bazaar. And yet here I was getting ready to spend the night with another man, a handsome, intelligent Egyptologist who seemed absolutely perfect for me. If I started dating Simon, I could possibly arrange to stay in Egypt somehow, and if we were married, I could live in Egypt. He had said it would take years to excavate Imhotep's mastaba, and I could be part of the incredible excitement surrounding this historic discovery, sharing my days and nights with a man who shared my same passion for ancient Egypt. It was such a perfect daydream that for a few seconds I actually managed to forget the sensual gift another man had given me last night in the bazaar as a promise of things to come…

I wiped myself clean, pulled my panties and shorts back up, and buried the scrap of tissue in the sand. There was no point deciding between Simon and the nameless stranger tonight. I had time, thank the gods. I had only just arrived in Egypt, yet already I had been here long enough to know that things would unfold as they were meant to. Here in this ancient land coincidences felt like part of a mysterious choreography intimately related to everything I had ever thought and felt and dreamed. And right now all I knew for certain was that the nameless man from the bazaar had given me very good advice—I had to remember my dreams, in every sense, and trust that they would come true, although how, and with whom, I could not yet know.

I rejoined Simon at the top of the steps leading down into the mastaba. He was holding the flashlight towards the ground, and to me it looked as though the golden disc of the sun had fallen worshipfully at his feet.

'Feel better?' he asked quietly.

'Yes, thank you. I'm ready for the burial chamber now.'

'Are you sure?'

His undertone told me I could expect to encounter a lot more than an empty sarcophagus down there. 'I'm sure,' I replied quietly.

Back down in the courtyard, Steve was encouraging the fire back to a more passionate life while Carol remained huddled beneath their blanket, her knees drawn up against her chest in an effort to ward off the desert chill. I tried to catch her eye, but she was looking at Steve, and I couldn't blame her. The way the muscles of his back rippled as he stoked the flames was rather engrossing, especially when I compared the sight to the cold black hole Simon was leading me towards.

'You first,' he said.

'Oh no, you first.'

His flashlight revealed worn steps descending almost at a right angle deep into the earth. Without hesitation, he started down them.

I followed carefully behind him. His shoulders blocked the light, so I descended mostly by feel, tentatively clinging to him the whole way down. We had only gone a few feet into the darkness before I found myself longing for the fire we had left behind, very much like a disembodied soul must miss its warm, pulsing heart. In a matter of seconds, the absolute darkness of this secret place—deliberately dug far from the sacrificial chamber where Ti's life-like form still stands within the serdab—made the comforts and pleasures of the courtyard feel distressingly, almost impossibly, far away.

It was a relief when we finally reached level ground, but there wasn't much else to feel good about. Until Simon grasped my hand, and his firm grip sent reassuring warmth through my whole body. I sensed he was not in the least bit nervous, and I found this mysterious inner male strength intensely attractive. We just stood there hand in hand for a moment, our eyes gradually adjusting as he thrust the beam of his flashlight into the pitchy gloom. The edge of the light revealed a massive structure looming against a far wall and I assumed this was Ti's sarcophagus.

'Was Ti encased in eight different coffins like Tutankhamun?' I asked, whispering respectfully.

Simon didn't answer as he led me deeper into this haunting

wound inflicted in the earth by Ti's stubborn desire to live forever.

I made nervous conversation, anxiously wondering just how far he was planning to take us down here, in more ways than one. 'I don't believe the Egyptians mummified themselves because they wanted to keep using the same body.'

'Then why do you think they did it?' He laid the flashlight down on the thick rim of the sarcophagus.

'I don't know.' I clutched myself as I shivered.

'Are you cold, Mary?'

'Yes a little.'

The steady beam of light flowing parallel to us gilded the edges of his silhouette and made it look like the darkness itself had taken form. A stab of fear intensified my excitement in a way I had only experienced the night before in the bazaar. And now I shivered again, this time from the thrill of desire that coursed down my spine to the dark opening between my thighs I could never see, only feel.

'Then brace yourself,' he warned quietly, grasping my wrists and gently forcing my arms out of their unconscious mummy-like pose over my chest. He raised them up over my head, and before I could wonder what he was doing, he reached down and pulled my shirt off. 'I want you,' he whispered, carelessly dropping my clothes onto the packed earth, and impatiently tugging my zipper down with a ripping sound that echoed sinisterly in the ancient tomb. 'Do you want me, Mary?'

'Yes...' I wasn't wearing a bra, and my naked breasts looked so flawlessly pale and firm in the darkness they might have been made of alabaster.

'Then I'm going to take you.'

'Yes,' I repeated helplessly, glad he wasn't giving me time to think about what was happening. It would be foolish for me to remain loyal to a nameless stranger, and yet I was irrationally tempted to do so, which made Simon's commanding attitude come as a relief.

He genuflected before me. 'Are you sure?' he asked even as he slid my shorts and panties down my legs.

By way of response, I stepped out of them, looking down at the dim light of his blond hair and remembering a dark head in a similar position. I wasn't sure, but I think a stab of disappointment became hopelessly confused with how much it inevitably excited me to have a handsome man's face so close to my sex lips. I didn't appreciate the careless way he abandoned my new white cotton panties to the black dirt of a centuries-old grave, yet I was grateful for the powerful current of his desire which made it easy for me let go of my heavy thoughts and just go with the sensual flow, submerging my body in these timelessly arousing moments deep in the earth.

'Oh Mary...' He grabbed me by the waist as his mouth fell hungrily on one of my nipples, making me gasp from the stimulating contrast between his warm lips and the frigid crypt. I surrendered to the supple arch of my spine by tossing my head back as he pressed me firmly against him while passionately suckling one of my breasts.

I was overwhelmed by a small storm of sensations that sent a hot flash of arousal down my body, instantly making the space between my legs warm and wet. His mouth was hot and alive compared to the cold still air of the burial chamber, and my naked skin pressed against his slightly rough jeans as he clutched my slender waist with hard, possessive fingers made me even more aware of how soft and vulnerable my young body was surrounded by timeless earth and unyielding stone.

I moaned as he transferred his attentions to my other achingly firm nipple, but I wasn't so much responding to the sweet pleasure of having my breasts so thoroughly appreciated as to the feel of my body, braced on the comfortable modern pedestals of my sneakers, willingly going completely limp in his hands. I deliberately didn't do anything except passively let him worship the lush charms of my flesh as he literally held me up with his hands and his mouth. I was seriously turning myself on imagining that stripped of all defenses my slender body was supported only by the irresistible force of his lust. His fingers digging into my skin promised that his cock would be just as hard and unrelenting as it thrust me into ecstasy's otherworldly dimension.

'Oh Mary!' he repeated eloquently.

I didn't respond, not wanting to break the submissive trance I was letting myself fall into; my back arched as I offered my breasts up to his deliciously devouring appetite, my head thrown back so all I saw were my own rousing dark fantasies.

He planted his hand against my upper back and straightened me up to face him. 'You're so fucking beautiful,' he said accusingly.

I moaned feeling bereft as he suddenly let go of me, but it was only so he could open his pants. I held my breath waiting to see what would emerge, and the pale shaft of his stiff penis as he pulled it out was all I could have hoped for. The mere sight of it made the hole between my legs feel even deeper and darker, desperately in need of his almost luminous erection to fill it and show me all the beautiful sensations buried within me.

'There's nowhere to lie down,' he said in a threatening undertone that made me shiver it got me so hot inside despite how cold my skin was. 'What do you suggest?' He stroked himself slowly, clearly enjoying the feel of my eyes on his cock.

Shivering again, I hugged myself in anticipation of feeling his long, thick erection sliding into my tight pussy, and because it was much more exciting not knowing how he would put it inside me,

I didn't answer.

'Turn around and bend over,' he ordered quietly, correctly interpreting my silence to mean it was his decision, 'and brace yourself on the edge of the sarcophagus.'

I didn't care that the stone scraped my skin a little. It was a small price to pay for the intense turn-on of being helplessly naked in such rough surroundings as I bent at the waist and gripped the edge of Ti's eternal resting place. I was surprised by how much it excited me that we weren't in a safe comfortable bedroom lying on a nice soft bed with silk sheets caressing our skins. In this impenetrably dark tomb all we had was each other, our two bodies embraced by elements hostile to our flesh bringing us more intensely together.

'Mm, yes, that's a good girl,' he murmured as I felt him step up tightly behind me. 'Arch your back just a little more,' he urged, resting his hand on the base of my spine and pushing down on it gently. 'That's it. Are you on the pill?'

'Yes,' I whispered.

'I'm glad, because I would hate not being able to feel you, and I want to feel you, Mary. More than anything right now I want to feel your pussy caressing every inch of my cock all the way down to my balls.'

I whimpered in an agony of anticipation as he caressed the cool moons of my ass cheeks with his warm hands, making me almost painfully aware of my wet, begging pussy made to wait for his penis. At last he began penetrating me, but so slowly I could hardly stand it. The teasing sensation of his head lodged between the lips of my sex gradually became the deepening pleasure of his hard-on forcing my clinging depths open around it, his rigid cock suffusing my belly with a penetrating warmth like a solid shaft of light magically illuminating the secret shrine between my thighs. When he was finally all the way in, it felt so good I moaned in protest as he remained buried motionless inside me for what felt like a small eternity.

'Oh yes…' he whispered, and pulled out all the way to start thrusting into me hard and fast. After his initial control he drove into me, beating his hips against mine as though his life depended on it, making my arms strain against the sarcophagus as every time he plunged I felt as though he was granting my body its deepest wish. 'You like it like this, don't you, Mary?'

I was in no position to argue.

'Do you like my cock inside you?' He rammed the question into me.

'Oh yes!' I gasped. He banged me from behind with such force that even my clitoris, technically left out in the cold, trembled in response to his virile onslaught, making the experience almost overwhelmingly pleasurable for me.

Sustaining his relentless rhythm, he demanded, 'Tell me how much you like it.'

'Oh God, I love it,' I obeyed breathlessly, 'I love it!'

It was true. I loved the sensation of his erection surging up into my body and granting me the blessed sensation of being full of a real man. Keeping my legs straight to help brace me as I held on to the edge of the sarcophagus, my back arched receptively to offer my slick pussy up to his deep, hard thrusts. It was an exercise I could have sustained forever.

'You have such a sweet little pussy, Mary, so tight and yet so deep, I can shove my cock all the way up inside you like this…'

I cried out from the excruciating pleasure as he illustrated his point and I felt the cool kiss of his balls on my hot vulva.

'I ram my dick all the way up into your sweet little slit and still barely touch bottom.'

'Oh God that feels so good, don't stop,' I begged, 'please!'

'Does it feel like I'm going to stop, Mary? Does my cock feel like it's anywhere near ready to stop fucking you?'

'No…' I groaned as he pulled out of me slowly, allowing me to relish the full rigid length of his erection as my innermost flesh seemed to swell worshipfully open around it. And then I whimpered from the torturous ecstasy as he plunged all the way into me again. His penis was so thick and rigid and planted so deep inside my flesh the fulfillment was excruciating, and yet there was still enough mysterious room left inside me to accommodate the thought of another man.

'Oh yes, yes!' I cried shamelessly, forgetting to respect Ti's ghost as Simon's hips started pumping again and the impression his hard-on made inside me became confused with the memory of a dark-haired stranger's head buried between my thighs.

'Mm, yes, Mary, come for me…'

'I can't…'

'You,' he stabbed into me accusingly, 'can't?'

'I have to touch myself!'

'I see.' He pulled out of me abruptly. 'Come here, baby.'

I obeyed him a little stiffly, straightening up and turning around to face him. For some reason it excited me that he was still fully clothed and I was completely naked except for my shoes and socks. It was perversely arousing to have my tender breasts and open sex exposed in a cold stone tomb while the naked soles of my feet were still protected by my sneakers, reassuring symbols of the fact that I could walk out of there whenever I wanted to; comfortable reminders that my body wasn't really the helpless vulnerable plaything of unseen forces that might be penetrating me in the form of Simon's powerfully virile silhouette.

He pulled me into the shelter of his arms. 'This is turning you on, isn't it?' he whispered, holding me close against him.

'Yes,' I confessed. 'I guess I have a kinky streak.'

'Well this is the first time I've ever had sex in a crypt, too, in case you're wondering.'

I wasn't, all I was wondering was if I would ever see the mysterious sheik from the bazaar again, and fully admitting this to myself while standing naked in another man's arms, I heaved a sad, frustrated sigh.

'I'm not finished with you yet,' he warned quietly. 'We're not leaving this tomb until I feel you come fully to life.'

He grasped one of my hands and led me in the direction the flashlight was pointing, its faint yellow light washing over what looked like a broken column. 'Sit on this and lie back,' he instructed.

The surface looked smooth enough, and just conceivably wide enough for me to obey him. I lifted myself gingerly up onto the pedestal, aroused by how cold and hard the stone was against my soft ass, and I was even more enticingly aware of my tender wet pussy lips as the bottom of my pouting little pudenda kissed the edge.

'Lie back,' he urged as I hesitated, stroking himself again even though his erection did not look in the slightest danger of diminishing.

I obeyed him with the thrill of longing to feel his cock stabbing me again. I was perched on the very edge of the broken column that was digging into my ass cheeks, and with my spread legs bent at the knees, the tips of my sneakers just barely touched the ground. My body felt excitingly soft and vulnerable lying against the totally unyielding surface, and any discomfort I felt was washed away by a flood of anticipation as I watched a broad-shouldered silhouette gilded by the light behind him step forcibly between my thighs.

I was infinitely glad he didn't say anything, which enabled my imagination to take off as I lifted my hand and touched myself, pressing the tips of two of my fingers against my clitoris. I caressed myself as only I know how watching a rock-hard shadow penetrating me, and as it slowly filled me, pleasure fully possessed me. The silence in the chamber was absolute beyond our excited breathing, and the soft wet sound of his balls slapping against me as he gripped the backs of my thighs, raising them around him so he could dive fast and hard into my juicing hole. I willed him not to speak—to remain a tall anonymous silhouette embodying the tomb's eternal penetrating power—as the soul of my flesh began rising between my legs, spreading the divine wings of an orgasm through my pelvis as his stone-stiff erection stabbed me over and over again relentlessly, sinking deep into my weeping pussy before pulling out again almost all the way, until I imagined that the pleasure of his full length rending me open would kill me as I started coming around it.

'Oh yes, Mary, come with me.'

I barely heard his voice as a soaring climax left my naked body lying across the cold stone; a willing sacrifice to the ecstasy dispersing all my thoughts in an upsurge of pure joy.

* * * *

Emerging from Ti's burial chamber, part of me concentrated on my footing, while the rest of me dwelled breathlessly on the things I had learned about myself clinging to the edge of a sarcophagus while being violently fucked from behind.

It was going to be hard to live with the knowledge that I was a lot kinkier than I had believed, judging from my morbid fantasy in the crypt that my helpless young body was being possessed by irresistible unseen forces embodied in Simon's forceful silhouette. I had imagined an Egyptologist would have sensitive, skilled hands (I had seen all those National Geographic specials in which archaeologists brushed dirt off long-buried artifacts with mind-numbing patience) but I had never suspected they would have such equally hard-digging erections that would help me unearth feelings and sensations I had not realized my emotions and my body were capable of.

Deep in languorous thoughts about the last timeless hour that would live in my memory forever, I collided with Simon when he suddenly stopped dead at the top of the stairs. Without turning around, he reached behind him, gripped one of my shoulders, and applied a pressure that indicated he wanted me to stay down in the tomb. Much as I had enjoyed everything he had done to me there, I was not willing to submit to this particular inexplicable desire of his, so I was relieved when he muttered, 'Too late' and completed his ascent up into the fresh night air with me following right behind him.

At first glance, I thought the three Egyptian men who had earlier delivered our hedonistic supplies had returned to take away the evidence of our decadence, but then I realized there were at least half-a-dozen native men crouched around the fire. As we emerged from the crypt, they stared at Simon and me as grimly as if we were actually rising from the dead, and their sober expressions made my light-headed sensual contentment feel so sinful I began to worry we had violated some sacred Moslem law by making love in a tomb. I sensed they all knew what had just taken place down in Ti's sacred resting place, and I was torn between feeling profoundly ashamed and elatedly wicked. Then I ceased being aware of anyone or anything else as a figure strode out of the mastaba like my best nightmare.

'Good evening,' my mysterious stranger from the bazaar said in a deep, quiet voice that carried effortlessly around the courtyard and seemed to echo in my very bones.

Tonight my handsome sheik from the perfume shop was wearing Western clothing that did a much better job of showing off his breathtakingly broad shoulders tapering down into narrow hips and long, strong legs. His full-sleeved white shirt was tucked into tight black pants, which in turn disappeared into knee-high black leather boots, and everything fit him so perfectly I found I could not fit anything else into my mind looking at him.

He strode right up to me as I stared at him with a relief that was mingled equally with disbelief, because this was the last place I had expected him to show up. Completely ignoring Simon's presence beside me, he reached down for one of my hands and holding it gently, raised it slowly to his lips. 'Allow me to introduce myself, Mary.'

In the shadows ebbing and flowing over his features like an amorphous tide controlled by the hissing fire, the scar beneath his mouth attracted me like the crescent moon with its sensually dangerous mystery. 'Sir Richard Gerald Ashley, at your service.'

'He's carrying a gun,' Carol suddenly announced in a tight voice.

I glanced over my shoulder, and saw my friend and Steve still huddled beneath a blanket, but apparently it wasn't just the cold they were protecting each other from now.

'It's a very small gun, just a toy, really,' Richard protested without taking his eyes off me or letting go of my hand. 'Very useful, however, against scorpions and,' he finally looked at Simon, 'other vermin.'

As if he had not heard or even seen him, Simon walked away in the direction of the fire, effectively abandoning me. The men who were crouched around the flames all leapt to their feet as he approached, but he simply strolled past them as if they too were invisible.

'Listen to me, Mary.' Richard slipped a heavy arm around my shoulders and drew me slightly away from everyone. 'I don't know what Simon has told you, but I'm sure it's not the truth, at least not all of it.'

There was an urgency below the surface of his calm voice that captured my attention even as I tried not to enjoy the weight of his arm too much, or the feel of his firm, muscular body against mine. 'So let me tell you what I know, Mary. I know your boyfriend is holding up the progress of Egyptology for his own selfish purposes—'

'He's not my boyfriend,' I interrupted him with what I felt was a very important fact.

He flashed me a smile that literally made me feel weak in the knees, which were already a little tired from my trudging across deep sand with a heavy backpack and from my recent erotic exercise down in the tomb. 'I'm glad to hear that, Mary, but you should never interrupt me.'

'I'm sorry.'

'Simon, the man whom I'm sure would very much like to be your boyfriend, is deliberately burying evidence that could throw immeasurable light on the field of Egyptology. He believes Imhotep's tomb is his to do with as he pleases, which I don't need to tell you is not the case whether he discovered it or not.'

'He doesn't believe that,' I argued even though in a sense I agreed with what he was saying. But I felt guilty about betraying Simon with my thoughts, so I reluctantly slipped out from beneath Richard's arm. It was more difficult pulling my hand out of his, however, like deliberately letting go of something I had always desired. 'Simon only wants to be able to finish his book on Saqqara without being—'

'Ah, so he has found the entrance. I was sure it wasn't just a rumor this time.'

'I didn't say...I...'

'Don't worry, love, you haven't betrayed him. I know about the photograph, and I would like to see it, if I may.'

'Why were you dressed like an Egyptian at the bazaar?'

This question helped me skirt the issue of the photograph, which would put me in the impossible position at the moment of choosing between him and Simon. I also wanted to know more about this man who felt so hauntingly familiar to my body even though there was no chance we had met before last night.

'Because I find it easier to mingle with the natives when dressed like one,' he replied, staring earnestly down into my eyes. He was standing as close as he possibly could to me, and I was letting him because I wanted him that close. 'The local culture is much more interesting when you truly open yourself to its unique pleasures,' he added softly.

I forced myself to take a step back, a little disconcerted by his penetrating regard and by the fact that I felt myself falling strangely against gravity up into his eyes. 'Is that how you found out I had the photograph,' I made an effort to organize my thoughts and continue the conversation so I wouldn't keep thinking about how good it had felt when his tongue was wordlessly circling my clitoris, 'because your disguise lets you in on all the good local gossip?'

My feelings were in turmoil. My brain wanted to mistrust him because Simon obviously didn't like him, and yet everything he said struck me as completely reasonable, not to mention the magnetic physical attraction I felt for him that made it almost impossible for me to think straight. I wondered if it was my body, so strangely and irresistibly drawn to his that was seducing my mind into believing whatever, and then another distressing possibility prompted me to demand, 'Did you have something to do with Steve's little accident? Were you trying to get a hold of—'

'I had nothing to do with whatever happened to Steve.' His mouth hardened and I suffered the impression that he was disappointed I had felt it necessary to ask him such a question. 'If I had wanted to steal the photograph, Mary, rest assured I would not have made such a mess of it.'

'I'm sorry,' I said quickly, 'I didn't mean to imply…I mean, I don't believe you're a thief, Richard, not at all.'

'Thank you.' While it lasted his smile made my heart feel wonderfully light. 'However, there are other interested, and much less ethical, parties than myself who would stop at nothing to claim such a momentous discovery for themselves. And also please remember, Mary, that it was Simon who started this little game. He was a fool to think he could keep such an important find a secret for very long.'

It hit me then that the man I had just made love to was not the man I was standing so close to now and had no desire to move away from. Perhaps Simon was a bit foolish, not just for thinking he could keep the discovery of Imhotep's tomb a secret, but because he had left me alone with an attractive, eloquent man whose low opinion of him was beginning to feel distressingly justified.

I looked behind me. Richard's native companions were squatting comfortably around the fire again talking amongst themselves, and Simon, I was shocked to discover, was sitting back against the mastaba wall comfortably wrapped in the blanket we had been sharing earlier. I couldn't believe it, and his complete detachment suddenly made me feel as if I were dreaming; it just didn't seem possible after everything we had done together down in

Ti's burial chamber.

Richard followed my gaze. 'How do you suppose he would react if I made off with you, Mary? Would he fight me for you, I wonder? Shall we test him?' Before I could respond, he swept me off my feet into his arms. 'My poor love, you look exhausted. What you need is a nice soft bed.'

I opened my mouth to protest, and discovered the rest of me had absolutely no desire to do so.

He carried me back towards the fire, whispering, 'Let's see if you're more important to him than that precious photograph, shall we?' He raised his voice challengingly. 'Mr. Taylor, I'll make a bargain with you. I'll let you have Mary, for the moment, if you'll let me take a look at that photograph.'

'Sorry,' Simon's apology drifted amiably across the courtyard, 'but I don't have it.'

'I know. Mary has it, but considerate young woman that she is, she won't let me see it without your permission.'

Comfortable as I was in Richard's arms, the silence with which Simon greeted this proof of my loyalty made me squirm indignantly. How dare he put me in this position? It didn't matter that I was finding it quite stimulating...

'I don't respond to coercion, Sir Ashley,' Simon replied at last. 'You can wait along with everyone else for the discovery to become public. That's assuming, of course, there is a discovery worth mentioning and it's not just another pedestal.'

'Simon, aren't you going to tell him to put me down?!'

'Why don't you ask him to put you down yourself, Mary?'

This was not the point, and yet he did have a point, and I was so furious with him for undermining my self-esteem by treating me so nonchalantly after fucking me so passionately that I couldn't think straight. I had to show him just how much his indifferent attitude was hurting me, or at least would have been hurting me if I hadn't felt so good in Richard's arms.

'The photo is right over there, Sir Ashley,' I said politely, 'so if you'll kindly put me down I'll...hey, stop them!' Clearly understanding English better than they let on, Richard's native companions immediately leapt to their feet and converged on our supplies like a pack of starving dogs.

Simon finally showed some emotion as he too rose abruptly. 'Mary!' he exclaimed, the blanket hanging from his shoulders like a kingly cape. 'You lied to me.' He sounded stunned. 'You told me you didn't have the photo with you.'

'Simon, I...' I didn't know what to say.

'Bass!' Richard's thunderous command magically dispersed the cloud of white robes from around my possessions. 'Mary,' he set me down gently, 'I don't want them pawing at your things. Would you please be good enough to fetch the photograph for me yourself?'

'You're only going to look at it, Richard? You're not going to take it?'

'I give you my word.'

One of the Egyptians impatiently kicked a fallen log back into the blaze as I reflected on the dancing, potentially destructive flames for a long moment before finally walking over to my back-pack, and slipping the photograph out from inside a zippered pocket. Then I counted to three and made a wild dash for the fire. Two of Richard's men attempted to intercept me, but I changed course and the sand cushioned my fall as with an eager hiss a flame licked the photograph painfully from of my fingertips. I watched the cartouche of Imhotep's tomb dissolve in a black wave, and then dozens of hands reached for me at once like a monstrous centipede landing on top of me.

'Get away from her!' Simon yelled.

'Mafish!' Sir Ashley's angry Arabic command was more effective. I was released at once, but the minute I got to my feet, Richard swept me up into the safety of his arms again even though they also felt dangerously good around me. 'That was beautifully dramatic of you, love. Still, I wish you hadn't done it. You've burned the only evidence of a potentially great discovery.'

He began walking towards the steps leading out of the mastaba's courtyard, his long stride unhindered by my weight. 'Nevertheless, the photograph is of no consequence anymore. The discovery will become public soon enough, and it has already led me to a far greater treasure.'

'Where the hell are you going with her?' Simon demanded, finally coming back to life.

'You can't kidnap an American citizen, Richard, put her down.'

'Who said anything about kidnapping her?' Sir Ashley replied without bothering to look back. 'She's coming with me quite willingly. Aren't you, Mary?'

'It won't work.' Simon sounded infuriatingly calm. 'I'm not telling you where the tomb is, so put her down or I'll have you arrested.'

'Arrested for what, for stealing her heart?' Richard started climbing the steps with me still cradled in his arms, forming the head of a procession of men that made me feel like a sacred offering, except that we were headed out of the mastaba where I was leaving a part of my heart in the form of a handsome Egyptologist I had just made passionate love with.

I craned my neck to look back down into the fire-lit courtyard, crying, 'Simon?'

'Don't be afraid, Mary,' he called up to me, 'he can't hurt you.'

'You're in much better hands now, love,' Richard assured me soberly.

It became so dark as we climbed towards the desert floor that all I could see were stars winking mischievously, or meaningfully, in his eyes, it was impossible to tell which. 'But you can't just take me!'

'I can't?' He sounded almost genuinely surprised that I would question is ability to do anything.

'No, you can't,' I insisted, yet I wasn't making the slightest effort to get away from him. In fact, I had my arms wrapped around his neck. I told myself I couldn't hope to fight him, so there was no point in doing so, but I knew this was a flimsy excuse for how excitingly happy he made me feel.

'I have no intention of letting you get away, Mary.'

I kept staring up the dark space where I knew his eyes were and at the stars burning in his gaze. They seemed to form hieroglyphic constellations my soul understood, and they told me he meant what he said.

'So...' I took a deep breath, 'you're going to hold on to me until Simon tells you where he found the entrance to Imhotep's tomb?' I was suddenly afraid that I was only a means to an end to him and that I was imagining everything else between us.

He did not answer as we reached level ground and I felt the dessert spread its majestic silence all around us.

'He won't tell you, Richard. He knows you can't keep me away from him. He won't tell you where the tomb is,' I insisted, more hurt than I cared to admit by the possibility that a major archeological discovery was all he was really interested in.

'Mary,' he lifted me up and set me down on a smooth, hard surface even my inexperienced bottom immediately realized was a saddle, 'don't you understand yet?' He helped me spread my legs and get one of them over the pommel so I was perched comfortably on the horse's back. 'It's you I'm after.'

* * * *

Despite the awe-inspiring beauty of a sky so full of stars it made me realize what I had been missing all my life living beneath the light pollution of a modern city, I was too confused and overwhelmed by recent events to really appreciate the sight. I was also scared of falling off the magnificent creature flexing its powerful muscles between my thighs. I had never ridden a horse before, and pounding at full gallop across the desert was a rough way to lose my equestrian virginity. I was very glad to have the white fence of Richard's arms around me as I leaned back against his solid warmth and clung to the pommel for all I was worth.

I had no idea where he was taking me, all I knew was that with every muffled beat of the horse's hooves I was farther away from Simon and all the incredible feelings and sensations he had unearthed in my flesh and psyche deep in a tomb. Naturally, I hadn't expected him to give in to Richard and reveal the location of Imhotep's tomb, but I didn't see why he couldn't at least have tried to prevent another man from carrying me away right under his nose.

He should have done something! He should have done something! He should have done something!

The damning statement beat through my head in rhythm with the horse's hooves. All I could see were stars above me, and Richard's rippling sail-like sleeves around me holding onto reigns that vanished into the horse's pale mane, streaming against the sky in front of me like a planetarium show of the Milky Way galaxy. The cold wind keened in my ears and made my face feel as if it were carved out of stone even as all the muscular life supporting me kept the rest of me comfortably warm.

My friends back at the office in Boston would certainly think I was making it up if I told them I had been abducted on horseback and whisked across the Sahara by a beautiful armed Englishman. I couldn't even picture myself telling the tale, perhaps because I had absolutely no desire ever to return to the fluorescent sterility of my office in the Prudential Tower. Just thinking about it was ruining the adventure, so I put incredulous co-workers out of my mind and immersed myself in the tumultuous present, where multitudes of stars overhead were an audience focused entirely on me and my life, which from the moment I landed in Egypt started becoming truly interesting.

'Where are you taking me, Richard?' I cried over the roar of the wind. 'To your gilded tent in an oasis?'

He laughed at my little joke, and the vibration of his chest against my back blending with the horse's surging motion between my legs was quite stimulating. In fact, it was just a bit too stimulating. My pussy was feeling even more sensitive than usual after Simon's rampant strokes down in Ti's eternal home, and with my legs spread open across the horse's surging muscles, my labia was responding to the hard, relentless caress of the saddle in a highly debilitating way. Unable to get a grip on anything with my feet, I had no choice but to tighten my thighs around the saddle in order not to slip off as I held on to the pommel for dear life—which had the effect of bringing the wickedly arched front of the saddle directly into contact with my clitoris. The unyielding pressure of the hard leather vibrating directly between my thighs was uncomfortable one moment and intensely exciting the next, as I struggled to reconcile my mind's opinion that it would be dangerous to give in to the pleasure with my body's insidiously sweet insistence that ecstasy is welcome under any circumstances.

'Richard, are we almost there?' I cried.

'No, we have a ways to go yet.' He didn't need to shout over the wind; he responded directly in my ear, and his deep voice flowing through me on his warm breath stoked the delight smoldering between my legs. 'Aren't you enjoying the ride?'

'Oh yes, I'm enjoying it too much!'

He chuckled again, and once more the vibration of his hard body pressed against mine contributed to the hot havoc between my legs.

'Oh God,' I moaned, 'can't we stop for a minute?'

'No, we cannot,' he said, and flicked the reigns so the horse picked up its pace.

My grip tightened convulsively on the pommel, which had the effect of jamming it directly against my clit in a deliciously painful way.

'Why are you fighting it, Mary?' His quietly reasonable yet deeply seductive tone seemed to rise straight out of my own soul. 'Let yourself go.'

'I can't let go, I'll fall!'

'You know what I mean, Mary, just let yourself go.' A commanding edge entered his voice that mysteriously sharpened the delight cutting up through my pelvis. 'Do it, Mary, I want to feel you trembling with pleasure against me. I won't let you fall, trust me.'

I could no longer resist what was happening. The sight of the stars burning overhead was becoming wonderfully confused with the feel of my own smoldering blood cells as the promise of a climax ignited the haunting branches of my veins. Suddenly I couldn't understand why I was fighting the effects of the rhythmic pounding against my vulva, and as the pleasure ascended inside me, I lost my fear of falling because even though I couldn't explain it I trusted this man implicitly.

'Oh yes, Mary, I can feel how close you are...look, can you see them, directly ahead and just slightly to the right of us on the horizon?'

I looked, and the sight became confused with the pleasure peaking inside me.

'Come now, Mary…'

My body obeyed him, and yet I somehow managed to keep my eyes open during the orgasm's devastating throes so as not to lose sight of the three pyramids of Giza silhouetted on the horizon. For a few physically transcendent moments my heart beat faster than the horse's hooves, and as it fluttered back down to a deeply relaxed and contented pace, I watched the pyramids slowly growing and swallowing more and more stars with their haunting dimensions. The sight filled me with a sense of well being so profound that my brain, desperately fishing for words to describe it, failed utterly.

'Good girl,' Richard murmured in my ear, then he didn't speak again as we approached the only remaining wonders of the ancient world. Now that I had given into the erotic pressure of the saddle against my pussy, it ceased to bother me and I settled comfortably back against him, relaxing my grip on the pommel somewhat as I settled into the horse's rhythm instead of fighting it out of fear of falling.

When we finally reached the base of the smallest pyramid we slowed to a swift trot, and I could only admire the confident way Sir Ashley maneuvered the horse over the rocky terrain as I heard his native minions clattering less elegantly behind us. And as we rode beneath it, the great pyramid's shadow darkened my mind in a mystical way I find it hard to explain now. The feel of Richard's arms around me deepened into a timeless embrace in which I forgot his name, which I had only just learned anyway, and it was as though I even forgot what my own name was supposed to be because names didn't matter at all, they were superficial and temporary and what we felt when we were together was destined to last forever…

I jolted back into my own tired and bemused identity as Mary Fallon, legal secretary enjoying an unbelievably eventful vacation in Egypt, when the horse trotted casually to a stop.

Behind me, Richard dismounted, and I literally fell out of the saddle and down into his arms. After that, I have a vague memory of lights washing over my closed eyelids in warm waves accompanied by murmuring voices, and then of being laid across a wonderfully soft surface my entire being sank into gratefully.

CHAPTER FIVE

In the morning, when I awoke to my naked body lying in a king size bed, my sore muscles were too grateful to permit me to worry about it just yet. According to my body's cat-like perceptions, it was better to be lying on a soft mattress beneath clean cotton sheets than wrapped in a sand-filled blanket on the hard ground.

I opened my eyes, but I didn't move for a while; I just enjoyed lying there, going over everything I had experienced in the last twenty-four hours. I had backpacked across the desert, dragged a well-developed young man into a tomb, made love in a dark crypt and been whisked away on horse back by an English lord beneath a universe burgeoning with stars. To think I had worried about missing my workouts at the gym while I was on vacation! And those were just the last twenty-four hours; even more incredible things had happened to me since I arrived in the land of the pharaohs.

Tentatively, I raised my head from out of a bower of pillows, and found myself face to face with a smiling alabaster bust of one of

Akhenanton's many daughters. She looked as happy as I realized I was feeling even though she would have had reasons to be concerned about her future, just as I did. She did not look at all worried about the fact that her father had thrown Egypt into chaos by replacing the worship of multiple gods with one Supreme Being. I, on the other hand, was trying not to worry about the fact that Richard's appearance in the mastaba last night had thrown my feelings into chaos by making it obvious I wasn't ready to devote myself to one man, not yet. I liked and admired Simon to no end, and my head said he was the perfect mate for me, yet the two times I had encountered Richard I felt as though every cell in my body was flung into orbit around him through irresistible magnetic laws of attraction I could not explain away, much less ignore.

The quality of the silence in the room told me I was alone, so I sat up.

Sky-blue curtains hung over floor-length windows. The sun penetrated the fine material in a luminous haze through which the white silhouettes of eighteenth dynasty dancing girls were visible, their hips swaying gently in the breeze from a central air-conditioner. On the nightstand opposite the one occupied by one of the heretic pharaoh's daughters sat a lamp I recognized as a copy of one found in Tutankhamun's tomb. It was shaped like three lotus blossoms growing out of a central stem, and the almost translucent white alabaster was undoubtedly a breath-taking sight in a dark room when it was lit from within. And it was no lifeless museum copy either. I could tell from where the stone became slightly more opaque at the base that it was actually filled with oil. Apparently, the room was decorated in the New Kingdom style, which was lovely, but I preferred Old Kingdom purity and boldness of line. The artistic style of Egypt's earliest dynasties was hard and confident, an arousing balance of physical sensuality and metaphysical conviction. In other words, I was not going to let myself be girlishly impressed by Sir Richard Ashley's seductive accommodations.

After making use of the bathroom (which thankfully was completely modern) I examined the rest of my beautiful room with restless delight.

A gilded wooden chest sat at the foot of the bed. Every inch of it was carved with exquisitely colorful bas-reliefs also dating from the eighteenth dynasty, and still exhibiting some of the artistic decadence instigated by Akhenaten even though the artist had ostensibly returned to the traditional style. It occurred to me that if I could find my clothes I could get dressed and leave, but I deliberately postponed looking for them. After all, Simon was probably still in the desert with Steve and Carol, not to mention that he had done nothing to prevent Richard from literally riding away with me, so he deserved to worry about me a little. Besides, I couldn't find a phone in the room, which meant there was no way I could call him even if I knew where to reach him. Apart from the bed, there wasn't a single modern object; even the nightstands were gilded shrines. There were two beautiful chairs made of a dark, gold-edged wood, their backs carved into figures of eternity—a handsome man with one leg bent beneath him in a deep genuflection and a large ankh, symbol of life, hanging from one of his outstretched arms. He was smiling peacefully despite the fact that he was clutching a snake in each hand, the two serpents rising stiffly on either side of him and curving above him to rest their heads on the solar and lunar discs.

After I had finished taking an appreciative inventory of my room, I began waking up to my situation. I couldn't be sure exactly what Simon's feelings were for me. There was no doubt about the fact that we had shared intense pleasure down in an ancient burial chamber, but sexual chemistry did not a relationship make, and in three weeks I was supposedly flying back to the States. Then there was the disconcerting knowledge that it was probably Richard who had undressed me last night, and I suspected my exhausted body had innocently enjoyed his warm caresses as he pulled off my shirt, then my shorts and panties…

This was the thought I had been avoiding since I woke up. How could I possibly have slept through a man carrying me up to his room, laying me on a bed and taking off all my clothes? It was true I had had an exhausting day and night, but I had never been so tired that I could sleep through the experience of someone handling my body. No matter how tired and sleepy I was, or how gentle he had been, I should have felt what Richard was doing to me and been aware of what was happening. I had not behaved in such a relaxed and unconsciously trusting fashion with another person since I was a baby and my father rocked me in his arms before laying me in my cradle, and I could not even begin to understand how it had happened to me now as a grown woman with an almost complete stranger.

I got back into bed, taking refuge from my thoughts—which were both strangely disturbing and exciting—inside the sheets' protective cocoon. My brain felt sluggish as a caterpillar heavy with the imminent glory of its metamorphosis into a winged being no longer subject to earthly laws. Whether they wanted to or not, certain caterpillars were meant to transcend their nature, and I sensed something akin to this happening inside Mary Fallon. The change inside me had begun the other night in the heart of the Kahn el-Khalili bazaar when a robed man I recognized before I even saw his face entered a perfume shop. I couldn't put my finger on the feelings Richard had awoken in my heart, but they were there, and they were growing. The vivid sensual dream I had had when napping in a mastaba haunted me like a vivid butterfly's wings in which part of me sensed a pattern that kept eluding my rational waking mind. Nevertheless, as I lay in bed in that modern hotel room decorated with ancient art, I became aware of the subtle but somehow undeniable fact that a mysterious new sense was blooming inside me…

Or maybe it was just the opposite, maybe I was losing my senses, abandoning myself to wanton excess here in this exotic land, breaking out of my snowy New England cocoon and flitting from man to man just like a wild butterfly. Perhaps Simon was right and I was sexually out of control.

But I didn't want to think about the bastard who had not lifted a finger to help me last night. How could he let another man carry away a woman he had just made passionate love to in a tomb? His behavior was so incomprehensible that I flung the sheets off me angrily and got out of bed again.

I had to wrestle with two dancing girls to get the curtains open.

My breath caught. The city of Cairo stretched out below me as far as my eyes could see, the domed spires of mosques, delicate and colorful as the distended throats of male frogs showing off, lending a unique quality to the urban sprawl. And even through the glass I could hear the faint insect-like drone of millions of people and terrible traffic.

The much louder sound of the doorknob being turned made me jump. For an instant I considered draping a curtain around me, but whoever was on the other side of the door paused just long enough to give me time to run back to the bed, and pull the sheets up over my chest as I sat up against the headboard.

Sir Richard Gerald Ashley entered the room wearing a smile on his lips that tripped up my heartbeats because his mouth looked so much like the one on the handsome figure of eternity.

'Good morning, my lady,' he said cheerfully, as he casually seated himself on the edge of the bed facing me. He was wearing a black silk ankle-length robe tied at the waist. The portion of his chest I could see was covered with a sparse bush slightly darker than his long hair, which he had not bothered to pull back in a ponytail yet, and its soft flow behind and over his shoulders made them look even stronger and broader.

'Good morning,' I replied sulkily, trying to hide how much his appearance affected me by deliberately refusing to call him my lord.

His smile vanished as he reached for me abruptly and yanked the bed sheet out of my grasp. 'So beautiful,' he murmured, gazing intently at my naked breasts. 'Just as I always imagined them.'

I raised the sheet defiantly back up to my chin. 'It isn't a good morning.'

'And why is that, dear?'

'You know why.' I stared back at him helplessly.

'Because I spared you a cold and uncomfortable night in a tomb with a man who doesn't really care for you?'

'Whether he does or not,' the casual way he stabbed me with this statement seriously hurt, but I kept my voice under control, 'I shouldn't be here right now and you know it, so I'm not going to argue with you, Richard.'

'Excellent, then we can have breakfast. I imagine you must be starving.' He rose. 'There's a dress in the closet. You may put it on if you like, although I would be delighted if you didn't. I'll be back in a minute.' He left.

The dress he referred to was long and sleeveless and made of nearly transparent white linen. I had just finished slipping it on when he returned leaving the door open behind him so two native men could wheel in a table laden with silver serving platters. They kept their eyes lowered, careful not to look at me as they positioned the table, and then set the two chairs carved with figures of eternity at each end. There was a crisp flutter of robes as they hurried out of the room, closing the door very quietly behind them.

'Mary, if you please.' Richard pulled one of the chairs out for me, his smile deepening as he gazed at me with an appreciation that was at once relaxed and possessive.

Beneath his regard my nipples got so hard they threatened to poke through the linen, which revealed my rosy aureoles like flowers blooming beneath a soft morning mist. Resisting the urge to cross my arms over my breasts, which would have contributed to my Egyptian appearance, I seated myself with all the slow, unhurried dignity of an ancient queen. 'I normally have a light breakfast,' I informed him somewhat haughtily.

'But you're not living your normal life at the moment, are you,' he pointed out, taking his place across from me. He then uncovered the platters one by one, and watching him casually set the silver lids down on the carpet, I thought of a god creating a domed city. He had ordered a traditional breakfast, and it took all my self-control not to look too interested as my sense of smell was assaulted by the sinfully delicious aroma of eggs over-easy accompanied by thick slices of bacon, hash browns and French bread still hot from the oven. There were little porcelain containers of butter and strawberry preserves, a glass pitcher of orange juice, a pot of coffee, what looked like real heavy cream, and a bowl of sugar cubes I thought would make ideal building blocks for an ant pyramid.

'Eat up, Mary you don't have to pretend with me.'

'What do you mean by that?'

'I mean you don't have to feign a lady-like appetite. I respect all your hungers, and the more intense they are, the better.'

I couldn't help but smile at this remark as I began filling my plate with gusto, because the truth is, I was starving.

'Coffee?' he inquired.

'Yes, please. But I'm surprised you didn't order tea, being a Brit.'

'Personally, I prefer coffee.'

'I'm sorry, I should have known there wasn't anything trite about you, Richard.'

'Thank you, Mary, that's very perceptive of you.'

'You sound surprised.'

'Not at all, on the contrary, it's to be expected.'

I had to swallow a decadent mouthful of runny egg yolks before repeating, 'Expected? How can you expect anything from me, Richard? You don't even know me.'

'I know you very well, Mary.'

'But we've only met twice,' I reminded him, trying not to think about how well we had gotten to know each other the first time in the bazaar, but that had only been our bodies.

'Are you sure about that, Mary?' he asked quietly, gazing into my eyes over the gilded horizon of his porcelain coffee cup.

I looked away. 'You forgot to include a hairbrush in your stage props.' I deflected his profound question with a sarcastic reflection, and immediately hated myself for it. Yet part of me was overwhelmed by how fast everything was happening and how intense it was. 'Or is it that I don't need a hairbrush because you want me to shave my head like an ancient Egyptian noble woman and wear a wig?'

'You can have—'

'Aha! You were about to say "you can have anything you desire", weren't you, which would be very disappointingly trite of you, Richard.'

'No, I wasn't about to say that,' he replied placidly, and sipped his coffee before continuing. 'I was about to say that you can have only what it pleases me to give you.'

'Oh.' I picked up my knife and started buttering my bread to hide how much I liked the sound of that. 'Well then, my lord, can I please have a toothbrush and some dental floss as well?'

'Certainly, my lady, especially if they will encourage you to smile more. You really are incredibly beautiful when you smile.'

'Unfortunately, your actions don't usually prompt me to smile, Richard.'

'But they have made you cry out with pleasure,' he reminded me.

I looked away shyly.

'If my actions do not make you smile, Mary, it's because you take them the wrong way. There's more than one way to perceive the same thing, and then there's a level of perception above all others that captures the full picture.'

'Like ancient Egyptian wall paintings.' I looked at him again eagerly.

'Exactly. And what does that tell you?'

'It tells me that intuition, inspiration, is the key, maybe the only key, to a higher level of perception.'

'Very good.' He set his empty cup down. 'So, forget for a moment what your brain tells you about me as a result of certain circumstances involving an arrogant Egyptologist and other distracting, but ultimately irrelevant, factors. What does your much more inspired intuitive sense say about me, Mary?'

I wiped my lips with the cloth napkin, my eyes fixed on the inverted pyramid of chest visible between the nocturnal folds of his robe. 'It tells me...'

'Go on, love, I know how you feel, I just want to hear you say it...you have to say it in order to fully realize it and accept it.'

'But that's just it,' I braced myself by looking into his eyes,

'I don't know what I feel.'

'Yes, you do, you just don't know what to think about what you feel, but we always know how we feel.'

'That's true.' I glanced across the room at the lovely face of Akhenaten's daughter. Whatever had happened to her in life, her soft, secret smile afforded me a glimpse into a dimension of being transcending every possible concern. Her smile was the visible expression of the absolute faith she had in her eternal nature, which made her perfectly comfortable with her body since her true self did not share in its limitations only in its pleasures.

'I feel like I know you, Richard,' I stated matter-of-factly, meeting his intensely serious and beautiful eyes again. 'My body knows you somehow. I just want to fall into your arms every time I see you!'

* * * *

An hour later, after I had brushed my teeth, enjoyed a long hot shower, brushed my hair until it was sleek and straight as an ancient Egyptian queen's, dabbed lotus oil on the back of my wrists and applied genuine black kohl to my eyelids, I felt ready for anything.

The girl gazing back at me from the mirror could easily have lived five thousand years ago. She was beautiful and intelligent, deeply spiritual yet also intensely sensual, and she had equal rights with men under the law...well, to a certain extent anyway. Even though she could own property, an ancient Egyptian woman could also be property, meaning a man was only allowed one wife, but he could have as many concubines as he could afford. Nevertheless, it had taken centuries for women to be treated with the same respect they had enjoyed in the Egypt of the pharaohs.

I spent a little more time than was necessary in the small

bathroom's shrine to the pleasures of the flesh. I was avoiding the conversation Richard had interrupted after my passionate confession by stating that we would continue it later after I had refreshed myself. I knew whatever he said would constitute a devastating assault on all my psychological defenses, and despite how irresistibly drawn I was to him part of me was still compelled to mistrust him because Simon did. Carol's boss was a down-to-earth scientist who had worked hard to get where he was. Sir Richard Ashley had probably been born with a silver spoon in his mouth with which he fed himself whatever fantasies pleased him. The suspicion gnawed at me that maybe he believed his soul had been around since the beginning of time because being wealthy he had too much time on his hands and didn't know what to do with himself in the present. Yet I was assuming a lot; he could also have made his own fortune. Not to mention that when I looked into his eyes the last thing I saw was a spoiled and deluded man—what and who I saw actually took my breath away.

He was waiting for me when I finally opened the bathroom door, pausing shyly on the threshold. The beautiful objects before me might have belonged to me thousands of years ago, and I suffered a feeling akin to déjà vu but much more powerful. It was as if this room were a tomb I had never left and my life back in Boston was only a dream I was having while I waited; waited to come alive again as who I really was.

'Mary,' Richard whispered, and it hit me that Simon would be content with my mind and my body but that this man was after my very soul.

He looked enthroned where he sat in one of the 'eternity' chairs. He had placed it in front of the gently swaying dancing girls, and positioned the other chair facing his at a slight angle. I got the impression he was granting me an audience, and it suddenly made me acutely aware of my barefoot and unadorned state. I was dressed like a servant or a very poor man's concubine without shoes or jewelry, yet this humiliating fancy was wiped out of my mind by the look in his eyes as I approached him. My skin was still slightly damp from the shower, and judging from his expression the fine linen clung to my body in all the right places. My nipples were standing at attention again, and there was nothing I could do about the way the dress got caught between my thighs as I walked, making me vulnerably aware of my labia's soft, slick lips as I seated myself. I gripped the chair's gilded arms and planted my feet side-by-side on the carpet, very conscious of the fact that I would have looked just like an Egyptian statue if I had bothered to smile.

'Since you have forbidden me to express any trite sentiments, Mary, I will not tell you again how beautiful you look.' The sash holding his robe closed had loosened somewhat and exposed more of his chest. 'You are an exceedingly rare vintage, Mary. I saw it in your eyes the other night at the bazaar. I've learned to glimpse a woman's soul in her eyes the way I judge a wine by the depth of its color,' his gaze traveled slowly down my figure, 'and by its legs.' He smiled softly as he looked at my face again. 'Your soul has been around for a long time, Mary, aging through wooden coffins the way a fine wine matures in oak barrels, and I have no intention of letting your intoxicating power go to waste.'

'I like that metaphor,' I replied guardedly. 'Or is it an analogy?'

'It was a compliment.'

I couldn't resist returning his smile. 'And not at all trite,' I observed.

'How much do you know about ancient Egypt?' he asked me abruptly.

'How much do you know, Richard?'

'A great deal. Are you familiar with the term Winged Sandals?'

'Aren't they what Hermes wore? But that's Greek mythology.'

'Full of entertaining stories, but a pathetic excuse for a religion, don't you think?'

'Absolutely.'

'Winged Sandals, Mary, were worn by the priests and priestesses of Anubis, although not literally, of course, it was simply the title given to people who possessed the ability to leave their bodies.'

'Really?'

'Really.' He did a good job of imitating my blunt American exclamation. 'It referred specifically to their ability to dream true dreams.'

'What do you mean by true dreams?' I was interested against my will, and tempted to tell him about the dream I had had while taking a nap in a mastaba, but I stopped myself. I didn't want to make this too easy for him. I wanted him to do his best to convince me of something my heart was beginning to believe even while my brain kept struggling to put it into words.

'Let's just say the priests and priestesses of Anubis were able to meet with each other on another plane of existence, or another frequency of being, if you prefer more modern terms. It's incorrect, however, to call it an out-of-body experience, because in reality we possess several bodies composed of varying degrees and concentrations of energy. The soul is as much a body as our flesh-and-blood vehicle, only it is much more sensual and powerful, to put it as simply as possible.'

'So, what you're saying is that the priests and priestesses of Anubis met on another frequency of being where everything is as fluid as it is in our dreams?'

'With the difference, Mary, that they were able to control what happened to them there. It was often their duty to help people whose unconscious fears manifested in unsavory ways while they were asleep, a time when even the most unimaginative human being becomes an infinitely creative artist. Whether they remember their dreams or not, everyone has an active nightlife.'

'You mean these priests and priestesses would enter other people's dreams?'

'They would meet them there. Yes.'

'And meet each other there too?'

'Yes. Imagine the possibilities.'

I was silent for a moment as I did so.

The sash of his robe came undone as he brought his left ankle up to rest on his right knee, and even though knew I was staring shamelessly, I couldn't raise my eyes from what I could now see hanging between his thighs.

'Is something wrong, love?'

'For Christ's Sake, Richard, I can see...you know.' I looked over at Akhenaten's daughter to avoid staring at the rather insultingly relaxed part of his anatomy he was deliberately exposing to me.

'The hypocrisy of our so-called normal social relationships is ridiculous, Mary. People have to learn to be more honest with each other. Does it really bother you that you can see my penis?'

'Yes, it does.' I stared indignantly into his eyes.

'Why?'

'Because!'

'That's not an answer.'

'Because it's not polite, Richard.'

'And why is that?'

'Oh, stop it, you know perfectly well it's not acceptable normal behavior.'

'I rarely find normal behavior acceptable in any sense.'

'Granted, but perfect honesty is a dangerous policy, Richard. We can't just do or say whatever we please if it's going to hurt someone else.'

'And how am I hurting you by just sitting here? Is there something about the male sexual organs you find offensive?' Leaning back in his 'throne' he uncrossed his legs and stretched them out before him. The robe got caught between them and almost fully revealed one of his strong thighs.

'It's not right,' I argued tightly, even though his beautifully large and shapely organ was no longer visible.

'You didn't answer my question.'

'No, there's nothing about the male sexual organs I find offensive.'

'Then is it my penis in particular that makes you uncomfortable, or that you didn't like the look of for some reason?'

'Of course not, it's beautiful...I mean...'

He gave me that breathtaking smile of his again. 'I'm actually doing you an honor by letting you see my most private parts, Mary. I want you to see them.' He lowered his voice. 'I want to feel your eyes caressing me. Our sexuality is a perfectly natural—'

'Now that's trite.'

He frowned slightly. 'Nothing could be more trite than Simon's behavior last night. He got what he wanted, and then...' He shrugged. There was no need for him to say more. 'First of all,' he went on after what for me was a painfully awkward moment, 'you should know that what you and your friends were doing in Ti's mastaba is illegal. I don't know who Simon had to bribe to get permission, but obviously camping out in a national treasure is against the law. Smoke from the fire you built in the courtyard can damage the paintings, and so on. Simon must be friendly with some rather corrupt members of the Antiquities Department to have gotten away with it. He obviously wanted to impress you. Either that or he has a kinky streak and prefers cold crypts to comfortable hotel rooms—No, don't say anything yet, please let me finish first. God knows I have nothing against kinky streaks, but I don't think one should be allowed to risk damaging priceless works of art just to indulge in them. Secondly, I didn't threaten anyone with a gun. Your friend observed one on my person and made unwarranted assumptions that I was going to use it to intimidate either Simon or Steve into revealing the location of the mastaba. Thirdly, I told you I had no intention of stealing the photograph, and I meant it. However, you denied me the chance to keep my word by burning it first. There, I trust you're a little less confused now about what happened. I wanted to give you the chance to correct the mistake I feel you're making by becoming involved with a man whose methods and morals are extremely questionable. I also wished to get to know you better, and I'm sorry if I misread your feelings last night. I sensed it was your desire to come with me. You're free to leave at anytime if that's what you wish.'

'It's not what I wish,' I murmured, staring down at my lap.

'I know it's not,' he said gently. 'But I get the feeling you need more time to think about things. I have some business to take care of. I can only hope you'll still be here when I get back, Mary. I'm sure you will be.'

* * * *

Richard left me alone again to ponder his words. It was wise of him, for the more I thought about what he had said, the more the handsome Egyptologist shrank in my esteem. I assumed I was in a suite at the Mina House hotel where my host had done a little redecorating with reproductions of ancient Egyptian pieces worth a small fortune in themselves. His Victorian ancestors had probably started an illegal collection of Egyptian antiquities.

Simon might have corrupt connections, but Richard had enough money to be emotionally corrupt in every sense.

Lying despondently across the bed, I began to understand what it felt like to be a royal mummy in her lovely tomb. I couldn't have been more paralyzed if I had been bound from head to toe in resin-dipped strips of cloth.

Most of me longed to stay with Richard and explore the mystical connection he was obviously implying we had, but another part of me wanted to return to Simon and our very real promising relationship. My tired muscles were also appreciating just relaxing for a while. Despite the recurring questions that seemed to be all the royal embalmers had left of my brain—Does Simon really care about me? Can I trust Richard even though he's decadently rich and I know nothing about him?—I dozed off.

I must have slept for a long time. When I woke, I sensed the day drawing to a close sooner than I had expected as the room swiftly darkened.

I discovered only the bathroom was wired up to the twenty-first century when I got up and tried to find a light switch, which explained the oil in the alabaster lamp and the black box of matches I discovered lying behind it. I couldn't find a papyrus with instructions on how to light it, but it turned out I didn't need one. The matches were long and the wicks floating in the dark oil sparked eagerly to life. The princess's smile also came hauntingly to life in the flickering illumination, her alabaster skin pale as a ghost's. The lotus lamp shone more and more beautifully as the shadows deepened around it, and gazing at it, I began seeing the lamp as a symbol of my own stubbornly positive heart surrounded by all the doubts and fears inevitably cast by the troubled world in which I lived.

Who did Richard think he was anyway? If I wanted to make a

mistake by getting involved with Simon—and so far it had been quite a stimulating error—it was my own damn business. Sir Ashley wasn't my father, and he couldn't justify his interference in my personal life by saying he was my friend, either. We had only met twice, for Christ's sake!

Seated on the edge of the bed, I glanced down at my hands clenched tightly in my lap, and suddenly I knew beyond a shadow of a doubt that I was somewhere else. I was someone else as for a subliminal instant the electrical synapses in my brain rearranged themselves and my pulse flew out of the branches of Mary Fallon's veins before fluttering back down into a whole other self.

My back straightened into the regal spine of a woman who knows time is circular because her own blood cells are the nature of time itself, and when the bedroom door opened suddenly, I rose and ran joyfully into the arms of the man who entered the room.

'Mary!' he whispered. 'I knew you would feel it, I knew it.' He stroked my hair. 'My beautiful one.'

His caress made my brain feel like a stone carried away on feelings too deep for words. It was a long moment before I reluctantly remembered that I was clinging to a rich Englishman, not an ancient priest of Anubis, and my arms slipped sadly from around him. I saw that his broad shoulders were set off by a short-sleeved white shirt, his black pants merged with the darkness, and his belt buckle glinted like fangs as he drew me towards the bed. 'How do you feel?' he asked gently.

'Stunned...I mean, I've had déjà vu before, but that was... my God!'

'Yes, I know, it's me, Nefermun,' he whispered, his breath warm against my temple, 'don't you feel it?'

'Yes.'

His strong arm around my shoulders inexorable as the law of

gravity, I sat down on the edge of the bed again. He stood facing me, and I watched in a contented trance as he unbuckled his belt and unzipped his pants.

'These are a lot harder to get out of than a linen loincloth,' he remarked, and I heard myself laugh quietly with him. 'Remember your dream, Mary?'

I looked up at his face, and the firm shadows of his features softly carved by the lotus lamp seemed to fill all the empty spaces inside me.

'Yes, I remember,' I said, and reached up with both hands so he could cradle the sacred gift of his penis in my cupped palms as he pulled it out of his pants. He was only partially erect, which gave me a chance to savor the warm tenderness of his smooth, circumcised skin over the unyielding strength of his stiffening length. Remembering the drop of semen that had glistened from the rift in his head and reflected the rising stars in my dream, I grasped the base of his shaft boldly with one hand, relishing how rigid it already was in my grasp. The elastic of his underwear was shoving his balls directly up beneath his cock, and I lifted it up out of my way to lick the delicate fullness of his scrotum, noticing with appreciation that it was shaved. I heard both surprise and pleasure in his moan, and deeply gratified by the sound, I immediately slid his erection into my mouth, sucking on his head for a second to moisten my lips and make it easier to slip their tight ring down his full length.

'Oh Mary,' he whispered.

I sensed him deliberately resist the urge to take hold of my head with his hands. Instead he kept his arms relaxed at his sides as his penis grew even harder against my soft tongue. I remembered my dream and the way I had caressed my lover's head with the back of my throat, a skill no man had inspired me to develop in this life until now, for no other cock had ever tasted so good to me. The flavor of his semen was just right, as though it had been made especially for my tongue and taste buds. So many times in the past the flavor of a man's bodily juices had deterred me from wanting to please him this way for too long, but Richard's pre-cum was the mysterious foam on the intoxicating pleasure I took in swallowing his erection whole over and over again, letting him ride my face as my head bobbed up and down in the room's deep shadows. Every time the bulbous tip of his rigid shaft sank down towards my virgin neck, the satisfaction I experienced in burying all of him inside me was much greater than the slight discomfort.

'Oh yes, you do remember, Mary.' His voice was as soft as his cock was hard.

I moaned in disappointment as he stepped back, sliding out of my devoted mouth. He shoved his pants and underwear down his legs, then just stood there looking at me.

Without even thinking, I sank to my knees before him, pulling off the black leather sandals he was wearing before tugging his pants all the way off him. They were heavy with his belt. I didn't just toss them aside; I laid them carefully down beside his sandals. Even though they were not a ritually blessed loincloth, they still belonged to him and therefore deserved my respect as symbols of the flesh his soul had chosen to wear in this world. Then, I stood before him and caressed the white shirt up his chest, savoring the complimentary contrasts of his tender flesh and the hard muscles beneath it. His skin was warm beneath the crisp coolness of his chest hair, which was just enough to give him all the exciting feel of a man without interfering with my kiss as I planted my mouth between the gentle swell of his pecs.

I felt his heart pulse beneath my lips, then he finished the job of pulling his shirt up over his head. Before he could toss it away,

I took it from him and spread it neatly over his pants. He was completely naked now, and I seated myself on the edge of the bed again to take him in. As with his features, the proportions of his body struck a chord of perfection deep inside me. His broad shoulders and chest tapered down to an ideally slender waist and hips supported by strong, long legs that were just the right pedestal for the crowning glory of his fully erect cock.

'You're so beautiful,' I told him.

'Now it's your turn to take off your dress and show yourself to me, Mary.'

I obeyed him gladly, enjoying the caress of the delicate material as I pulled it up over my head. I draped it beside his clothes on the floor, and then stood at once proudly and shyly before him. He had already seen my naked sex close up at the bazaar, but this was the first time I felt the warm touch of his eyes on my breasts, and all the rest of me.

'You are even more beautiful,' he said. 'Lie back across the bed, my love.'

My love...the words seemed to give me a delicious shove across the firm mattress and make it easy for me to get comfortable against the pillows. He joined me on the bed by crawling onto it on all fours like a sleek, powerful animal; a jackal with a long black snout and sharp, gilded ears—

—I cry out in terror, and then whimper in intensely confused relief when instead of sharp teeth sinking into my skin I see a man's ringed hands gently grasp my ankles and spread my legs. It is a Priest of Anubis kneeling between my thighs, and his erection promises me as much pleasure as I can bear. Then I look up past his broad shoulders and see his shaved skull gleaming in the lamplight.

'E'Ahmose!' I sigh.

'Nefermun.'

He spreads his body over mine without letting our skins touch, the strong columns of his arms rising on either side of my breasts as he gazes down at my face.

I grasp his cock like a dagger in my hand and arch my back, lifting my hips off the bed, urgently begging him to stab me with his full, rending length.

'No,' he says firmly.

I let go of his beautiful rod knowing I have done wrong, that it is not my place to force his entry into my achingly empty passage. He will determine the moment and the pace of the penetration knowing that the longer he makes me wait the more receptively open I become to him and all his desires. So I distract myself by caressing his shoulders and breathing in the scent of his warm skin, a stimulating combination of maleness and the oils he uses to shave, as well as to anoint his skin when serving the god in the sacred heart of the temple only he is allowed to enter. And like the divine altar, the space between my legs is always mysteriously burning for him, especially when he is inside me and stoking my need for him almost unbearably.

'Oh yes,' I breathe, 'thank you, my lord!' as he finally grants the moist lips of my opening the promising kiss of his head. But then he seems content to remain planted there, enjoying the desperately juicing embrace of the entrance to my flesh.

'Oh E'Ahmose, you are being very cruel tonight.'

I fling my arms up over my head so as not to grasp the firm cheeks of his ass and push his fleshly column down to the very foundations of my being.

'And you are enjoying it, my love,' he lets me have a teasing bit more of his erection, 'as you enjoy everything I do to you.'

'Please, my lord,' I beg, writhing my hips against the leopard-skin and subjecting myself to the sweet torture of his rampant cock stuffing the mouth of my hole and stirring up my lust for his full length even more.

'Stop that, Nefermun,' he chides me sternly, but even in the dark chamber I can see the smile in his eyes, 'or I shall make you wait until the next full moon to feel the ray of my love inside you.'

'I can only hope my lord will not be so cruel to his devoted consort and priestess.'

'Your hopes and dreams are as dear to my heart, Nefermun, as the silent voice of the god, so I will give you what you want now, and ask only that you savor the blessing of our union without moving, so that you can fully experience your innermost self merging with mine on every level.'

'Yes, my lord,' I whisper, but then almost forget my promise when he begins sinking inside me and the longed for pleasure scatters my thoughts like so many grains of wheat drifting away on an ever-deepening fulfillment.

'Open your eyes, Nefermun and look into mine.'

I obey him, and the ecstasy becomes even more profoundly intense when his penetrating stare merges with the experience of his erection slowly stabbing me. When he is fully submerged between my thighs, he bends his arms and opens his mouth over mine, thrusting his tongue between my lips in time with his body beginning to beat against me, so that it is all I can do to consciously observe the overwhelming sensation of our becoming one with each other.

I wrap my arms around his chest and pull him down on top of me, loving the powerful weight of his body and the feel of his warm, tender skin over the implacable heart of his manhood pumping between my legs.

I gasp when the feel of long hair flowing down his back surprises me.

'Don't speak!' His whisper is timeless as the wind echoing through the ages in the spiraling shell of my ear.

I don't feel the need to understand what is happening. His driving energy is all I care about as my awareness of everything becomes almost wholly concentrated in my sex. My thoughts are replaced by the sensation of my vaginal muscles contracting and expanding around him in the most intimate caress possible, enabling me to thoroughly experience the full length and breadth of his cock breaching my tight yet welcomingly wet depths. And every time I tighten my inner muscles the exercise tugs on my clitoris, sensitizing it to the rhythmic friction of his thrusts opening me up. His erection just barely brushes my glowing seed as he digs deep and hard into my cleft, determined to wrest the earth-shattering bloom of a mutual climax from our flesh. I can feel my body beginning an ascent that is exactly the same even though every time I close and open my eyes I see a different room around us and feel a different surface beneath us.

He pulls out of me abruptly. 'Turn around,' he commands.

Without hesitation I roll over on the soft skin and gladly offer this virile priest the smoldering shrine of my pussy from behind. Kneeling and spreading my legs, I arch my back as deeply as possible, thrusting my ass up into his hands so he can brace himself by clutching my soft cheeks as he plunges back inside me. But when I bury my face in the animal skin, breathlessly accepting his aggressive thrusts, it is Richard's voice I hear behind me, 'Oh yes, Mary…yes…' for in this position his cock slides effortlessly into my slick passage all the way down to his balls. Long hair or a smoothly shaved skull, a thin mouth or full lips, it doesn't matter. The only thing that matters is how good it feels as he channels all his strength into possessing me, until his erection finds the divine core of ecstasy buried deep in our flesh by the grace of the gods and that only he has the power to access for both of us. 'Come with me!' he orders.

I reach down beneath me, find the swollen bud of my clitoris and obey him instantly, my cries of pleasure harmonizing with his groans as his cock pulses deep between my thighs, suffusing my belly with the uniquely fulfilling warmth of his cum.

He remained buried inside me for a long moment after the wave of our pleasure ebbed, leaving us breathing hard on the soft shore of the bed, on which the sensual animal skin had been replaced by sterile white sheets. The great loss I experienced as he finally pulled out was assuaged by the knowledge that I would feel him inside me again. I knew now that we had been meant to come together like this for longer than I could literally remember, and I could only hope we would be able to continue feeling each other like this forever.

'Come here,' he said tenderly.

I sat up, and found myself falling languidly and comfortably into his arms as he lay back against the pillows, cradling my head comfortably on his shoulder. 'Tell me what you just felt, Mary, and what you saw.'

'It was only my imagination, I'm sure,' I mumbled, loving the sensation of his warm, strong body lying pressed against mine. 'I have a very vivid imagination!'

'I'm sure you do, but it wasn't your imagination this time.' He used the firm but gentle tone of an adult addressing an uncertain child. 'Now tell me what you believe you only imagined.'

'I saw you, and a man who wasn't you, and yet it was you, he just didn't look like you do now.' I knew my grammar was hopelessly sloppy, but that seemed irrelevant in light of what I was trying to describe. 'His head was shaved and he was a priest, a priest of Anubis because I saw a jackal…'

'Yes,' he whispered, 'a wearer of the Winged Sandals.' Sliding lower on the bed, he turned on his side to face me, his arms coming around me as his eyes looked straight into mine. Tiny golden lotus blossoms floated in his irises, reflecting the alabaster lamp. 'And in the past he found you the same way I found you now.'

'And how did you find me now?' I asked softly, knowing the answer but scarcely believing it.

'I found you through dreams, my love.'

'You mean you're psychic?'

'I am when I'm dreaming. We all are, we just don't remember it, usually.'

The golden lotuses floating in his dark stare affected my blood like moons stirring up my desires again in a way I had thought possible only in dreams. 'Richard…' There was so much I wanted to ask him I found I couldn't put a single question into words.

'Yes?'

'Do you love me?'

'You know I do,' he planted his lips against mine, 'Nefer-marymun.'

CHAPTER SIX

I helped my priest of Anubis put his clothes back on as best I could. He had to handle his tight black pants, but I found the ritual of assisting him in donning his clothes again strangely pleasurable and relaxing. The act helped create a bridge between the devastating pleasure we had just experienced together, and whatever was to come next. I was at once relieved and slightly disappointed that the only thing he had planned for the moment was dinner. After he watched me slip back into my dress, he took my hand and led me out of the tomb-like room into his own adjoining suite. The lotus lamp we left burning behind us was lovely, but there's nothing like electricity to steady the nerves, and my mystically shadowed brain needed all the light it could get.

'Are we eating downstairs in the dining room?' I ventured to ask, but since he had not provided me with a less revealing garment, I rather doubted it.

'A dining room crowded with tourists is hardly the place to talk about the real Egypt, Mary.'

This man had a way of saying 'no' I could only admire. 'I'm all ears,' I declared, which was not true, for he had just made me intensely aware of other more intimate parts of my body. Now that I had seen and felt him naked, he looked better to me than ever, and I watched him hungrily as he seated himself in a delicate chair resembling a sugary confection, that amazingly enough supported his considerable muscular weight. He picked up the white gilded receiver of a French phone and proceeded ordering dinner from room service in as much detail as a pharaoh commanding a legion of cooks, his black pants such a stunning contrast to the room's airy blue-and-white décor that I felt slightly disoriented. It was as though the door between our two bedrooms was a portal in time through which we had traveled centuries in the second it took us to cross the threshold from ancient Egypt to Edwardian England.

I leaned back against the dresser, growing increasingly light-headed. Looking around the room, I suffered the disconcerting impression that nothing in it was actually solid. Everything appeared to be really there, edges were sharp and focused, but somehow I knew it was only because I was aware of them. When I looked away the blue-and-white tones would dissolve into formless waves of energy again. I had read somewhere that electrons act as particles when they're being observed, but at all other times they behave like waves.

'Dilwaatee minfadlak.' Richard slammed the receiver down with satisfaction.

I nearly jumped out of my present skin.

He looked over at me tenderly. 'Come here.' He patted his dark lap. 'Why are you so far away? We have a lot to talk about.'

That was the understatement of centuries. I was bound to him like a patient to a doctor since only he could possibly explain to me what had just happened between us. 'I would prefer to stand for the moment, thank you,' I said. 'My head feels like it's about to disconnect from my shoulders and fly away like a Ba bird.'

He laughed. 'You're quite a lovely bird.'

'I wasn't referring to British slang.'

'I know that,' he said patiently. 'You were referring to the fact that Egyptians often depicted the soul as a bird with a human head.'

'I'm sorry, of course I knew you knew that, I just feel very weird...I don't feel like myself.'

'No pun intended?' He sounded serious, but his eyes were smiling.

I returned the smile with my lips, but my confusion was growing exponentially and inevitably making me anxious.

'Please, my love, come here.' He patted his thighs again with both hands, his brows furrowing slightly as if he couldn't possibly think of any reason why I would refuse.

Before I knew it, I found myself perched on his firm thighs with my wrists resting on his strong shoulders as I held on to the excitingly strong yet tender column of his neck. 'What did you mean when you said you found me through dreams, Richard? Is that how you knew I'd be in the bazaar the other night?' I met his earnest stare with my own, once again admiring the golden rim around his pupils that made me think of sunflowers growing in the heart of his irises, which were that inscrutably beautiful color between slate-gray and the deepest green possible.

'I thought you remembered your dreams, Mary.'

'Yes, but up until recently, they've only been dreams that had nothing to do with my real life.'

He shifted my weight on his lap, not because I was too heavy for him but to hold me even closer. 'Until recently?' he prompted, his expression neutral, but I could sense how much he wanted to hear what I was about to say.

'Until I arrived in Egypt. But I think you knew that.'

'I think I did, I just didn't know whether you remembered. I hoped you did.'

'Richard…' I said weakly, because his hand slowly caressing the side of my thigh was making it difficult for me to concentrate.

'Yes, my love?'

'Was that you?' His rhythmic caress was hypnotizing me. 'Was that you in the dream I had in the mastaba?'

'You mean the dream in which you were lying on a leopard-skin couch with your favorite cat in a room open to a garden on both sides and I came to you?'

'Silhouetted against the sunset…'

'Yes, I suppose I was, since I came in from the garden.'

I asked breathlessly, 'And what did I call you?'

His mouth tilted subtly up at both ends, giving his smile the enigmatic cast of an ancient statue. 'You called me E'Ahmose, which means Born of the Moon. You named your cat after me, my beloved Nefermun.'

I planted my lips against his, the only possible response to undeniable proof that he had entered the profoundly intimate space of my dreams with the same effortless power that his erection penetrated my flesh. His tongue thrust civilly but demandingly into my mouth, and I felt both of us pouring our souls into the kiss through the strong, supple, sensitive and agile muscle buried beneath our lips. So many things were expressed without words, swiftly and magically, while at the same time so many urgent, passionate questions were asked in this kiss, that I finally let go of the confused shipwreck of my rational thoughts and surrendered to the overwhelming knowledge I was in love with this man. I was drowning in him, utterly losing myself as I let go of the fear that what I felt between us wasn't real but only a deluded desire to believe in true love and that it lasts forever.

I surfaced reluctantly from our deep and complex kiss. 'Do you expect me to believe all this?' I gasped. 'How did you even know I was in Egypt? Are you playing with me, Richard?'

'Let's see, which question would you like me to answer first? I'll start with the last one, which is a clear indication that Mary Fallon is still fighting Nefermun. I am not playing with you, and you know it. A dream told me you were in Egypt. I didn't know what your name was, or exactly when you would be arriving, or even what you actually looked like, but I knew you were coming to Egypt. You told me so yourself. And after that it was pure choreography that helped bring us together, all with the first step of Simon's wild inspiration to stash the photograph in your luggage. Obviously he was being influenced by forces beyond his control that meant for us to come together again.'

'What do you mean I told you I was coming to Egypt? How could I have told you if I didn't even know you?'

'Our souls have met countless times before in dreams. I know you don't remember, but you did tell me, or rather, Nefermun did.'

'But my name is Mary.'

'I'm sure you've read Shakespeare.'

'"What's in a name"?'

'Actually, more than you realize,' he blithely contradicted himself. 'You need to answer to Nefermun again to truly be yourself, Mary.'

Even though it made me feel strangely off balance again to do so, I let go of his neck and got up off his lap. 'Nefermun,' I echoed, tasting the syllables on my tongue and trying not to like them so much. 'She's who you're in love with, not me.'

'You're being ridiculous.'

A blend of anger, impatience and disappointment darkened his expression for a moment that made me feel foolish indeed, for this was not the sort of reaction I wanted to inspire in him. There was a perversely stubborn and suspicious streak in me, bred by a number of previous disappointing relationships with men that had nothing to do with how I really felt about love, or about this man in particular. 'That was not Nefermun- talking, was it?' I asked by way of apology.

'No,' he stood up, 'it wasn't.' He pulled me into his arms and let me feel the hard bulge between his thighs pressing into my soft belly as he spoke. 'The way I see on the other side is more complete than my waking consciousness, Mary, and yet it's also not quite so defined, or definite, I don't know how else to express it. It'll take time to try and describe it to you. But for now, just answer me this. Do you normally let total strangers kiss you,' he was referring to our meeting in the bazaar, 'and go down on you?'

'Of course not! But nothing that's happened to me since I arrived in Egypt has been normal.'

'Thank the gods for that, hmm?'

He was teasing me, but his supernatural interpretation of the chemistry between us was too serious for me to respond lightheartedly. 'How can I believe this, Richard?' I begged to know. 'How can I really believe my dreams aren't just my imagination, and that it's not just a coincidence you had a similar dream? How do I know— I didn't want to ask this, but I had to. 'How do I know I didn't mutter in my sleep last night when you carried me up here?'

He let go of me. 'Are you accusing me of lying to you?'

His mouth was so hard I suddenly understood the meaning of pharaoh's crook and flail—I had just been in the wonderful crook of his embrace, now his frown felt like a flail applied directly to the haunting muscle of my heart. 'No,' I said meekly.

'That's what you implied, that I learned the details of the dream you had in the mastaba from your sleepy mutterings last night and used them to seduce you into believing we had dreamed together.'

I was appalled, because that was exactly what my statement had implied, and yet I didn't really believe that about him at all. 'Perhaps,' I looked earnestly up into his eyes, 'I should make more of an effort to behave like Nefermun for a change. Whether or not I really am her reincarnation is another matter altogether. The point is she's much more like I imagine myself being. I'm beginning to realize there are aspects of Mary Fallon that I don't really like that I was never really aware of before and that I should stop indulging and identifying with. Nefermun feels a lot wiser, and a lot less stressed out. Um, does that make any sense?'

He drew me into his arms again and held me close, laying my cheek against his chest and resting his hand on my head. 'It makes perfect sense, Nefermun. And remember, the only proof you need of anything is how you feel deep down in the very heart of your soul, forget what your rational mind or the rest of the world tell you that you should feel.'

'Yes!' I sighed.

'Now stop thinking about it,' he urged gently, 'and let's just relax together for a while and enjoy the lovely dinner I've ordered for us. I think you'll appreciate the wine I've selected to go with it.' He let go of me and turned towards a door I assumed led out into the corridor.

Right on cue, there was a polite knock. I hadn't heard a sound outside in the hall. Maybe his hearing was keener than mine, or maybe...I'd never actually known a person who possessed any kind of extra-sensory perception, and I couldn't help wondering how it worked. What was his range, so to speak? And more importantly, how was it possible for me to resist a man who could sense what I was thinking and play my feelings like an instrument?

He went to open the door, and two native men promptly wheeled in a couple of tables. Richard spoke to them in Arabic, and I gathered something he had ordered was missing. A second later I discovered what it was when another man literally ran into the room cradling a black bucket of ice containing a bottle of white wine. He set down his precious cargo on one of the tables, and I swear it was not my imagination that he winked at me before he left because I thought I recognized him. The other two waiters hung around for a moment while Richard made sure everything he had ordered had been prepared to his specifications, then they too left the room without ever once looking at me. I might have been a ghost for all the attention they paid me.

My emotions were suddenly a sickeningly mixed brew. Battling with the elation the appearance of one of Simon's native assistants naturally aroused in me was annoyance. I had been bottled up in a room all day long like a genie in her bottle, yet at the moment I had no desire to leave and return to my insultingly cool-headed Egyptologist. I couldn't be sure, but I suspected he was spying on me through his hired hand, making sure I was all right, which I suppose I should have found flattering, but instead it only made me more anxious than I already was. I did not doubt the bottle Richard had ordered was expensive, and now a wild thought ruined how eagerly I had been anticipating a glass of wine. I wasn't sure it was safe to drink. What if Simon actually believed Richard was keeping me here against my will and his smiling lackey had slipped something in the wine that would render my host sleepy enough to let me to get away? It was a totally crazy idea, but then again I was in Egypt, where anything seemed to be possible, and the fact was, the bottle had already been opened. (I wasn't thinking straight enough to consider the fact that if the wine had indeed been spiked with something that it would have the same effect on me, hence defeating Simon's purposes, whatever they might be.)

'Come, Mary,' Richard said, smiling over at me from beside the feast awaiting us.

'It looks wonderful,' I declared even though nothing was visible except the covered silver serving platters like the domed rooftops of a city famous for its culinary arts. I didn't know what to do. The bottle was already in his hand. 'Does the hotel usually open your wine bottles for you?' I asked. 'I mean, shouldn't they bring it up to your room sealed, then open it and let you taste and approve the vintage?' I seated myself watching him pour a small amount of the wine into his glass.

'That would be the proper procedure,' he agreed. 'But I'm sure it's fine.'

I held my breath as he took a sip. Surely his cultivated palate would detect a foreign substance?

'Mm, very nice...I'd like to propose a toast.' Apparently satisfied with the quality of the vintage, he filled both our glasses. 'To us,' he intoned soberly, 'and to every other us we've ever been and ever will be.' He raised his glass and waited for me to follow suit.

I did so, but the instant the crystal rim touched his lips, I leaned over the table and passionately knocked the glass out of his hand.

* * * *

After dinner, Richard rewarded me for my loyalty with heavy golden bracelets inlaid with lapis-lazuli. He slipped them onto my arms, and for a moment they felt a little too much like shackles I had perversely chosen over freedom, but only for a moment.

However, my gesture had not pleased him at first since he had believed it my rude response to his romantic toast, and the look in his eyes after I knocked the glass out of his hand is one I prefer to forget. When I quickly and breathlessly explained to him there was a chance the wine was drugged, he laughed and kissed me on my highly imaginative forehead. 'I don't think so, love,' he assured me. 'Simon is simply making sure you're here with me and that you're all right. It's common knowledge I have a Suite in the Mina House.'

When he was finished with me, I stood motionless as a mannequin displaying a style that was popular millenniums ago and which is still fashionable with women whenever they want to dress up dramatically and exotically. The full-length mirror he positioned me in front of made it quite clear that I made a beautiful Egyptian princess. An exquisite copy of a belt I recognized from a book on Middle Kingdom jewelry made of tiny golden fish linked together swam around my hips, and draped over my chest and shoulders was an amazingly light collar composed of red-and-blue faience beads. I held my breath as my host suddenly genuflected before me, but it was only to slip gilded sandals on my feet that matched the thick bracelets on my arms. Then standing behind me again, he gently placed a golden filigree crown on my head carved in the form of a delicate vine decorated with tiny carnelian flowers.

'Are we going to a costume party?' I heard myself ask dryly as I pretended not to be impressed with Nefermun's beauty. I knew it was my body, Mary Fallon's body, reflected in the glass, but it was an ancient soul I glimpsed staring back at me with a depth of confidence and a profound sensual ease I did not possess in this life except in my fantasies.

'Yes, as a matter-of-fact we are.' Richard stood with his hands lightly gripping my bare upper arms and his eyes holding mine in the mirror. 'A private party.' His white shirt could have been made of the finest linen, and his long dark hair resting on his broad shoulders before flowing down his back was certainly Egyptian enough.

I managed to keep my voice steady. 'This is just a little strange, Richard.'

'I sense Mary Fallon and Nefermun at each other's throats, and Mary is afraid of losing a part of herself in awakening another, but there's no need to be afraid, trust me.'

I clung to his voice, which was both infinitely soft and firm, listening to what he had to say for all I was worth, whoever I was.

'Nefermun is an ancient priestess. Mary Fallon's personality was shaped by the twentieth century, and so she believes her rational mind is to be worshipped above all her other feelings and perceptions. But pure reason is a limited, fear-ridden deity, my love, and I know your heart is pure and powerful enough to see past the pragmatic, money-worshipping culture into which you happened to be born this time around. Do you understand what I'm saying to you, Nefer-marymun?'

'Yes!' I whispered fervently. 'You make complete sense to me, Richard. Your mystical beliefs strike me as totally logical.'

'That's because they are, logic of a higher order. Do you like your new name, Nefer-marymun?'

'Yes, it feels right.'

'Mm...' He pressed his hard-on against me, cradling it in the small of my back. 'You feel right, just right.' He turned me to face him abruptly, his possessive grip tightening on my arms. 'Nefer-marymun,' he whispered.

'E-Ahmose.'

I savored the ancient name on my modern tongue and liked how sweet and familiar it tasted. Our breaths wrestled together for a moment before his lips pinned mine down and slowly parted, teasing me with the promise of his tongue and another deep, spiraling kiss. Then I was distracted from our silent conversation by the feel of his hand lifting my dress up in front, and slipping between my legs. I moaned into his mouth as he cradled my soft, sleek pussy in his hard palm, feeling my naked sex lips bloom eagerly against the pressure of his skin. I sincerely hoped that what lay in his future was touching me like this again and again forever. I cried out softly as he thrust his index finger into the moist heart of my vulva while at the same time gently crushing my clitoris beneath his thumb. The summit of my mound was caught in the vice of his grip. The pleasure was almost painfully intense as his hard thumb rubbed up and down against my clit, his finger penetrating me rhythmically.

'Oh God, stop,' I begged.

'Why?' he whispered against my cheek. 'Doesn't it feel good?'

'Oh yes, too good…'

He laughed. 'How can anything feel too good, Nefer-marymun?'

'I don't know!' I wrapped my arms around his neck and clung to him. The sharp ecstasy cutting up through my pelvis made me feel as though he was lifting me off the floor in the devastatingly powerful cradle of his thumb and forefinger.

'I want you to come for me again, my love. Soon you'll learn to come without touching yourself,' he promised. 'The more times we come together and you let go of all your tensions, the more sensitive your clitoris will grow until it learns to respond to the subtle friction of my cock as much as to the slightest touch.'

'Oh God,' I groaned, loving what he was saying as much as what he was doing, though I still felt it was too much pleasure too fast for my body to handle. Then I let out a small scream when the door leading out into the hall crashed against the wall as someone kicked it open.

Simon's man cut a menacing figure in a long black robe, and there was something threateningly sinister about the white crescent of teeth he flashed Richard.

E'Ahmose, Priest of Anubis, did not react as I expected him to by pulling his hand out from between my legs and letting my dress fall around my ankles. Instead he behaved as though we had not even been interrupted.

'Richard,' I gasped, 'there's a man—'

'You're going to come for me, Mary,' he said calmly.

I glanced over at the intruder, whose initial defiant grin was dimming to a look of disbelief as he eyed my naked thighs and Richard's hand working between them.

I had never been in such a position before, and something strange was happening inside me. I realized with a shock that it was seriously turning me on to be skillfully fondled by one man while another man watched. Our observer's stare penetrated me at the very heart of the pleasure I was feeling from Richard's relentless caress. My defenses collapsed around me. Overwhelmed by how strangely aroused I grew when we were no longer alone, I came.

'Mm, yes, that's it,' Richard purred in my ear as I climaxed in his hand, burying my face in his neck so as not to witness my own wanton behavior.

It was a loss when he pulled his hand out from between my legs. As he took a decisive step back, my arms slid reluctantly from around him.

His eyes held mine as he slipped his glistening index finger between his lips and sucked off my juices before facing the man standing motionless in the doorway, as if paralyzed by what he had just witnessed. Richard crossed his arms over his chest and regarded our dumbfounded audience with an expression that appeared passive, but the contained power I sensed in his absolute control thrilled me.

'It appears Simon is not man enough to come for you himself, Mary,' he observed, his voice ominously civil. 'But now his servant has, I think, a very meaningful message to deliver to his master.'

Suddenly the Egyptian seemed to fly into the room in his billowing black robes like a huge raven cawing angrily in Arabic.

I had no idea what the man was saying. Richard's voice captured all my attention as he drew me into the safe harbor of his arm and whispered urgently in my ear, 'Go, Nefer-marymun! Find your way back to your friend and your sexy Egyptologist and think about everything you've felt here with me, and everything I've said, then make your choice.'

'But I don't—'

He shoved me gently away from him. 'Go now.'

'But I don't want—'

Simon's man stepped between us.

'Richard, I can't leave like this!' I was referring to my scanty ancient attire, of course, but especially to all the feelings he had stirred up inside me that beat like fists against my chest, my heart racing in protest at being nipped in the bud like this.

'Go, Mary,' he insisted, his eyes beautifully hard, 'I'll come for you again when you've resolved the conflicts inside you and divested yourself of everything, and everyone, you really don't need or want.'

'But—'

'Go, my love, now.'

Nefermun obeyed E'Ahmose's command at once, overriding Mary Fallon's desire to linger uncertainly in the doorway. I knew in my heart that what he was telling me to do was necessary, but I didn't want to leave him, not now after what both his personalities—the powerfully erotic priest of Anubis and the romantically skilled Englishman—had made me feel in that bedroom lit only by an alabaster lotus lamp. But even as I ran impulsively down the corridor in search of an elevator, I knew I had felt a similar reluctance to separate myself from Simon after everything he had made me feel down in Ti's burial chamber. Nefermun might understand E'Ahmoses's logic and motives, but I, Mary Fallon, definitely resented Richard for essentially kicking me out of his room just after giving me a violent orgasm in front of another man. Nefermun might not mind that her nipples and pubic mound were enticingly visible through the finely pleated long white dress, but I certainly cared about exposing myself to all of Cairo like this.

I stopped to wait for the elevator. I had no desire to leave Richard, but if it was true he had loved me through the ages, then he would come for me again soon enough, just as he had said he would. Yet simply because we were in Egypt did not give him the right to behave as despotically as a pharaoh! Nevertheless, he was right. I had to make my mind up about Simon, and to do so it was necessary for me to see him again. My intense attraction to Richard could not be denied, but neither could my feelings for Simon.

I kept glancing back in the direction of Sir Ashley's suite expecting Simon's messenger to appear and lead me safely back to Carol's place, but the door-lined hallway was as still and silent as the corridor of a tomb. I wondered what had happened to him and wondered if I should be concerned about Richard, until I realized how foolish that was. My Priest of Anubis could take care of himself; it was Simon's servant I should have been concerned about, but I was too busy worrying about myself right now.

I let two empty cars come and go before I finally accepted the fact that no one was going to escort me home or anywhere else. I still had no idea what had become of Simon's man (maybe he'd flown out a window) and I was sorely tempted to return to Richard's room and demand he let me put on my normal clothes, yet Nefermun would not let me do it. I stood with my arms crossed over my chest as though posing for my own mummy, and I imagine my eyes looked as big and dark and profoundly uncertain as a Roman mummy's sarcophagus. I don't think I had ever appreciated the expression 'torn inside' as much as I did in those moments. But three times must be the charm, because when the elevator doors parted again I stepped into the thankfully empty car.

The whole way down I dreaded other guests would get on and that I would be unable to escape their incredulous stares, but I was spared this embarrassment. There was no way I could avoid being seen down in the lobby, however, and as the doors sighed open, I braced myself for peoples' reaction to my appearance. Forcing my arms down to my sides, I stepped stiffly out onto the polished marble floor. Fortunately, I was relatively familiar with the layout of the Mina House, having had dinner here with Simon and Carol, and I headed purposefully towards the entrance trying my best to avoid eye contact with anyone. Then I realized that although everyone I passed noticed me and often stopped to stare at me, no one actually seemed shocked by my appearance. In fact, everyone smiled when they saw me, and when they whispered amongst themselves, pointing in my direction, it was with a respectfully subdued, almost reverent, curiosity. Well, of course, I was in Egypt; they probably thought I was on my way to work somewhere playing Cleopatra.

Nefermun did not mind being the center of public attention, and so I let her take over, or rather I let her possess me as I walked confidently, I can almost say regally, across the slick stone floor in my gilded sandals, my back straight and proud. My stiff shoes made a delicate clicking sound, and I was amazed by how well they fit me, which in turn led me to admire Sir Richard Ashley's powers of observation. I had not noticed him looking at my feet at any point during our first meeting in the Khan el-Khalili, but he had obviously gauged my shoe size that night and procured these sandals for me in the interim.

I had almost made it to the front doors when I was intercepted by a group of jovial Japanese businessmen who swarmed in on me hungrily, all of them wielding cameras that buzzed and clicked around me like insects capturing my image from every angle. It was impossible for me to shoo them away, and I saw no point in ruining their fun by crossing my arms over my chest and attempting to cover my nipples—which felt hard as stone against the veil-like dress—so I let them have their delighted fill of me. I painted the appropriate smile on my lips as flashes exploded in my face with the blinding power of suns going novae.

When they finally lost interest in me and walked laughingly and triumphantly towards the front desk to check in, I stumbled slightly on my way out the front doors. At last I found myself out in the cool night air, and even though it was heavily perfumed with car exhaust, it still tasted delicious to me after being cooped up inside all day in my tomb-like bedroom.

I was immediately surrounded again, this time by cabbies all dying to take me wherever on this earth—or beyond it by way of passionately reckless driving—I wanted to go. It was only then that it hit me like a block falling off the pyramid that I didn't have any money on me, American or Egyptian. I debated whether or not to run back up to Richard's room and demand cab fare. Charm alone, extensive as it was in my nearly transparent attire, wasn't enough to get me across the Nile to Carol's apartment, and yet the robed men eagerly orbiting me didn't seem at all concerned by my lack of a purse.

I shook my head. 'No money, sorry.' I raised my empty hands dramatically in front of me. 'Nothing. Mafish.'

They didn't seem to understand me, perhaps because I was wearing golden bracelets and a shimmering golden vine crowned my dark hair. I had assumed Richard adorned me with costume reproductions of ancient Egyptian jewelry, but I began to suspect I had underestimated his tastes and the value of his gifts when one of the drivers tried pulling one of my bracelets off, quite unconcerned about taking my whole arm with it if necessary. Since I was not about to let him have it, I found myself moving in the direction of the street and what I assumed was his cab, at which point he let go of me, grinning happily. That's when I realized he hadn't actually been trying to steal my jewelry; the gesture had been his rather primitive but admittedly effective way of letting me know I could pay my fare with the bracelet. Much as I hated to part with my lover's gift, Sir Ashley had given me no choice but to fend for myself as best I could, so I let myself be enthusiastically ushered (politely shoved) into the back seat of the small car. I forced myself to relax against the seat, and then clung to it as we shot away from the curb like a bullet released from a gun into Cairo's rushing bloodstream of traffic that glowed with the white and red cells of countless headlights.

'Ala-tool?' My chauffeur grinned back at me. 'Urrayib? Bi-eed, beautiful princess?'

I had to tell him where I wanted to go. The only problem was I had no idea since I didn't know Carol's address by heart. 'The American Embassy,' I improvised. They would be able to give me my friend's address, or at least her phone number so I could call her, and hopefully she would be home and be able to give my driver directions. I would tell the people at the embassy that Carol and I had been at a costume party and that she had left with someone else forgetting I didn't know the way back to her apartment. It was a lame story, but much more believable than the truth.

'American Embassy one bracelet,' my driver stated emphatically.

'Half a bracelet,' I haggled, 'and the other half when you get me to my friend's apartment.' I spoke slowly, praying he would understand me. 'I have to go to the embassy because I lost my friend's address.'

'Yes,' he nodded, 'embassy first to obtain address, then friend's apartment.'

'Exactly!' I was infinitely relieved he understood English.

'Beautiful princess's crown for whole journey!'

'Oh no, only one bracelet, and count yourself lucky.'

'Two bracelets,' he bargained cheerfully.

'One bracelet.'

'Oh very well, aywa!' He flung his hands up in mock exasperation as he agreed to my terms. The car swerved violently, leaving my organs floating in one spot as my skeleton shifted into another, yet my Egyptian driver appeared unaffected by the laws of gravity as he calmly took hold of the wheel again with one hand while at the same time lighting a cigarette with the other.

Now that business was taken care of, we sped along in a comfortable silence punctuated by the burning red tip of his cigarette rising and falling, rising and falling...Occasionally, he glanced at my face in the rear-view mirror, and my enigmatic smile as I thought about my new name, Nefer-marymun, must have made him feel as though he was transporting an ancient statue.

It was dawning on me that Richard was perhaps attempting to escalate my transformation into Nefer-marymun by sending me out into the world without any of Mary Fallon's clothes or possessions, thereby forcing me to identify with my ancient self, whose mysterious strength I would have to call upon to help the nervous and stressed out legal secretary from Boston deal with such adverse circumstances. Nefer-marymun could handle a night alone in Cairo without any money or a passport, wearing only a transparent dress and priceless jewelry, because somehow she knew everything would be all right, she just had to help Mary believe that and stay calm.

The little car came to an abrupt stop beside a small guardhouse outside the gates of what I could only hope was the American Embassy.

My driver quickly got out to open the back door for me, and I caught him intently studying the effect of the cool night air on my nipples as I emerged. Once again, I crossed my arms over my chest. I wished Richard had been kind enough to provide me with a flail I could use to defend myself if necessary.

I found myself in a small antechamber furnished with a handful of very uncomfortable looking chairs. There was a wall directly across from me whose blank facade was broken by a screened window. Behind the fine metal web sat a young Egyptian man in uniform whose eyes widened in disbelief when he saw me appear before him like a vision from the ancient past, or a drunken hallucination, depending on whether or not he happened to have a bottle hidden in his desk. He shook his head swiftly back and forth like a wet dog, and rubbed his eyes like a sleepy child, but I refused to go away. Finally accepting the fact that I was real, he barked an order over his shoulder. Two more uniformed Egyptians immediately appeared behind him, and stared at me open-mouthed.

My driver stepped up beside me and began speaking rapidly in Arabic.

I fervently hoped he was explaining my situation to them, and careful not to uncross my arms, I tugged on his sleeve. 'I need my friend's address, my American friend's address. Her name is Caroline Jordan.'

'Could you please repeat that?' The man seated at the desk requested in perfect English.

I was so relieved I was going to be able to communicate that I relaxed my royal mummy's stance. 'I need my friend's address,' I repeated. 'Her name is Caroline Jordan. She lives in the foreign residential area...well, in one of them. We were at a costume party...'

He listened to my tall tale with a slight smile on his lips (I preferred not to think of it as a smirk).

'And the problem is she left with someone forgetting she hadn't written her address down for me,' I concluded.

'I see,' he said, and there was no question about the fact that he could see, that they could all see, my most intimate assets. 'And how do we know you are really a friend of this young woman?'

I had dreaded this question, for I had no way of proving it. 'Well, you can call her and ask her. I mean, she should be home by now.'

'Do you have her telephone number?'

'No, that's why I came here, because I don't have her address or her number.' My patience was beginning to wear as thin as my dress.

'Do you not carry a purse, miss...?'

'Fallon, Mary Fallon.'

'May I see your passport please, Miss Fallon?'

'No, you may not,' exasperation replaced my anxiety, 'because I don't have it. I don't have anything.' Nefermun wouldn't have needed a passport to travel through Egypt, I thought testily.

He glanced up at the men flanking him as if to say, 'Can you believe these crazy American girls?' before resuming his polite interrogation and lascivious examination of my nipples. 'Was your purse stolen, Miss Fallon? Do you need to file a report with the Tourist Police?'

These were perfectly reasonable questions, and yet I found I could not answer them. 'No, it wasn't stolen, I…I accidentally left it in a tomb, but my friend found it, and it's back at her apartment now, where I would very much like to be, so can you please—'

'I thought you said you were at a costume party.'

'Oh God, I was, it's a long story, believe me. Can you please just look up her number and call her for me? She'll verify who I am.'

Suddenly, an impatient stream of Arabic welled up out of my driver, who had obviously lost his patience with the embassy officials. I had no idea what he was saying, but I was hopeful his tirade would get me what I needed. Finally, one of the men behind the screen disappeared, and I endured an awkward moment avoiding two pairs of dark eyes boring through my dress until he returned a moment later carrying what looked like a thick phone directory.

The young man in charge flipped through it casually, deliberately taking his time. He would also have found what he was looking for a lot faster if he hadn't kept glancing at me, even though his eyes never made it up as far as my face. Finally, he picked up a pen and wrote something on a notepad. He tore off the bottom of the sheet, and slipped it beneath the screen.

My driver promptly snatched up the scrap of paper covered in swirling black lines I sincerely hoped were Carol's coordinates.

He clutched the vital information to his chest, muttered something in Arabic to the officials, and grabbing my arm yanked me back outside.

Once again I found myself in the cockpit of a little Egyptian cab, and discovered it was time to pay my fare.

'I take bracelet now,' my escort stated firmly, 'then I deliver you safely to friend's house.'

I couldn't argue with him after how helpful he had been, so I slipped off one of the bracelets.

He snatched it out of my hand, and it vanished into the folds of his robe so swiftly I suspected some of his ancestors had been tomb robbers.

I recognized the foreign residential section the moment we entered it, and my heart began fluttering like a butterfly perching on all my nerve-endings in turn as Simon's sunny blonde head drew nearer. I hadn't realized how much I wanted to see him again, and I was dismayed by my elation, which Nefermun felt was a betrayal of Richard. Then a circumstantial net was flung over my pulse when I realized I was on my way to Carol's apartment, and that Simon would not even be there. I probably wouldn't even see him tonight, and yet I absolutely had to see him; I couldn't possibly wait until tomorrow. I had left my beautiful priest of Anubis, so I was going to see that damned Egyptologist tonight if it was the last thing Mary Fallon ever did. When she went to bed tonight, it would not be alone like a mummy retiring to her cold sarcophagus. 'No way!' I vowed out loud.

My driver jumped in surprise at my sudden outburst and his cigarette fell from between his fingers into the folds of his robe. He let go of the steering wheel, searching wildly for it with both hands, and as a result the little cab began veering from one side of the street to another like a drunk scarab beetle.

'Look out!' I cried, because we were headed straight for two palm trees and the space between them was definitely not wide enough to accommodate us.

The Egyptian triumphantly placed the cigarette's crumpled body back between his lips, and casually saved us both from a fiery death at the last possible moment.

Suddenly, it didn't seem so vital to me that I see Simon tonight; it would be enough if I managed to remain in the same dimension with both him and Richard—although I was sure E'Ahmose could find me in the next world should my cab driver end up taking me there.

A few minutes, and dozens of sultry daydreams later my kamikaze cabby announced, 'Beautiful princess's apartment!' as we screeched to a halt so abruptly I nearly dove into the front seat.

I quickly opened the door and stepped out onto the safe sidewalk. 'Shukron!' I gasped.

'Kuwayyis.' Grinning, he walked ahead of me towards the building and held open the glass door leading into the lobby.

'Shukron,' I said again, politely tying to get rid of him since I could find my own way from here, but he simply nodded enthusiastically, and I started up the stairs with him trailing on the heels of my gilded sandals. He escorted me all the way up to Carol's apartment, where he abruptly stepped in front of me and knocked loudly and peremptorily on the door demanding that whatever infidel lay behind it let the beautiful princess in at once. At least that's what I think he said; it was hard for me to make sense of his passionate mixture of Arabic and English, all I know is it sounded wonderfully dramatic. However, there was no response whatsoever from within the apartment.

'It's no use,' I told him. 'Either Carol isn't home or she's taking a nap, which would be just as bad. She sleeps like a fairytale princess and it would take a lot more than banging on the door, or a kiss from a handsome prince, to wake her.'

'Princess?' He looked astonished. 'Another princess inside?'

I laughed, trying the doorknob. It turned like a charm and I nearly tumbled into the living room.

By the time I found my balance and turned around to thank my driver for all his help, he had vanished as silently as a genie.

I closed, and carefully locked, the door behind me. It was still relatively early, yet the apartment was dark and silent as a tomb. Carol wasn't losing any sleep over the minor matter of her best friend being swept away on horseback across the desert by an armed man. It was more likely however that she was out with Steve. It was also possible she was out with both Steve and Simon. Or maybe she and her adorable boss were out alone together somewhere fondly hugging each other again in my absence.

I refused to pursue the catty thought. The truth is, I really didn't care where anyone was, because I suddenly became aware of a void inside me that had nothing to do with the empty apartment.

'E'Ahmose,' I whispered into the dark room filled with modern furniture that struck me as totally lifeless compared to the lovely objects I had been surrounded by all day. 'Oh, Richard,' I sighed, 'why did you make me leave you? So I would miss you? So I would realize how much you already mean to me?' Well, I had to admit it was working, and if this temporary separation deepened the bond between us, then I told myself the desolation I was suffering now was more than worth it.

I made my way down the hall by feel. Carol's bedroom door was closed and it appeared to be just as dark on the other side. I opened the door a crack and peered into the impenetrable gloom. 'Carol?' I called softly.

'Mary,' she replied at once sounding strangely breathless, 'you're back!'

'Yes, I am. May I turn on a light?'

'No!'

'Why not?'

'Because she's not alone,' an amused male voice replied.

'Oh, God, I'm sorry.' I quickly closed the door again and retreated down the hallway.

The guestroom was as dark and cold as a crypt, which felt just about right at the moment; I deliberately didn't turn on a light. Just able to make out the soft sarcophagus shape of the bed, I went and sat despondently on its edge. I was the one who had two men fighting for me, at least metaphorically, yet here I was sitting all alone with my beautiful sexy outfit going completely to waste.

A deep moan behind me made me leap off the mattress. 'Who's there?' I gasped, almost knocking over the lamp on the nightstand in my haste to switch it on.

For an instant I was half blinded, but I had no problem making out the body that suddenly sat bolt upright on the bed as though resurrected by the power of Re even in his humble form of an electric light bulb.

'Nefertari?' Simon's eyes were huge and strangely blank; his irises really might have been made of lapis-lazuli. 'The beautiful one has come back to me,' he muttered, reaching hesitantly towards me as though I was an apparition he couldn't actually hope to touch.

Only then did I realize he merely appeared to be conscious. Amused that my eloquent Egyptologist also talked in his sleep, I took hold of him by the shoulders. 'Simon, wake up.' I shook him gently.

His head fell forward, and then snapped back up again. 'Mary?'

He gazed sleepily up at my face before his gaze traveled slowly down my body. 'Jesus,' he whispered, 'I must still be dreaming.'

'No, you're not,' I assured him, standing up straight so he could feast his eyes on me, especially on my firm breasts flatteringly outlined by the transparent linen.

He caught hold of one of my wrists, and pulled me down onto the bed with him. 'You must be a dream,' he muttered, crushing me passionately against him.

'Simon, I can't breathe.'

'But you don't need to breath, Mary, you're only a dream, and dreams don't breathe.'

'I'm not a dream,' I insisted, trying to push him away.

He relaxed his vice-like embrace, but refused to let go of me. 'If you're not a dream, why are you dressed like an ancient Egyptian princess?'

I wondered if he was still half asleep because his reasoning powers seemed a bit groggy. 'Sir Richard Gerald Ashley dressed me like this.' It titillated me to say the full name of his current incarnation, which was not as romantic as E'Ahmose, Born of the Moon, but still possessed a dignity worthy of how magnificently intelligent and beautiful he was, in my opinion.

Simon did not so much let go of me as push me away from him, and the look in his eyes told me he was wide awake finally. 'That bastard,' he said through his teeth.

'I don't have a problem with it,' I remarked lightly, admiring one of the gold bracelets I still had left. It was decorated with a geometric rendering of lotus blossoms formed by inlaid blue and red stones I could not identify but that were beautiful enough to be precious.

Simon snatched my wrist, and raising it between us studied the bracelet himself. 'He gave you this?'

'Yes, and my crown, too.' I touched the delicate vine reverently. 'And my belt.' I looked down at the little golden fish swimming around my hips. 'Isn't it beautiful? And my collar.' I caressed the controlled explosion of primary colors resting against my chest. 'And my sandals.' I extended one of my slender legs and displayed my gilded foot.

'Thanks for the inventory.'

'My pleasure. They look real, don't they?' I couldn't resist asking. He was an Egyptologist, so he should be able to tell. It wasn't the monetary value of the ancient-style jewels that interested me; I was looking for evidence of the value my so-called Priest of Anubis actually placed on our relationship. If he had showered me with costume jewelry, my faith in his timeless feelings for me would suffer a disappointing blow.

Simon studied my face for a moment , and I sensed him determine that my curiosity had nothing to do with money as he frowned down at my collar, and then rubbed one of the little fish dangling from my belt between his thumb and forefinger. 'They're either real or very good imitations, but I suspect they're real,' he concluded.

My respect for him deepened as he gave me a totally objective assessment of the valuable gifts another man had given me.

His shoulders slumped as though he was suddenly exhausted. 'He's rich as a pharaoh,' he added despondently, and his head fell heavily into his hands.

Respect naturally flowed into concern. 'Are you all right?' I asked, gently resting my hand on one of his thighs. He was wearing khaki slacks and a matching shirt that made him look every inch the handsome Anthropologist.

'I'm fine,' he muttered, then suddenly looked up at me askance. 'Why are you here, anyway?'

'Because this is Carol's apartment and I'm staying with her?'

He sat up again. 'Why didn't you stay with Richard?' he demanded bluntly.

'Did you send one of your men to spy on me?' I continued our tradition of answering each other's questions with more questions.

'I wanted to make sure you were all right. Obviously,' the ghost of a sneer touched his lips, 'there was no need for me to be concerned. I should have known it wasn't true.'

'That what wasn't true?'

'I thought you said money didn't mean anything to you, Mary.'

'It doesn't,' I insisted. 'I could care less that Richard is rich.' I winced. That was the second time in one night my grammar had left much to be desired.

'Then what is it about him you can't resist, the size of his dick?'

I slapped him.

He caressed his cheek gingerly. 'I'm sorry, Mary, that was way out of line. You have the right to see whoever you please.'

'Apology accepted,' I declared magnanimously.

He smiled. 'Thank you, princess.' Then he frowned again as he observed my erect nipples nearly poking through my dress. 'If it turned you on to slap me,' he said very quietly, 'please feel free to do it again.'

I glanced self-consciously down at my breasts. I couldn't say I minded how much attention they had received lately, but I was becoming a bit concerned about the constant state of arousal my body was experiencing since I'd landed in Egypt. It made resisting a handsome man's advances very difficult, and in this case impossible. When Simon grasped both my arms and pulled me to my feet, I meant to protest, but the lips on my face remained sealed as I felt the lips of my sex gape open willingly. He pushed me back against a wall, and the trace of anger in his lustful stare made me even wetter.

'So, how far did you go with him?' His voice remained dangerously quiet as he cupped my breasts in his hands through the dress and bounced them up and down slowly, almost as if weighing my character along with them.

'All the way,' I confessed, and cried out from the excruciating pleasure as he gave my soft mounds a punishing squeeze.

'Did you suck his cock?'

I met his eyes. 'Yes.'

He released me to unzip his pants. 'Then you won't mind sucking mine now, will you?'

I shook my head. 'No, please, Simon, I'm really tired.' This was true. I didn't have to tell him I just wasn't inspired to worship his penis as I had Richard's.

'You're tired, are you?' He didn't sound convinced, but he zipped his pants back up as though he were. 'Too tired to stand for a little while?' He reached down and deftly undid the clasp of my fish belt, letting it fall to the floor with a delicate ringing sound that echoed in my nerve-endings.

'No, I guess not,' I said, wondering what he had in mind.

I found out when he knelt before me and impatiently shoved my dress up my legs. The soft material formed a cloudy halo around my hips as I willingly spread my legs just far enough to accommodate his face between them. I couldn't believe another attractive man was eating me out hungrily, and yet my pussy had no problem accepting more stimulating attention. Holding my dress up out of his way, I stood motionless as a statue being worshipped. I watched his blond head for a while as it worked between my thighs, but then I just stared straight ahead into space like a true princess accepting the passionate devotion of one of her many subjects. His tongue was technically as agile as Richard's and yet somehow not as skilled because he wasn't as sensitive to the escalations and fluctuations of my pleasure. For a breathtaking moment his mouth would fondle my clitoris in just the right way, but then suddenly it would move on and the glorious current of a climax would ebb again, making his oral attention as frustrating as it was enjoyable.

Mary Fallon would have felt guilty about how long she was letting a man work on her like this, but Nefer-marymun was thoroughly and selfishly enjoying herself. I could see my reflection in the mirror over the dresser, and the delight lapping between my thighs felt like a fitting reward for how strikingly beautiful I looked, the blond head between my legs an infinitely more priceless gift than the jewels I was wearing. Then he abruptly brought his right hand into play, almost savagely thrusting two fingers up into my wildly juicing slit, and I saw the lovely statue in the glass come alive as I cried out in ecstasy.

He worked on me longer than any man ever had, and yet I couldn't come. Every time I felt the current of an orgasm rushing towards his sucking mouth and cresting tongue, it flowed disappointingly away again as I thought of Richard E'Ahmose, mysteriously more alive inside me than the physical pleasure another man was struggling to give me. Finally Simon stood up slowly in defeat, wiping his mouth on the back of his sleeve. I was so wet, I felt as though I had come close to drowning him without even climaxing.

'I'm sorry,' I murmured, letting my dress slip down my legs. 'But it's usually hard for me to come like that.' I kept telling him the truth, but only half of it. It was hard for me to come like that except with Richard.

'I enjoyed it very much, Mary.'

'Me too,' I said quickly.

'Yes,' he smiled ruefully, 'I know. But you warned me you were tired, and I still insisted on taking advantage of you. I'm the one who should be apologizing.'

Suddenly I wondered: what am I doing? I was blowing my chances with a handsome Egyptologist who was clearly interested in winning my affections, because I was perversely obsessed with a decadently rich Englishman obsessed with the occult. 'Oh Simon.' I slipped my arms around his chest and rested my cheek against his hard shoulder, 'I'm so confused.'

'Just give me a chance, Mary.'

I stepped back so I could look up at his face. 'Of course,' I said.

He returned my earnest regard with a long unreadable stare. 'We're both tired,' he concluded at last. 'Do you mind sharing your bed with me, or should I go sleep out on the couch?'

'Of course I don't mind.'

'Then take off your jewels princess, and let's hit the sack.'

CHAPTER SEVEN

The next day dawned bright and beautiful (nothing unusual in Egypt) and found me sitting at the dining room table with my chin in my hands half hypnotized by the twin serpents of Simon's lips as he talked, and talked and talked. This time he was wide awake, only now he was in danger of putting everyone else to sleep.

Still, he had put his tongue to such good use again that morning that part of me was feeling open to whatever he had to say. I had awakened as his golden head had sank between my legs, and then it was as if the sun had slowly risen inside me, I'd felt his warm tongue dipping and swirling. He'd quickly coaxed a sweet climax from my sleepy clitoris, in a sense catching it off guard before it had time to tense up in response to my thoughts of another man.

Now the four of us, Carol and Steve and Simon and I, were sitting around the polished mahogany table that belonged to the nameless American diplomat who owned this generically furnished apartment. We had enjoyed a light breakfast of toast and preserves and were lingering over second helpings of coffee, which I had brewed good and strong—except for Carol, of course, who was drinking her proverbial tea.

I glanced at Steve, admiring his recuperative powers—I still hadn't seen him wearing a shirt. Carol wanted to hear all about my 'adventure' with Richard, but Simon obviously didn't, which is probably one reason he kept talking. If I hadn't found his subject matter so interesting, his evasiveness might have annoyed me.

While we'd prepared breakfast, Carol had filled me in on what had happened after Richard carried me away on horseback. She confirmed that Simon had indeed sent his man to the Mina House to make sure Richard had taken me there. She also thought it highly significant that her boss had not gotten any work done yesterday. 'Let me tell you, Mary,' she'd whispered conspiratorially over the toaster, 'ever since I started working for him, absolutely nothing has kept him away from Saqqara for even half a day. Once he had a fever and yet he and Steve still went out to work. He must really have feelings for you. He stayed here waiting for news of you all day. I think he was hoping you'd show up like you finally did, and I think he had one too many scotches because he fell asleep in the guestroom where you found him. Now, quick, tell me what happened with Richard!'

But I hadn't had time to comply with her request; bread doesn't take that long to toast and both Steve and Simon came to hover hungrily in the doorway.

'Advances in modern neurology prove the ancient Egyptians understood the workings of the nervous system,' Simon informed us now, staring deep into my eyes, 'as well as the different relationships between the areas of the brain and how they control all our bodily functions.'

'Is that so?' I prompted.

'Yes.' He spun his empty coffee cup around and around as he spoke like a miniature parody of a flying saucer. 'That's so, Mary.'

I had to bite my tongue to keep from saying, 'Nefer-marymun, if you please.'

Carol placidly sipped her Green Tea.

Steve's face and inevitably bare chest were now hidden behind the tiny black hieroglyphs of The New York Times.

'As modern studies progress in such areas as the psychological aspects of healing and the effects of sound-waves on the body,' Simon went on as if everyone were listening attentively, 'even the incantations used in ancient healing methods can receive serious consideration. Ultra-sound is commonly used in advanced surgery today. May I have some more coffee, please, Mary?'

'Certainly, Simon.' I smiled at him sweetly, picked up his cup and returned to the kitchen with it.

'I need more tea,' Carol declared, following me. 'Tell me!' she whispered. 'Did you sleep with Richard?'

I smiled beatifically as I refilled Simon's cup. 'What do you think?' Unfortunately, he took his coffee black, because cream and sugar would have given us an excuse to linger in the kitchen.

'I think you definitely slept with him.'

'I think you're definitely right.'

'Mary!' She looked genuinely shocked. 'You're sleeping with two men at once?'

'I didn't plan on it,' I started back out to the dining room, 'it just happened.'

'What just happened?' Simon inquired suspiciously.

'Excuse me,' Carol said stiffly, and a moment later I heard the bathroom door close firmly behind her. I knew from past experience that she would not emerge from her humid haven for at least half an hour.

'Nothing,' I said, my smile and voice so sweet they more than made up for the lack of sugar in his coffee.

He stared fixedly at my face as I seated myself again. 'This process of gradual upgrading,' he continued where he had left off, 'has been taking place in every specialty within the field covered by Egyptology.'

'That's fascinating,' I said truthfully, yet it was also true that his monologue was starting to bore Nefer-marymun.

'Just how much the Egyptians and other ancient cultures knew about astronomy,' he seemed content to have only me for an audience, 'is finally being recognized by even the most conservative historians now.' A curl of his lip indicated what he thought of these academic turtles.

'Yes, I know, it's called Archeo Astronomy, isn't it?'

'Very good, Mary.' His passion for the subject kept him from sounding condescending. 'But what's even more interesting is that advances in high energy physics, molecular biology and even genetics can be applied to ancient creation myths which at first seem so alien and arbitrary.'

Steve snapped the Times down onto his lap. 'Get to the goddamned point,' he said, winking at me sympathetically as he folded the newspaper. 'You're putting the poor girl to sleep.'

'The point is, I believe there was once a great doctrine in which science, religion, philosophy and art were all fused into a grand synthesis,' Simon at last came to his impressive conclusion. 'And I believe this fusion, and the mysterious power latent within it, was responsible for the temples and pyramids of ancient Egypt.'

'Amen.' Steve slammed the newspaper down on the table before him as though swatting a fly that had taken the form of a period finally punctuating Simon's endless speech. 'Now let's get down to business, shall we?' Impatiently, he smoothed his hair back away from his forehead, and I noted it was no longer full of sand. I couldn't help thinking that his bare chest was not very businesslike, but he folded his hands before him on the table as seriously as an executive vice president in a conference room.

'What the hell are we going to do about this bastard, Simon?' I could only assume he was referring to Sir Ashley. 'He knows we've discovered the entrance to Imhotep's mastaba. The crazy bastard's rich enough to dabble in whatever profession he pleases, and right now, unfortunately for us, it pleases him to be interested in ancient Egypt.'

'Which he seems to know a great deal about,' I remarked.

'Listen to her,' Simon said, 'she sounds as though she enjoyed her stay at the Mina House.' The fact that he was suddenly referring to me in the third person gave away how angry he was even though his expression and the tone of his voice were perfectly civil. 'I hear Sir Ashley has a suite on the top floor decorated with an extensive collection of ancient artifacts as well as more contemporary antiques. It must be lovely.'

Steve asked me quickly, 'Do you have any idea how he knew about the photograph, Mary?'

'Yes,' I replied, my stare locked with Simon's in the painful way fingers stick to ice, 'he dreamed about it.'

'What?' Steve sat back in his chair. 'He dreamed about it?'

'That's what he told me.'

'And you believed him?' Simon asked, but it sounded more like an accusation.

'He appears to be somewhat psychic,' I replied evasively.

He turned his head and stared out the living room window at the clear blue sky.

'He told me he sometimes has true dreams,' I added quietly, but it would have felt like betraying Richard to say more.

'Go on, Mary,' Simon urged while continuing to stare impassively out at the heavens. 'I know there's more, and there's no reason you shouldn't tell us.' He met my eyes again abruptly. 'Is there? It's not exactly a secret that Sir Ashley is interested in the occult, like so many of his wealthy British predecessors.'

'You're right, there's no reason I shouldn't tell you. After all, everyone believes whatever they want to.' I was talking fast, irritated that his skeptical attitude had the power to make me question all the fervent feelings I had experienced with Richard. 'Sir Ashley believes he was once a priest of Anubis and a wearer of the Winged Sandals,' I blurted.

'Winged sandals?' Steve repeated blankly.

'Yes, Winged Sandals,' Simon echoed. 'Interesting. And I suppose that you, Mary, are his long-lost priestess?' His eyes shone like mirrors reflecting the sky, giving nothing away while making me see my poetic emotions as mere character flaws it was necessary for me to outgrow.

'That's what he would like me to believe,' I replied guardedly, and was humiliated by the realization that I had sunk completely back into Mary Fallon's rationally limited perceptions and forsaken Nefermun along with my deepest feelings, simply because I had no way of proving them. Yet even if there truly was something supernatural going on between Richard and me, Simon was the last person I wanted to be talking to about it.

'Let me get this straight, Mary.' He drained his third cup of coffee as though he needed every drop of caffeine to deal with Sir Ashley's deluded dreams. 'All day yesterday you sat in a room filled with copies of some of the treasures that might be found in an Egyptian tomb, and in the evening, Richard wined and dined you while very politely suggesting you had been lovers in a past incarnation, more specifically wearers of the Winged Sandals, and that dreams had led him to you again after countless centuries?'

I was aghast. Put that way, Richard's methods seemed so cheap and obvious that I felt my self-esteem plummeting into the dimples of the Egyptologist's maddeningly superior smile. At least Mary Fallon did. Nefermun and Nefer-marymun were both furious that someone was discussing Richard in such a disrespectfully judgmental fashion, blithely making light of his profound conviction in the immortality of the soul and the deathless power of love simply because they did not share in his beliefs.

'He left you there all day so you'd begin to feel like a mummy in her tomb,' Simon went on smugly, undoubtedly encouraged by my troubled expression. 'There wasn't any electricity, nothing modern in the room at all except the bed, and the central air-conditioner, of course. Am I correct?'

I nodded, too upset to speak.

'He hid your clothes and forced you to dress like an ancient Egyptian princess—'

'Excuse me, but he didn't force me to do anything.' I came back to life. 'I want to make that perfectly clear. He behaved like a perfect gentleman the entire time.' That wasn't exactly true, of course, but everything he'd done had pleased me and that was the truth.

'So you willingly left the mastaba with him?'

'Yes, I did.' I couldn't lie. 'Not that you were doing much to stop me,' I added petulantly. 'But you're right, he did all those things you described, and when it got dark I had to light a lotus flower lamp. And you know what? It was beautiful. I enjoyed every minute I spent at the Mina House.'

'And he showered you with jewels,' Simon reminded me. 'No woman ever born ever complained about that. They're beautiful copies of ancient pieces made of real gold and lapis-lazuli and other precious stones. You should see them, Steve. They're exquisite reproductions of Middle Kingdom pieces.'

'Well, what do you expect,' his assistant scoffed, 'the ass-hole's richer than pharaoh.'

And it seemed to me that these grant-dependent American anthropologists were decidedly jealous of the Englishman's financial independence.

Simon smoothed his hair back away from his face with both hands so forcefully it made his skull look gilded. There was a thin line of tension carved horizontally across the center of his forehead, and another smaller line was etched between his eyebrows, the only visible signs of the slight hangover he must have been suffering after drinking half a bottle of twelve-year-old scotch. Then suddenly he laughed, a harsh, disturbing sound.

'What's so funny?' I demanded.

'Carol, oh, Carol?' Steve called plaintively. 'Where are you, honey?'

'I'm sorry, Mary.' Simon's soul suddenly returned to his glassy eyes as his long fingers began fiddling awkwardly with his empty cup again.

'Sorry for what, for not doing anything to stop me from leaving the mastaba with Richard?'

His eyebrow arched again in that infuriatingly superior way. 'But I thought you said you went with him willingly, Mary?'

'I did.'

'Then there was no need to stop anyone, was there?'

'Oh, forget it! Is it true we were breaking the law by camping out in Ti's tomb?' I desperately changed the subject.

All the warmth vanished from his eyes again. 'You'd better decide right now what side you're on, sweetheart.'

I should have been prepared for the challenge, but I wasn't.

I had been postponing the moment when I would have to choose between these two men and both of them had captured my imagination and my feelings in devastatingly exciting ways. But now the moment had come, and I couldn't seem to find my voice. I was looking directly into Simon's eyes, but I was seeing a dark room lit only by a golden lotus lamp and feeling the strong, bare arms of a man reaching for me as the sunset burned like the blood of all the gods behind him and my blood purred joyfully through my body as he kissed me…

'Shit,' Steve whispered, 'he got to her.'

'Mary?'

That was all Simon said, but the concern in his voice broke a mysterious dam inside me. With a wild rush of verbs and adjectives, I heard myself trying to describe the dream I had had in the mastaba and the mystical feelings and visions Richard inspired in me.

'He must have drugged her,' Steve concluded cynically.

I shook my head. 'No, he didn't, and I had the dream before I even met him.'

'The dream you were having in the mastaba when I woke you,' Simon remembered out loud.

'Yes.'

'Then he must have hypnotized you somehow.' Steve stubbornly insisted on believing Richard had coerced me into desiring him. 'Either that, or you have an overactive imagination that's easily influenced by—'

'Excuse me?' I snapped.

'Or it could have been a genuine mystical experience,' Simon conceded with suspicious good grace. 'But whether you and Richard were acquainted in a past life is irrelevant now, Mary.'

'That's right, because whoever he was in the past, if you believe in all that reincarnation crap,' Steve threw in with admirable objectivity, 'in the real life present, he's a bastard, plain and simple.'

'Reincarnation is not crap.' Carol had returned. She seated herself beside Steve again looking as fresh as a dew-covered lily with her long braided hair hanging in a thick stem down her back.

'Let's not get into a metaphysical discussion.' Simon crossed his arms and relaxed in his chair. 'Mary is simply trying to decide who to trust in the here and now.'

'I never said I didn't trust you, Simon, and Richard has a right to believe whatever he wants to.'

'What's going on here?' Carol demanded with unusual firmness. 'What did that man say to you, Mary?'

'I have a feeling he threw dirt, or more appropriately sand, at my personal and professional integrity,' Simon told her soberly—and he certainly was sober this morning.

'And you believed him?' Carol accused me.

'Look, they asked me how Richard knew about the photograph, and I told them, he dreamed about it, but I have no idea if he was lying or not.'

Nefermun angrily squeezed my heart as I said this, but I desperately wanted this conversation to end. I wasn't ready to choose between Simon and Richard, not yet; I needed more time to think, or more importantly, to feel.

'Some people really do have extra sensory perceptions,' I added, 'it's not impossible whether you care to believe it or not. And I certainly don't see how playing with my head could possibly help him steal your discovery of Imhotep's tomb, which is what I assume you think he's trying to do. Yet I don't see why he would even bother. He's not an Egyptologist, and you told me yourself the Antiquities Department will be all over the find once it's made public.'

'Or maybe he thinks he's the reincarnation of Imhotep and

doesn't want us violating his eternal resting place.' Steve's sarcasm was so intense he almost sounded serious. 'Maybe he's deluded enough to imagine he has occult rights to the mastaba.'

'Yes, and maybe he's anxious for you to begin digging and it's the delay that's bothering him,' Carol elaborated as though her lover really were serious. 'Maybe he feels his powers will be enhanced once his mastaba comes to light.'

'Carol?' Steve waved his hand in front of her face. 'Earth to Carol.'

'This conversation is degenerating fast,' Simon observed.

I looked at him, and was surprised to sense he was disturbed, not about me, and my shifting sensual and emotional loyalties, but about something else, something he felt powerless to control. Maybe it was the hangover, but I didn't think so. I was already sensitive to what went on inside him, his thoughts and feelings were like waves beating against the shore of my awareness, and I sensed now that Carol's fancifully occult diagnosis actually bothered him. I remembered then what he had just been saying, that ancient Egypt was once a place where science, art and religion were a sensuous, powerful whole, and this would have been particularly true in the Old Kingdom, in which Imhotep's reputation was that of the wisest man of his time. If all aspects of life had at one time been a seamless whole, then wisdom would also have meant power, magical power of unimaginable proportions. Or perhaps it wasn't so unimaginable and this sundered union was still reflected in the Great Pyramid and all the feelings it still inspired in people.

I suddenly realized Simon and I were staring deep into each other's eyes, and the way his sky-blue irises shone above the horizon of his smile was all the proof I needed that he had been thinking very much the same thing I had.

* * * *

Carol and I were to be rather unceremoniously dropped off at the Cairo Museum, where Hamud would pick us up later that afternoon. Steve and Simon were returning to their work in Saqqara; sunburns and minor hangovers were not about to slow them down. They would return to Cairo in the evening, and the plan was that after they showered and changed we would all go out to dinner (not at the Mina House) and enjoy some of the city's more exotic nightlife (I refrained from mentioning even to Carol that it would be hard to top the exotic evening I had spent with Richard, a.k.a. E'Ahmose, in a bedroom filled with ancient works of art).

I doubted Simon would be in any condition to stay out late tonight—the line across his forehead had been deepening by the second—but it would be fun to watch him try. I was deliberately forcing myself to remain lighthearted. I knew where to find Richard and he knew where to find me, and if all else failed we could always meet up again in a dream. For now I was glad of the brief timeout I was being given. It is an understatement to say I was a bit overwhelmed by my experiences in the Mina House, and Simon's inexhaustible tongue had gone a long way to convincing me that it was in my best interests to honor his request and give him a chance. Nefermun was not so easily swayed, however, and my soul felt painfully torn. I knew the moment I met Simon that he was perfect for me, until Richard strode into my life in the bazaar and I was possessed by the feeling that we had always known, and desired, each other.

I really wasn't in the mood to visit the Cairo Museum, but I didn't say so because what I was in the mood for couldn't be expressed in mixed company. In my opinion, the long sunny afternoon would have been much better spent in a dark bedroom.

The question was with whom. As Carol was quick to point out the second Steve and Simon were out of earshot, I couldn't sleep with two men forever. Maybe a tour of lifeless artifacts was just the thing I needed to cool my blood a little, which would hopefully help me think straight and decide once and for all who I wanted to be with, Simon or Richard-E-Ahmose.

The Cairo Museum is a vast, multi-story warehouse-like building depressingly lacking in atmosphere and brimming with treasures. Egyptian civilization lasted thousands of years, but in the Cairo Museum no distinction is made between the different eras and dynasties; beautiful Old Kingdom pieces sit next to decadent Roman imitations. The ground floor of the Victorian building is a veritable forest of statues. Amidst colossi with legs as thick as tree trunks and shoulders the size of boulders, sit smaller, amazingly life-like pieces. As Carol and I wove our way between them, I was particularly drawn to the sculpture of a scribe with his scroll open across his lap. The folds of his soft belly were accurately and humbly depicted, and his smile was so breathtakingly alive I seriously wanted to get to know him. I could feel his love for his work as a scribe, and it might almost have been the centuries unrolling in his lap as he looked up for a moment to rest his shining black eyes.

Carol and I wandered from room to room, admiring art while daydreaming about living, breathing pieces of work. I assumed she was thinking about Steve, and I had the binary suns of Richard and Simon forever in my mind...although with his long dark hair and mystical powers Richard was more like a mysterious black hole to which I was irresistibly drawn.

'You know, Carol,' I joined her in her contemplation of a poorly drawn papyrus of the Ptolomeic era, 'Sometimes I wonder about Lillith, Adam's first wife, you know, the one who got kicked out of paradise for some reason or other.'

She gave me her undivided attention, which was rare for her. 'Why?' she demanded as though her whole life depended on the answer.

I noticed that the armed security guard standing in the doorway was giving us both his undivided attention.

'I don't know…' My train of thought turned a conceptual corner and I almost lost track of it. 'I just can't help wondering why no one ever talks about her. You'd think the first real woman, the woman created by God at the same time as man who wasn't just part of his rib, you'd think she'd be important, wouldn't you? Lillith, the first real woman, got kicked out of paradise for some reason and Adam was left with Eve, who wasn't his equal or his soul mate because she was made from his rib, and look what she ended up doing. I mean why is Lillith—?'

'Mary, what the hell are you trying to say?'

'Carol, do you realize there really haven't been any religious figures for women to identify with, at least not that I can think of, since the Egyptian goddess Isis, and the Christians cleaned her up immediately, adopting her as the Virgin Mary. They actually took ancient statues of Isis sitting with her baby Horus, the falcon god, and turned him into Jesus, but Isis was no virgin…although she did conceive Horus with Osiris after he was dead and she found all the pieces of his body the evil Set had scattered across the world except for his penis, but that doesn't make her virginal, just totally, magically, sensual.'

'You're seriously attracted to Richard, aren't you?' She translated my lame theological rambling into a succinct and significant fact.

'Very attracted. I've never been so literally drawn to a man in my life, and yet I'm afraid it might only be a physical—'

'You're incapable of only feeling something physical for a man and you know it, Mary. You always end up falling in love with the guys you sleep with.'

'Mm, yes, that is a problem.'

The security guard took another step towards us.

Carol moved over to a papyrus display case a little farther away from his smoldering interest. 'It's our genetic make-up,' she went on quietly. 'How quickly and intensely a woman gets attached to a man dates back to prehistoric times when men had to get as many women as possible pregnant to procreate the race, and women tied them down in order to raise these children and create a safe environment.'

'Working for an archaeologist is really bringing out your long-buried academic side, Carol, but I think you're suffering from a lobotomy of the imagination looking at the relationship between the sexes so, so naturalistically.' I had no idea if that was actually a word and I didn't care. 'The relationship between men and women is also metaphysical. The sun doesn't need the earth, but the earth and all its beauty wouldn't exist without the sun, and all that cosmic male-female principle stuff.'

'But what purpose would all that fiery burning power serve if it wasn't to create and sustain life?' my friend pointed out astutely. 'Men need and want women just as much as women need and want men.' She glanced over at the guard. 'Let's get out of here. He's getting up his nerve to talk to us and these papyruses aren't that interesting anyway.'

I followed her out of the room. 'So how was it with Steve?' I felt guilty about not asking her before, having been selfishly wrapped up in my own affairs.

'It was really great.'

'Would you care to elaborate? I'm your best friend, remember.

What did you do together?'

'Well, everything, I guess.'

'Wow. So, are you just getting him out of your system like you did Simon or do you really like him?'

'I think I love him.'

'Really?'

'Yes!' she sighed.

CHAPTER EIGHT

We spent most of our time at the Cairo Museum in the jewelry room.

I meditated for a good while on a colorful pectoral of Horus spread out on black cloth in which each tiny inlaid stone was a feather. The piece's stylized realism was strangely uplifting; it was both a detailed representation of a falcon and a symbolic image of the human soul. At its best, ancient Egyptian jewelry is visual poetry. Yet the beautiful pectoral struck me as dead lying inside a sealed glass case. The bird's outspread wings needed a heart beating beneath them to bring them to life. The necklace was meant to be worn against a man's chest, and I couldn't help imagining how good it would look framed by Richard's powerful pecs.

The fact did not escape me that it was not Simon's chest I pictured. I felt like a detective gathering evidence in the form of all my fleeting fantasies, trying to crack the case of which of the two men stalking my thoughts had truly captured my heart and not just my lust.

'Carol,' I whispered, 'I think those two guys over there have been following us.'

'Just ignore them.'

Was it my imagination, or did one of them look familiar? They were dressed in western clothing today, but that didn't mean they couldn't be two of Richard's servants. I could almost swear I had seen them crouching around the fire when Simon and I emerged from Ti's burial chamber. My pulse sped up at the possibility Richard was keeping an eye on me. 'Let's walk away and see if they follow us,' I suggested.

'Whatever.' She shrugged. 'Hamud will be here soon anyway.'

The two Egyptians did indeed follow us out of the jewelry room, but they were hard-pressed to keep up with us. Two slightly overweight men could not hope to match what Carol and I called our 'Boston walk', developed out of necessity when traveling from a train station to our destination in wind-chill factors that often plummeted well below zero.

We ran up a long flight of stairs, competing with each other to see who was less out of breath at the top. 'You might as well see the Mummy Room while you're here.' Carol's voice was admirably steady after the exertion. 'You have to pay extra, so maybe they won't follow us in there.'

Beneath the glass roof lay rows of glass cases displaying mummies in varying stages of preservation or decay, depending on whether you see the glass as half full or half empty. Some were nothing but blackened skeletons, yet a few, horribly enough, retained a semblance of life.

'Carol, this is sick,' I muttered, sticking close to her fresh, living body. 'And here they come. I guess they consider us worth the price of admission.'

Our pursuers had the audacity to grin at us as they entered the Mummy Room.

I ignored them as I paused over the remains of Seti I, the best looking mummy ever found, in my opinion. I enjoyed a sobering moment of communion with the long dead pharaoh. In the presence of this once strikingly handsome man, I lost my sensual appetite for a few moments, which broke my stimulating connection with both Richard and Simon and left me standing alone beneath the blue sky, remembering the intense love in E'Ahmose's eyes when we were lying in each other's arms.

'Good bye, Seti,' I whispered, caressing the glass over his face. 'And thank you.'

'Hamud should be here by now,' Carol said, 'let's go.' We wove swiftly between the mummy cases, and it was fun racing each other down the stairs then across the main lobby into the sunlight.

I groped in my purse for my sunglasses, and slipping them on, I spotted the large blue Chevrolet waiting for us at the bottom of the steps, parked directly below us at the curb. 'I want to buy something in the gift shop,' I declared.

'Forget it,' Carol snapped. She knew I wasn't really interested in the little tourist trap. 'We're leaving.'

I shrugged, and followed her down to the car. Even if Richard was having me followed, there was no point in standing around waiting for his men to spot us again, so I slipped compliantly into the back seat.

Carol sat up front with the grinning Hamud, and glanced sternly at me over her shoulder. 'You have to decide between Richard and Simon right now, Mary.'

'Right this minute?'

Hamud gazed curiously at my face in the rear-view mirror.

I frowned back at him playfully. 'He didn't have to choose,' I pointed out. 'How many wives does he have anyway, two, three? So why can't a woman have two men?'

His gold tooth flashed in the sunlight. 'Room for one more,' he announced.

'Shut-up, Hamud,' Carol said fondly. 'Mary, you have so much in common with Simon. You seem perfect for each other. You're the only person I know who actually likes listening to him talk. I don't think you should risk blowing your chances with him by letting some crazy rich Englishman turn your head. I realize Simon is dirt poor but—'

'Carol, Richard is not crazy, and it's not about the money. You know me better than that.' I slumped down in the seat so I was no longer reflected in the rearview mirror. 'Would you tell your chauffeur to keep his eyes on the road, please.' Without him seeming to pay any attention to its progress, the big car was swerving like an enchanted snake through the basket-like metal weave of bumper-to-bumper traffic.

'You have to be careful, Mary.' Carol was working herself up into full lecture mode. 'I know you're on vacation, but how you behave now can affect the rest of your life.'

The temperature in the car was plummeting by the second; Hamud enjoyed basking in the air-conditioner's Arctic breeze.

'You know what you said this morning about Richard and Imhotep's tomb, Carol, that he was anxious for Simon to start digging because he feels his powers will be enhanced once this mastaba comes to light?'

'I have no idea where that idea came from,' she admitted, sounding proud of her occult reasoning powers.

'Well, wherever it came from, I think Simon took it seriously.'

'No way.'

'The look in his blue eyes after you suggested it, it was like catching a glimpse of the sky the way it looked thousands of years ago before the pollution of cynicism.'

'That's a beautiful image, Mary, I think you're in love with him.'

'He's not your normal academic Egyptologist.' I ignored her romantic conclusion. 'I get the feeling he's trying to decode Saqqara's symbolism, not just create a detailed record of the bas-reliefs in each mastaba for posterity. I'm beginning to suspect all those beautiful bas-reliefs are equations and that there's an actual power hidden inside them.'

We were driving along the Nile now and the pyramids were visible on the opposite bank, small and far away yet still awe-inspiring.

'I think Simon is worried that Richard believes in the synthesis he was talking about this morning,' I went on enthusiastically. 'I think they're actually both after the same thing, but in different ways.'

'Imhotep's mastaba, or you, Mary?'

I let my feelings purr around this question for a moment. 'No, it's more than Imhotep's mastaba. Richard doesn't believe he's Imhotep's reincarnation. He's not some New Age flake, trust me on this one. I know for a fact that he believes his name was E'Ahmose, which means Born of the Moon, and that he was a priest of Anubis. I really don't think he's lying about his psychic powers either. He says he has true dreams, and I believe him.'

'Because you desire him.'

'No, because he knew what I dreamed the other day when I fell asleep in the mastaba. He described the details of my dream to me exactly—but now you made me forget what I was going to say. Where was I?'

'I have no idea.'

'You suggested that Richard wants to tap into Imhotep's power once his mastaba is unearthed. Imhotep was high priest, he designed the entire Zoser complex at Saqqara, the Step Pyramid and everything.'

'I know, Mary,' she sighed, 'I work there. Richard wants to be a maker of stone vases, too?'

'What?'

'That's the only one of Imhotep's titles I remember Simon ranting on about because it sounded so funny coming after all those other pretentious ones.'

'Would you please be serious, Carol. I feel like I'm on the verge of understanding something very important here.' I was struggling to give birth to a theory straining the parameters of my rational mind. 'Imhotep designed the Zoser complex and built it himself,' I went on. 'High priest wasn't just a prestigious title given to someone who burned incense and chanted meaningless spells, not if the synthesis of art and science and religion Simon was talking about this morning really existed. A high priest of ancient Egypt would have commanded literal, physical forces because he fully understood who, and what, he was. He would have believed beyond a shadow of a doubt, he would have known in his being in a way we've lost the ability to know, that his soul was an indestructible energy and his physical body merely a garment his naked power had slipped on for a while. The gods of Egypt are all symbolic expressions of the different stages involved in pure energy, or the pure force of life, taking form and becoming matter. Modern physics is saying the same thing in different ways, and I think the Egyptians believed that the creation of the universe is directly related to the human soul and its development, which means—'

'We're home,' Carol announced, sounding infinitely relieved.

'You can finish telling me all this later.'

* * * *

Back up in the guestroom, I was hit by a wave of restlessness that made the blank white walls of the modern room feel like an empty shell. I collapsed onto the edge of the bed, and fell heavily back across it to stop myself from calling a cab to take me to the Mina House hotel. Now that I had consciously made my choice, every second I spent away from my beautiful E'Ahmose felt like a century. And yet reason told me to keep my date with Simon, even if it was only to politely inform him that I was in love with Richard.

Carol was running a bath for herself, which meant I had more time on my hands than I knew what to do with until it was my turn to bathe and dress for dinner. I told myself I should enjoy the time alone, but it was impossible to relax feeling as though I had expensive champagne flowing through my body instead of blood. I was so intoxicatingly in love with Richard E'Ahmose the possibility of choosing Simon instead felt like a silly hiccup I had indulged in. The truth was, part of me had known from the moment I saw Richard's face and heard his voice in the bazaar that my heart and soul were lost to this enigmatically sexy stranger, and only my ridiculously rational mind had continued considering Simon.

I rolled restlessly over onto my stomach remembering the last time I had done this, and the hot stab of desire I experienced between my thighs made me moan into the mattress. Then I heard Richard's deep voice in my head saying, 'Remember your dreams, Mary…' and suddenly I knew I had a possible way out of the cage-like guestroom, less alive than an ancient Egyptian tomb which had at least been decorated with vibrant scenes of life. I would take a nap. I would try to fall asleep and see if I could meet my Priest of Anubis again in a dream. I hadn't seen him last night after I went to bed, but Simon had been lying next to me, and my uncomfortable awareness of his naked body kept waking me up throughout the night. There was nothing to prevent me from falling into a deep sleep now.

I got up and quickly stripped off my clothes, including my panties. I felt it was important to completely open myself to the purely sensual dimension I was consciously seeking to explore. There was no avoiding the slightly gritty feel of the polyester comforter as I lay down again, but I closed my eyes determined to ignore this reminder that I was in the twenty-first century. I had thought it would be difficult to fall asleep since I was feeling so strangely on edge, so it was a pleasant surprise when I felt my limbs growing gratefully heavy, and sinking into the bed in the unmistakably delicious way I knew would soon drown the constant chatter in my head and enable the deepest parts of me to drift off.

A loud beating sound directly above me startled me into sitting up.

'Meooow!' E'Ahmose the cat yowls in frustration that all the birds have gotten away from him again.

I blink, dazzled by the light and all the vibrant colors suddenly surrounding me. Then I realize it is the spirit of the setting sun sparkling across the water trapped in my dark lashes as my vision slowly comes into focus. Tall papyrus stalks form natural dark-green columns on either side of the river, that narrows to an intimate channel here in the place where we like to come fowling. The excited feline looks like a living figurehead with this front paws perched on the prow of the boat, but it is the tall, tanned man through whose legs I am able to see my cat who captures all my attention. Only a short white loincloth interferes with the sinuous flow of his muscles even as it enhances the bronzed smoothness of his skin. His back is to me, but every cell in my body recognizes his, and seems to course more joyously down the haunting tributaries of my veins at the sight of him. Part of me is surprised by the white cloth giving his head a square regal look, but the rest of me feels wonderfully relaxed where I lay across a Nile-blue cloth embroidered with tiny white gazelles leaping across it. The finely woven linen covers a thick grass mattress, and is littered with dark-gold cylindrical pillows made from a lion's skin stuffed with goose feathers.

'Come back to me, my lord,' I say plaintively, hungrily admiring his long, strong back.

'Just one last throw,' he replies, 'so my namesake does not die of frustration.'

I know he is referring to the excitedly taut figure of my cat at the prow of our small boat, drifting with the current along the eastern shore as close as possible to dense marshes alive with nesting birds.

'If you do not aim your shaft at me soon,' I tease, lying back languidly, 'it is I who shall die of longing years before our eternal home is finished, and then what will you do with my body?'

About a dozen birds abruptly explode from the marshes and, my heart racing, I watch with pleasure as my lover casts his spear into the heart of the wildly beating flock with the controlled power I am forever longing to be the victim of. It seems a small but wholly fitting tribute to his cat-like speed and grace when one of the winged creatures drops straight down from the sky at his sandaled feet, his weapon thrust deep into its delicious little body. He just has time enough to pull the small spear out of the dead bird before the four-legged E'Ahmose sinks his fangs into what he obviously considers his rightful prey, and hauls it triumphantly away to his place at the head of the boat.

The tall, two-legged E'Ahmose turns towards me, smiling. 'There,' he declares, kneeling on our make-shift bed, 'that demanding animal of yours is satisfied for the moment, so now I can concentrate on the much more arduous task of satisfying you, my love. It will take more than one thrust to quiet your wild desires, Nefermun.' He spreads himself on top of me as he speaks, aligning his sex with mine, and he is so much taller that I find my face on a level with his heart, which feels just right since it is his presence in the world that puts a smile on my lips, and makes me glad to open my eyes every morning as I inhale the subtly invigorating scent of his naked body lying beside me.

'Oh my lord!' I hold on to him, suddenly afraid the gods will take him away from me as jealous punishment for worshipping their priest more than them. 'Promise you'll never leave me, E'Ahmose.'

'Sweet Nefermun,' he kisses my forehead, effortlessly banishing the demons of my frightened thoughts as he lifts his body slightly off mine to find the opening in my pleated garment, 'we will be together forever,' he parts my dress as I unpin his loincloth, 'in this world and in any other Re shapes for the pleasure of our flesh through the soul of the gods.'

I do not need to reach down and guide his erection into my slick burrow, for his rigid length makes its way effortlessly into my tight channel. I sigh happily, raising my legs and wrapping them possessively around his hips as he begins thrusting hard, the full weight of his body pinning mine down beneath it. This evening there is no torturous savoring of the moment of union; his face buried in a lion-skin pillow, he penetrates me fast and furiously, concentrating on the divine exercise of driving his cock as deep into my body as possible even while pulling it almost all the way out, subjecting me to the exquisite agony of his head parting my labia and his rampant penis, solid as a god's golden phallus, rending me open time and time again. I love it when he possesses me like this, seemingly without a thought for my feelings, which inexplicably stokes my excitement almost more than when he is being a patient and considerate lover. I love the experience of his firm muscles straining against my soft curves trapped beneath them. I love the sensation of his balls slapping against my drenched sex blending with the sound of the river lapping against the hull as I sense my flesh becoming deeper and deeper for him. And yet I am also his vessel contentedly riding the current of the pleasure I can give him simply by lying passively beneath him. Then I lift my legs high and spread them wide so as not to hinder the violent choppiness of his hips as an orgasm carries his soul away like a powerful undertow , and leaves his helplessly gasping body lying motionless in my arms.

CHAPTER NINE

'Mary was saying something really strange in the car today,' Carol remarked at dinner that evening.

Simon looked even worse than I had expected he would; he could barely keep his eyes open, which made him look intensely angry, or maybe he was angry, with me, because he could sense I had already chosen Richard over him.

I nearly hadn't recognized Steve at first because he was wearing a shirt, and judging from his expression it had been hand-woven in a monastery of self-flagellating monks. The top three buttons were undone, yet he still kept tugging on the collar to get the starched rim away from the back of his sunburned neck.

Not surprisingly, neither Simon nor Steve reacted to Carol's vague statement. The former was enjoying his 'hair of the dog' with a vengeance, and the latter was too busy writhing like a caterpillar struggling to find a way out of its cocoon. And I for one was too busy missing Richard, or E'Ahmose, or was there a difference?

The only way I had been able to console myself after I awoke from my second amazingly vivid dream of the man I had loved centuries ago was to choose a white dress for the evening that was the closest thing I owned to an ancient Egyptian gown. The halter top set off my shapely shoulders, and made a bra impossible, but I was no longer shy about showing off my lovely nipples. The dress clung gently to my curves and ended at mid thigh, enabling me to show off the legs so many men had admired in white high-heeled strap sandals. And since I didn't feel it was right to wear the jewelry Richard had given me while I was supposedly out on a date with another man, I hadn't adorned my body with anything at all. Only my nails were still sporting an expensive French manicure that I frowned down on now, thinking that the delicate almond polish I had seen in my first dream might be more interesting.

'I love the way everyone just ignores me,' Carol declared petulantly.

'Sorry. What did you say, honey?' Steve made a noble effort to concentrate on something other than his physical misery.

'Oh never mind.' She pouted.

'She said "Mary said something very strange in the car today".' Simon said. 'Which means it probably made profound sense,' he found the energy to add.

'Thank you,' I chimed in. 'I rather think it did. I was just telling Carol that I don't believe your book is a mere documentation for posterity of Saqqara's bas-reliefs. I believe you're studying them the way a physicist would work on an equation. I think you're trying to decode their symbolic language because you believe the Egyptian's had access to a very real physical power resulting from the synthesis of art, science and religion that you were talking about this morning, a force mankind lost when it concentrated on developing the rational part of the brain that can't see how, on an invisible level, everything is a mysterious whole.'

His eyes opened almost all the way, but remained fixed on his drink. 'Now is not the time, Mary,' he said wearily.

'And why isn't it?'

'Because the show is about to begin.'

A milky spotlight suddenly spilled between the two rows of tables and a loud, rhythmically pulsing music burst out of hidden speakers, making further conversation impossible. There was the trill of a tambourine evocative of Hathor's sistrum, and then a vision sashayed into the light—a woman trailing golden gossamer-thin veils like hazy morning sunshine flowing over her green bra flowering with red tassels that danced against a snowy field of naked flesh. In her navel gleamed a dark-red jewel held magically in place as her belly undulated and rippled in enviably supple waves. Her luxurious black hair was pinned up away from her face but allowed to tumble freely down her back. Her unveiled features were heavily but tastefully made up, and her bone structure was strikingly beautiful.

After the inevitable stab of jealousy, I allowed myself to succumb to the dancer's spell. It was amazing how she could jiggle her hips and make a supple wave out of her soft yet toned belly, and coordinate these tantalizing displays of erotic skill with the graceful motion of her arms as well as the precise steps of her bare feet. It made me wish I possessed such athletic control of my torso so I could treat Richard in private to this enticing visual display of a woman's mysterious inner muscles. The firm control the dancer had over her softly undulating curves beneath the expressive arcs of her arms symbolically transformed her whole body into a woman's sexual organ rippling and contracting, yielding and tightening around a man's erect force while her lovely face smiled rapturously and her arms slipped lovingly around him. I was entranced by the spectacle of a professional belly dancer practicing her art, not in the way a man would be, but because it filled me with a sense of my own feminine power.

After her performance, the applause lasted a long time, during which I was surprised and annoyed to catch Simon and Steve whispering to each other, obviously deep in a conversation that had been going on for a while.

'I'm going to the Lady's Room,' Carol announced.

'I'll go with you,' I said. Richard would not have ignored the sensual dance, I was sure of that, and Simon plummeted another notch in my esteem because he obviously had.

'…From the Antiquities Department,' I heard Steve murmur as I got up to leave the table.

'Maybe, but they can't do anything,' Simon replied, looking smug. 'Even if they've heard the rumors, it's illegal to torture us to try and find out the location.'

'Yeah, but they'll be watching us like vultures, and the minute they figure out where the entrance is, they'll bury us in red tape and nationalist rights and hand it over to their own archaeologists on a silver platter.' Steve looked particularly handsome when he was angry. 'A few of them are sitting over there at the bastard's table right now. We'll never swing the excavation rights, never.'

I hurried after Carol, who had been born with a honing device for bathrooms; she always knew where to find them no matter where we were. 'Richard's here!' I whispered.

'What?' She stopped dead. 'Where?'

'Somewhere…oh, my God, there he is!'

'Mary, you're here with Simon. Remember?' The painful strength of her grip on my arm made me wonder why she hadn't gone into sculpting as well as painting and photography. 'Don't even look at him!'

'But he's so beautiful!'

'"The devil is a charming man",' she quoted glibly, literally dragging me towards the bathroom.

'I don't believe in the devil, Carol.'

'Which makes it all the easier for him to get you.'

'You don't believe in the devil either, for Christ's sake.'

'I know, but I have to say something to stop you from making a fool of yourself. Weren't you scared when he carried you off on horseback? You don't know anything about him except that he's rich.'

'And smart and handsome and great in bed and—'

'So is Simon.'

'Yes,' I wrenched my arm out of her grasp, 'you would know that, wouldn't you.'

I shoved open the bathroom door, frightening away the young Egyptian boy who had been standing just inside it serving as a living towel rack in exchange for baksheesh. When I stormed in, he raced out waving all the white flags of his towels in a terrified surrendering of space to the angry foreign woman.

I slammed into one of the stalls and began relieving myself not just of wine but of the ridiculous jealousy that had possessed me, especially considering the fact that it wasn't Simon I wanted. I knew it now beyond a shadow of a doubt. Twenty-four hours away from Richard had been almost more than I could stand, and my dream of E'Ahmose and Nefermun fowling and fooling around in the marshes was still so fresh and vivid in my mind it hurt. When I realized Richard was in the nightclub with me, the joy that suffused my whole being felt like my heart bursting free of all the minor doubts bandaging it. I had recognized the quality of the joy from my dreams—a happiness as subtle and yet as obvious and wonderful as the sunrise. It was Richard I wanted to spend the rest of my days with, Richard, handsome and intelligent and sensitive enough to consider the possibility that he had lived before. Simon was also extremely bright, and his theories about ancient Egypt were marvelously profound, but I felt there was something missing when I was with him. He believed magical things about ancient Egypt yet failed to apply it to the present and to his own life. He prided himself on the fact that he was a hard-working anthropologist and not just a rich eccentric like Sir Ashley.

Yet it seemed to me that unless you embraced the reality, the fact, of mystery as an undeniable aspect of life, you could never truly be a great scientist. Simon was a wonderful man (although I didn't agree with the selfish way he was covering up a monumental discovery) and Mary Fallon would probably have been happy with him, but my deepest self, Nefermun, would have remained unfulfilled. My true self, the woman I had always imagined being, the intensely sensual yet also deeply spiritual woman waiting curled up in my chest like a sleeping cat dreaming of what life could really be like with the right man, Nefer-marymun would never have been born. Nefer-marymun would never have had a chance to begin realizing herself if I had not met Sir Richard Gerald Ashely. And we would never have met at all if he had not seen me in a dream and traveled across the world to find me against all rational odds.

'Mary?' Carol called plaintively from an adjoining stall. 'Are you all right?'

'I'm fine,' I said cheerfully. We flushed in tandem, and smiled at each other as we washed our hands, forced to shake them dry as the living towel rack had fled. 'I've made my choice, Carol.'

She looked at my face in the mirror, her eyes wide with anticipation.

My smile deepened.

She sighed, 'Richard.'

'Yes. I know you think I hardly know him, but the truth is, part of me knows him better than anyone I've ever met before and I think than anyone I ever will meet. He's my destiny, Carol. I've never felt this way before. Things just got complicated because I happened to meet Simon first, and he seemed so perfect for me that my brain wouldn't let me shake that initial impression and take Richard seriously. You see, my mind mistrusted our irresistible attraction to each other. I thought maybe it was just a sexual thing, but that's because our bodies were responding to the mysterious magnetic attraction between our souls. I don't know if it's true or not, Carol, but with this man I can truly sense I've lived before and that love really is forever, and that no matter how many times love changes form, it never dies.'

Her eyes were shining. 'I think I'm going to cry,' she warned.

'Oh Carol,' I slipped an arm around her shoulder, 'don't worry, Simon won't be that upset, he—'

She shrugged my arm off angrily. 'That's not why I'm crying!' She sniffed dramatically. 'It's just so beautiful!'

I laughed. 'It's a beautiful mess I've gotten myself into. That damned photograph complicated things even more. It's strange that my finding my soul mate is coinciding with the discovery of Imhotep's tomb.'

'I believe you love Richard, Mary, but are you sure you can trust him?'

'Carol, I could ask you the same thing. Are you sure you can trust your boss, and Steve for that matter?'

'Steve's the one we found lying unconscious in the desert, not Richard,' she reminded me sharply.

'He told me he had nothing to do with that.'

'And of course you believe him because he's your soul mate. But what are you going to do now? You came here with

Simon tonight.'

'I know.' I bit my lip wondering what was the best way to handle the situation.

'You have to come back to the table with me, Mary, you can't be so rude as to—'

'I know,' I repeated. Now that my mind had finally caught up with my heart and soul, every second I spent away from my beloved E'Ahmose was torture, but Simon had already ordered my dinner and I liked and respected him too much to just blow him off. But when we emerged from the bathroom, it was Richard's seated figure my eyes were drawn to.

'Come on, Mary.'

'I'm coming,' I said, but I lingered in the corridor leading on one end to the bathrooms and on the other to the exit.

Richard was talking to the man seated beside him, but suddenly he turned his head and met my eyes as though he had felt the touch of my longing on his skin. Beneath his intent stare my knees began to feel weak, and I had no idea how I was going to convince them to carry me back to Simon instead.

When two black-robed men gently took hold of both my arms and began escorting me towards the exit, I was more relieved than anything. I had fully intended to do the right thing and return to Simon's table to politely break up with him, but it seemed the decision was being taken out of my hands, and I was glad. The moment I became aware of Richard's presence in the club, my body began suffering something akin to physical pain fighting the irresistible need to move towards him and fall into the orbit of his arms. And when our eyes met across the dark room, I knew he felt the same way about me.

I had no idea how he had communicated with his men so quickly, but there was no doubt in my mind or in my heart that it was two of his servants leading me out of the building. Outside, I saw people glance curiously at the young woman walking between two unusually large Egyptians in elegant black robes, but all I cared about was the fact that any moment now Richard and I would be together again. I did notice, however, that the door one of the men opened for me belonged to a long black limousine, and the bare skin of my arms and legs appreciated the exquisitely soft leather interior as I seated myself.

Only a few heartbeats later, the door opened again so Richard could slip in beside me. Almost at once, the gleaming vehicle flowed away from the curb as smoothly as a whale diving into the twisting currents of dark alleys, as the lights of Cairo glimmered like moonlit foam behind us.

* * * *

Beneath his black suit jacket my priest of Anubis was wearing a sleeveless white T-shirt tucked into black jeans, and the sight of his strong bare arms as he slipped off the jacket struck me as the hieroglyph spelling out how much I loved this man. He leaned forward in the seat to press a button in the space-age console before him, and a bottle of Champagne appeared as if by magic followed by two crystal flute glasses. The interior of the limousine was incredibly spacious; I think it was bigger than my living room back home. I gladly accepted the glass he offered me, and watched in appreciative silence as he filled it with the glimmering liquid. My hand trembled slightly, but it wasn't the car's fault; the ride was so smooth we might have been flying away from the club on a magic carpet.

'Thank you, sir,' I said formally.

He touched his glass to mine. 'My pleasure, Nefer-marymun.'

I took a sip. 'Mm, this bottle must have cost your chauffeur's entire month's salary. It's divine.'

'A compliment and a criticism all wrapped up in one.' He chimed his glass against mine a second time. 'Neatly done.' He smiled.

'I wasn't criticizing you, Richard.'

'I know you weren't, you're just socially conscious. I respect that.'

'Were you born into money?'

'Yes, and as a consequence people tend to assume I was handed everything on a silver platter.'

'Were you?' I sipped my champagne contentedly; it was wonderful just getting to know him better.

'Yes, I suppose I was.' A shadow of concern dimmed his smile. 'Does that bother you?'

'Not at all. I don't believe character is determined by circumstances, not to the extent modern psychology would have us believe, anyway.'

He touched his glass to mine in a third toast. 'You're as wise as you are beautiful, Nefer-marymun.'

'Well, I'm getting there,' I said humbly, draining my glass.

He promptly refilled it, his slate-green eyes inscrutably dark in the limousine's luxurious twilight.

'Why, Sir Ashley,' I drawled with an exaggerated southern accent, 'I do believe you're trying to get me drunk.'

'Have you eaten yet tonight?'

'No.' I felt a stab of guilt. 'Simon had ordered me dinner, but…' I took a long, numbing swig of the fine champagne to forget about the man I had just left stranded in a restaurant along with my best friend and her date.

'Was I mistaken?' he asked quietly.

'Mistaken about what?'

'When our eyes met in the club, I sensed, I knew, you had made your choice, Mary.' He drained his own glass abruptly. 'Was I mistaken?' he asked again even more softly.

'No,' I whispered fervently. 'But I was planning to go back to Simon's table and tell him politely, somehow.'

'I sensed you were torn.' He refilled his glass. 'And I hope you'll forgive me for sparing you an uncomfortable scene that in my opinion wasn't necessary. Mr. Taylor doesn't really care about anyone except himself and his career. He'll be fine without you.'

'That's a bit harsh, don't you think?'

'Not at all, just the sad truth, and I'm glad you haven't eaten tonight. A ritual should always be performed when the gross process of digestion isn't interfering with higher functions.'

'Ritual?' My empty stomach contracted uncomfortably around the portentous word.

'Yes, my love, a sacred rite that will help Nefermun come fully to life inside you and enable you to truly begin living as Nefer-marymun.'

I discovered my throat was suddenly too tight to swallow the fine champagne. 'What exactly do you have in mind, Richard?'

'If it's all right with you, Mary, I'd like you to spend part of the night in a pyramid, the pyramid of Unas, to be precise.'

I laughed. 'Are you joking?'

'No, I'm not.'

I still couldn't quite make out the expression in his eyes, but I could sense my reaction had disappointed him somewhat. 'I'm sorry, Richard, it's just so...unexpected.'

'You should learn to expect the unexpected, my love, always. But it really shouldn't be so unexpected. The final stage of initiation for priests and priestesses of Anubis consisted of spending whole nights alone in the heart of a pyramid.'

'Alone? Did you say alone?'

'You're co cute.' Smiling indulgently, he caressed my cheek with the fingertips of his free hand in the way that made me feel infinitely precious. 'Don't be afraid, I'll be with you in the beginning, and at the end.'

'Richard, I—'

'Hush.' He gently placed his index finger over my lips. 'You know Nefermun wants this more than anything and that only Mary is getting the jitters.'

I looked deep into myself while gazing into his shadowed eyes and realized he was absolutely right, as usual.

'It was fun fowling in the marshes this afternoon, wasn't it?' he asked casually, and his smile deepened as I nearly dropped my glass.

'You were there?' I breathed.

'Yes. I'm so proud of you, Mary,' he added seriously, 'you've come so far so fast, no pun intended. You're so close to finding the key that will unlock abilities buried deep inside you. That's why I arranged for this ritual tonight, because you're ready.'

'Ready for what?'

'To slip on some Winged Sandals, my love.'

* * * *

I discovered during the long ride to Saqqara that eating was not the only thing prohibited before an important ritual. We spent a good part of the journey kissing and caressing each other, but that was as far as Richard would allow us to go. The sexual act, he told me, was an important part of the rite, and we couldn't waste any of our vital energy ahead of time. His mystical logic made perfect sense to me, especially when his tongue was passionately explaining it to me without words, and wondering what exactly he had planned was getting me so wet my pussy felt hotter and deeper by the second. I moaned, desperate to feel his magnificent penis opening me up as it filled me completely, but for the moment I was content to settle for the hard hand he thrust between my thighs to cradle my smoldering sex.

'Please,' I begged, clinging to his shoulders and kissing the deliciously firm yet tender side of his neck.

'No,' he whispered, his breath hot on my temple as he pulled gently on my hair to lift my face up to his again, 'not yet.'

I gasped when he pressed the heel of his hand against the infinitely sensitive seed of my clitoris through my cotton panties, and began moving it up and down slowly. 'Do you like that?' he whispered in my ear.

'Oh yes, don't stop.'

'I can't let you come,' he warned.

I leaned slightly back in the seat and caressed his hard arm down to his wrist, pressing his hand even harder against my clit. 'But I want to come,' I said softly, longingly.

'You can't,' he insisted even as he kept moving his hand relentlessly against me, 'not yet.'

I felt increasingly desperate for him to take off my panties and slip some of his fingers inside me at least, but he knew if he went so far that I would climax around his penetrating digits, so he deliberately left the frustrating white bandage of my panties covering my aching sex even as he kept rubbing my knob with the heel of his palm, at once cruelly teasing me and thoroughly pleasing me.

'Oh God, stop,' I begged breathlessly. 'I'm going to come if you don't stop!'

'No, you won't.' He kept up his subtle rhythmic caressing of the crown of my sex where my pleasure was growing and swelling, threatening to reach a peak from which all my feelings would plunge into a shattering climax. 'I'm going to bring you to the edge, Mary, and you're going to hold yourself there.'

'Oh God, I can't.'

'Yes, you can.' His voice was as firm as the base of his hand beneath which he was expertly massaging and stimulating the divine little seed of my flesh. 'You're going to poise your body on the brink of pleasure, Nefer-marymun, and let the promise of it suffuse your entire being, not just your body.'

'Richard, I can't do it, I can't!' I flung my arms up over my head and held on to the back of the seat as I gazed down the length of his arm. It was so straight and hard I thought of the serpents the god of eternity grasped in his hands, and I felt the beginning of an orgasm licking my clit like a hot tongue threatening to fork through my veins as a searing pleasure. 'You're just too good!' I gasped. 'You know just how to do that.'

He laughed beneath his breath, but his voice was serious. 'When you're sure, absolutely sure you can't take anymore without coming, tell me and I'll stop.'

'All right,' I lied.

'I'm trusting you not to let yourself come, Nefer-marymun.' He looked into my eyes. 'It's important, and trust me, the pleasure you'll experience later will be more than worth the struggle now.'

'But I'm so wet…' My white panties were clinging to my labia like a thick mist coating a flower's rosy petals. A climax was inexorably taking root between my legs and sending delicate yet deliciously strong tendrils of ecstasy up through my pelvis.

'Mm, yes, you are, very wet,' he agreed. 'Your pussy is so hot and wet my big cock would sink all the way down inside you with just one good hard thrust.'

'Oh Richard…Richard!'

He pulled his hand out from between my legs.

'Oh nooo!' I wailed.

The limousine came to a stop.

'We're here, my love.' He smoothed my dress down over my thighs again. 'You did very well, and now you're nicely primed for what's to come, no pun intended.'

'I hate you.' I pouted.

He laughed again quietly.

* * * *

I carried my high-heeled sandals across the sand during the brief trek to the pyramid of Unas, legendary pharaoh of the Old Kingdom. Every inch of the interior of his pyramid was covered with hieroglyphs known as The Pyramid Texts, which in later dynasties came to be called The Book of Coming Forth By Day, better known now as The Book of the Dead. It was Unas who first used these complex hieroglyphic formulas to render himself immortal, and it was in the heart of his pyramid temple that Richard intended to perform our ritual. I still had no idea what he had planned, and I distracted myself from trying to imagine it with academic thoughts that soothed my nerves. It had always struck me as rather inaccurate to call pyramids tombs. Unas had had no intention of 'resting in peace' inside his burial chamber, which was actually more like a launch pad to eternity. The mummy that was left behind could be likened to the discarded stages of the first Apollo rockets, a necessary part of the mysterious vehicle of spiritual growth but one that was nevertheless expendable, although it was true that great care had to be taken in how it was discarded in order not to short-circuit the divine journey.

'What are you thinking, Nefer-marymun?' Richard's deep, quiet voice seemed to rise all the way up into the pulsing sky and fill the universe with his uniquely stimulating personality.

'Oh nothing,' I replied, 'just some crazy stuff about mummies and rockets.'

'What?' He laughed, squeezing my hand, which he had not let go of since we left the limousine and he began leading me across the sand.

I explained my thoughts to him, and somehow refrained from asking him what exactly the ritual we were about to perform would entail.

'That's all true,' he agreed, 'although it is a rather unwholesome mixing of metaphors.'

'Talking to you is so much fun, Richard.'

'Just talking to me?' he teased.

Finally, unable to contain my curiosity and anxiety a moment longer, I blurted, 'What are we going to do inside the pyramid? You mentioned something about spending part of the night in there?'

'Yes, that'll be part of it. You need to spend part of the night alone in a pyramid.'

'But I don't want you to leave me alone in there.' I had been hoping he really hadn't meant the alone part.

'Yes, you do.'

'No, I don't.'

'Forget for a moment what Mary Fallon thinks and ask Nefermun what she wants.'

I bit my lip to keep from retorting, 'But they're the same person!' knowing full well this was not exactly true, and much as I hated to admit it, after a few uncomfortable minutes of soul-searching, I realized he was right—Nefermun was looking forward to the haunting challenge of being left alone inside a pyramid at night.

* * * *

I suffered the nervous thrill of a conspirator when we arrived at the entrance to the pyramid of Unas and were greeted by two of Richard's servants, possibly the same two who had escorted me out of the nightclub. I couldn't help noticing their long black robes were finer than anything Simon's men ever wore. It was a strange moment for what I knew mentally to suddenly kick in as a visceral knowledge that the man I loved was filthy rich. I had never considered the size of a man's bank account when assessing his worth, so perhaps it was poetic justice that my soul mate just happened to be wealthy.

'Are you ready, my lady?' Sir Ashley asked me with an intense formality that launched a flock of butterflies in my belly.

'Yes, my lord.' I really liked the sound of that.

One of his men handed him a lantern. 'Hold on to my belt,' Richard instructed me, and I dutifully followed him into the pyramid.

When we emerged from the uncomfortably claustrophobic passage, I had to bite my tongue. Richard had pointed out to me that the fumes from the fire Simon had lit in the courtyard of Ti's mastaba could potentially damage the bas-reliefs, yet his servants had lit four bronze braziers supported on pedestals inside the burial chamber of Unas containing some of the oldest and most sacred hieroglyphs in Egypt. This was such a prime example of double standards that I couldn't keep my mouth shut. 'Richard, won't the fumes from these fires damage the priceless Pyramid Texts?'

'They're being sucked out through a small tunnel by that battery-powered fan over there.'

'Oh.' I smiled, very pleased that my ancient priest had not become a modern hypocrite.

'But it was good of you to ask, and I would not even have considered doing this if I didn't feel you were worth the time, trouble and risk.'

'Thank you.'

He came and stood before me. 'My pleasure, because now we're going to prime the space.'

'Prime it?' I whispered, desire stirring in my belly like a snake, as my arms slipped around his neck and I tilted my head back for his kiss.

'Sexual energy,' he reached up and grasped my wrists, 'is unbelievably potent, Mary.' He gently removed my arms from around him.

'Wasn't there some crazy scientist once who tried capturing sexual energy in a box?' I asked.

'Yes. He had some interesting ideas, but he was, as you said, crazy. You look beautiful in this dress, my love, nevertheless, it must come off.' He took me by the arm and led me over to the large sarcophagus.

I had seen the Pyramid Texts in books countless times, but in reality, and experienced as a whole, they were much more striking. Lovely, exquisitely rendered hieroglyphs still alive with traces of color covered every inch of the walls, so that we were literally embraced by magical incantations.

Richard pulled off his shirt, and I followed his cue by undoing the clasp on my halter top and exposing my breasts.

'Leave your heels on,' he instructed as he kicked off his black sandals, and then quickly removed his pants and underwear while watching me slide my dress down my legs.

Tonight our clothes formed an unceremonious heap on the packed sand of the profoundly still chamber, the soft crackling of the flames in the braziers only enhancing the centuries-old, millenniums deep silence.

'No, I'll do that,' he said as I made to remove my white lace bikini panties.

He hooked his thumbs into the delicate elastic, and caressed the sides of my legs as he slowly pulled the skimpy garment down to my ankles, holding it open so I could step out of it in my high-heels.

I waited for him to compliment my legs, and was strangely pleased that he didn't. I could see the appreciation in his eyes, and that was more than enough. It was as if he knew that I knew I had great legs and had been told so countless times before, and his telling me now would be just another penny tossed into the fountain. In these uniquely special moments in the heart of a pyramid, his remaining silent before all my visible charms not only made him stand out from all my other lovers, it was somehow also proof that his feelings for me ran so deep there was no need for him to indulge my vanity.

'I want you to lie back on the sarcophagus, Mary.'

He grasped me around the waist as he had in the bazaar, and lifted me onto the edge.

I lay back across the cold stone lid of Unas's sarcophagus. Once again, I surrendered to the arousing sense of how soft and vulnerable my young flesh seemed surrounded by crushing layers of rock; rock that was in turn surrounded by the impenetrable darkness of a desert night trembling with a multitude of stars. And even while I couldn't see them, I felt those stars mysteriously reflected in all my nerve-endings.

The Englishman, who I knew from my dreams had once been

a Priest of Anubis, climbed onto the sarcophagus lid with me. In the flickering shadows, the long black hair he wore tied back, made me sense a jackal's tail. He crawled towards me, then over me; the sinuously strong lines of his body captivating me as he moved down towards my pussy and dangled the stiffening length of his penis directly over my mouth.

I craned my head up for the feast, and moaned as I failed to catch his head between my lips.

'No, keep your arms down at your sides,' he instructed, 'and use only your tongue.' He parted my thighs and buried his face between them as his cock filled my mouth.

I moaned again and again as he grew inexorably thicker and longer.

In this position I had no way of preventing the tip of his erection from burrowing into the sensitive space of my throat and I was glad. I was beginning to love the excruciating sensation, especially when soothed by the soft pleasure of his tongue licking my labia, preparing me for its relentlessly skilled siege of my clitoris, and I knew from experience it would surrender explosively to him in the end.

I loved having his thighs framing my face as he crouched over me, his knees braving the unyielding stone as I rested comfortably beneath him. I was amazed by the fact that I loved everything about him; there was nothing about this man that didn't turn me on, and I could only admire how well he coordinated twirling his tongue teasingly around my clit with sliding his dick in and out of my mouth, every few strokes letting me suck gratefully on his head so I could swallow his pre-cum.

His obvious enjoyment of what I was doing to him tasted so delicious to me I even loved the feel of his semen trickling down my throat, knowing that with any other man it would only have been an exercise in not choking. I had to control my gag reflex now, but it was worth it in order to please him as deeply as he was pleasing me. His lips and tongue never stimulated one spot on my pussy for too long, and yet they also never moved on too soon either. He always sensed when I was ready to follow the elusive current of pleasure to another glowing peak in the delta of nerve-endings flooding me with delight, the sweet thrill of his tongue's caresses deepening in rhythm with his erection rising in and out of my other warm wet hole.

He seemed to know when my clitoris had reached the crucial smoldering point and was ready to be set ablaze by a climax, because that's when he concentrated his attack, stoking my nub with serpent-like flicks of his tongue as his hips picked up their pace. He began urgently stuffing his cock all the way into my mouth, selfishly riding my face, and I came helplessly in response to the overpowering sensations penetrating me at both ends that made it impossible to resist the ecstasy ripping through my body. His erection muffled the screams struggling to rise out of my throat, as my clitoris seemed to burst open against his tongue like a juicy grape, the utterly intoxicating bliss of my orgasm flowing straight into his mouth. Breathless seconds later, the foaming wave of his cum broke on the back of my tongue and I felt we were literally drowning in each other.

When it was over, he slid his still rigid length slowly out from between my lips, then lifted his body off mine and gently drew my head up onto his thighs as he knelt behind me.

'You did very well, Mary,' he said quietly, brushing strands of my dark hair, sticky with the evidence of his pleasure, off my flushed cheeks.

'That was incredible, Richard.'

'Has a man ever come straight down in your throat like that?'

'God no.'

'Then why did you enjoy it with me?'

I looked up into his eyes. 'Because I love you.'

He bent over and kissed my forehead. 'I've been waiting a long time to hear you say that,' he whispered, and then abruptly left me lying naked across the sarcophagus. 'Stay where you are,' he commanded, picking up his black underwear and slipping it back on.

'But—'

'Not buts, not tonight anyway.' He cast me a teasing smile as he put on his pants.

Part of me wanted to bolt up anxiously, but I didn't, I just lay feeling wonderfully languid and relaxed against the cold, hard surface, enjoying the contrast of the warm light pulsing against my lids as I closed my eyes for a moment, then opened them again to gaze contentedly at one of the walls covered with hieroglyphs. I could scarcely believe I was looking at the famous Pyramid Texts, the earliest example of Egyptian funerary writing, and forever one of its finest.

'It's time.' The bare chest and arms that stepped into my field of vision certainly seemed to belong there. 'I'm pleased to see you don't appear at all nervous.' He regarded me soberly, and in the flickering lamplight his hair, which was now only pulled back loosely, formed sleek black wings around his face. 'Could it be the tense and anxious Mary Fallon was at last swept away by her intense orgasm?'

'Yes,' I sighed.

He placed a large, warm hand on my chest just above my breasts. Very slowly, barely touching me, he caressed my body down to the highly sensitized space between my navel and my clitoris. 'I want everything from you, Nefer-marymun.'

'You have everything, Richard.' I gazed hungrily up at his powerful torso. No elaborate pendant interfered with the clean lines of his chest, truly giving him the forceful aura of an Old Kingdom priest.

He leaned over me. 'Your body isn't all I want from you,' he whispered, his lips brushing my forehead again, and when he suddenly cradled my hot, slick pussy in his hand, my moan of pleasure echoed around the ancient chamber. 'You're special enough to come with me into another dimension, my love. The physical consummation is only the beginning of equally vital levels of union to be realized between us. The experience I'm about to thrust you into is one you'll never forget.'

He removed his hand from between my thighs and took a step back. Then he retrieved his shirt, slipping it back on before picking up the lantern he had brought into the pyramid with him.

For a mere second, I felt myself turn into Mary again, my body tense against the unyielding stone. But Nefermun was anticipating the sacred challenge to come, and she held Mary back.

The flickering light in the chamber darkened ominously when E'Ahmose walked over to one of the lamps and blew out the flame. 'I'll guide you by going ahead of you, my love,' he informed me cryptically, 'but you have to follow me yourself.' He spoke casually, as though we were merely planning a little car trip together.

'Richard, what are you doing?' I watched in growing trepidation as he moved to the opposite corner of the chamber and extinguished a second lamp. Now only two were left passionately fighting off the darkness. 'You didn't mention anything about leaving me alone in the dark, Richard,' I protested childishly.

'Don't be afraid, my love.' He repeated the endearment knowing it would soothe me as well as give me strength. 'Part of you recognizes this ritual of initiation. All priests and priestesses of Anubis had to go through this. It's necessary to immerse yourself in total darkness so the lines between your flesh and your soul are erased, which will help you become aware of your other, higher, senses.' He did not blow out the third flame but instead gently snuffed it out between his thumb and forefinger.

A host of restless menacing shadows was born around the last remaining lamp, and I don't think it was my imagination that they all appeared to be reaching for me like threatening fingers hungering for my dimly luminous flesh. 'Richard?!' I made a supreme effort not to let terror take complete hold of me.

He quickly returned to my side. 'The ability to dream true dreams is buried within you, Nefer-marymun.' His expression was kind but stern, and he did not touch me again. 'I'm going to help dig it out of you. What would otherwise take months might under these precise circumstances, and in this mystical place, take only a few hours. Your dreaming skills are not as developed as mine in this life so I'm appointing myself your teacher.' He turned away again and extinguished the last flickering lamp so the chamber was lit now only by his lantern.

'Richard, you're actually going to leave me alone here in the dark?' I was proud of how remarkably calm I sounded. 'Without any matches so I can re-light the lamps, I mean, just in case?'

Keeping his distance, he looked over at me where I lay on top of the sarcophagus. 'You won't need to light them,' he assured me. 'You're perfectly safe in here. My men are outside the pyramid and I'll be close by, closer than you think. I'll be as close as your heart, my love. Use your pulse like wings to lift you out of your fear into the dimension of your true self, Nefer-marymun.' He bent over, preparing to enter the passage leading out of the room. 'Only your body is tied to its limitations,' he told me over his shoulder, 'the rest of you is absolutely free and as powerful as your imagination.

I'm confident you'll find the door inside you that will bring you to me.' And with these final, impossibly positive words, he crouched into the passageway and left me alone in the dark.

CHAPTER TEN

My Priest of Anubis was right. I couldn't move a muscle I was so terrified of the absolute darkness. My feelings were running around each other like crazy and they felt just as real, or even more so, than my own skin now that I could no longer distinguish the borders between my inner and physical self.

I tried to forget the fact that the part of me named Mary Fallon slept with a nightlight back in her North End apartment. It was a lovely clear glass nightlight I had purchased at Bed, Bath & Beyond for $9.99 in the shape of an elegant seated cat. I thought of her as the Egyptian cat goddess Bastet and she kept me safe at night by holding the darkness at bay, sort of like a metaphysical curtain hook draping gentle, luminously edged shadows around me.

Yet even when Bastet wasn't plugged in, the darkness back in Boston was never as impenetrable as this thanks to street lamps. I had never known such a complete and utter blackness could exist as the one my beloved E'Ahmose plunged me into when he left with the lantern. The second he left I knew that I either panicked completely or stayed utterly calm, because only one or the other extreme was possible in the black hole that sucked all my thoughts and feelings out of me until they seemed to sinisterly fill the room around my helpless body.

I would either come out of this experience a better, stronger person, or I would faint from terror and sleep through the ordeal, it was my choice. Richard was waiting for me in a dream, but I would never be able to meet him there if I simply passed out from fear. I had to be brave. I had to take a deep breath and force my tense limbs to relax against the stone. I had to tell the cowering child inside me that I was not in any danger just because a silent, lifeless blackness was pressing against my skin. I was in the heart of a pyramid alive with beautiful hieroglyphs, hieroglyphs that guided the soul through all the necessary steps involved in becoming one with Re's eternal light and life.

I thought about the sun, I pictured it burning in the sky and tried to imagine its warmth caressing me the way Richard's hands caressed me. I could not let myself be mad at him for leaving me alone like this because I knew his intentions were good, and I was also genuinely concerned that any negative vibes I sent out would develop an objective life of their own around me. It seemed entirely possible to me that my thoughts could use the darkness to take form, so I had to keep my imagination as positive as possible.

No longer even dimly able to make out the borders of my flesh, I suffered the impression that my thoughts weren't imprisoned in my mind at all but were actually milling around me. It was an unnerving concept since I had seen too many horror movies in my life; my heart and soul were nowhere near as pure as an ancient Egyptian's would have been. I felt my brain perversely reigning over a veritable kingdom of nightmares swirling around me in an invisible psychological storm even as I tried to think calmly and rationally.

The air in the chamber was oppressively still and there wasn't even a whisper of sound, which made my quiet breathing seem unnaturally loud. The silence weighed as heavily as the inert hand of a mummy resting directly against my heart, my mind a Pandora's box abruptly flung open by the absolute absence of light and sound.

I can control this experience, I thought desperately, but my voice sounded impotently loud in my head. I didn't dare actually speak out loud for fear of calling attention to myself and encouraging one of the vague atrocities occupying the burial chamber with me to attack, which made me realize I was not really in control of myself at all. I knew for a fact that I was completely alone, yet I could not shake the horrible feeling that my vulnerably naked body had become the center of a demonic crowd.

I can control this, I repeated again with more determination. Darkness is not evil, I told myself sternly. And suddenly, in a blessed wave of remembering, Egyptian cosmology came to my rescue. A voice that was mine and yet stronger than mine recited words that seemed written in a luminous script before me: Darkness is the primeval clay of the universe from which I can shape whatever I desire. My mind is the Lotus bud that rose from the dark primordial waters of Nun and flowered into the divine light and life of consciousness.

By leaving me alone in here without any means to rekindle the lamps, Richard had made it clear that if I wanted light, it would have to shine from inside me.

I don't remember exactly when I began sensing the hieroglyphs carved into the chamber walls were subliminally supporting me. Picturing their hard, confident lines surrounding me somehow helped me get a grip on my irrational fears. They enabled me to reign in my wildly out of control feelings and focus my thoughts.

It just so happened I had read a translation of the Pyramid Texts on the plane from Boston, and now I 'entertained' myself by mentally reciting the fragment I remembered: Draw the bolt! Open the door to heaven! Open for Unas! The doors are open over the fire of spirit...Arise Horus born of the flame...clearing the way that he may pass...

This had to be the inner door Richard had referred to, the 'bolt' was fear, and until I found the strength to draw it, the way to heaven and the luminous flame of my invulnerable spirit was closed to me. Lying naked across the lid of a sarcophagus in a pitch-black burial chamber, my soul understood and appreciated this ancient invocation in a much more intimate and vital way than just casually reading it on a plane. All I had to do was lighten my heart by letting faith burn away the fears clogging my metaphorical arteries, or something like that.

At some point, I found myself not only forgiving Richard for leaving me here alone in the dark but actually thanking him for forcing me to face myself as I never had before. And remembering the way he had looked at me after we made love on this very same sarcophagus lid banished the demons haunting me and filled me instead with a reassuring sense of his presence. Suddenly, the darkness was not a formless threat, it was the mysterious depth of his love embracing me.

'I love you, E'Ahmose,' I dared to whisper the truth out loud. 'I love you, Richard!'

Eventually, amazingly, I felt myself drifting peacefully off to sleep. He had promised he would lead the way into our shared dream, and I didn't want to keep him waiting too long.

I can feel the heat of the sand through my gilded sandals. My power is a presence surrounding my body and I am fully accompanied by it now as I walk deeper into the temple. Re descending behind me caresses my bare shoulders with his penetrating heat, a little less ardently in the dry season. I am wearing only jeweled sandals and a pure white dress, for one can take only the magical flesh of one's soul into the darkness ablaze with dreams. I know the rite in which I am to participate is performed every cycle on the night the divine crook of the crescent moon first appears in the evening sky, and I am looking forward to it, as I look forward to everything with E'Ahmose.

I sensed myself shift restively against the cold stone on which I was lying, refusing to let go of the priestess walking through the temple merely to indulge a few minor physical discomforts.

Nefermun has reached the hall growing vast stone papyrus stalks where Re stretches long golden arms between the columns to embrace the priests and priestesses of Anubis preparing to worship his dark spirit.

Vividly painted hieroglyphs bloom metaphysical vines all the way up to the star-covered ceiling as in a final flood of light, the god completes his circuit of the heavens and plunges into the black earth.

In the same instant every man in the hall spreads himself on his back across the stone floor covered with blood-red runners, while every woman lets her dress feint into a pool of moonlight next to the body of her lover.

I am one of these women, and for a few moments I gaze around me at my sisters. They are all beautiful in their own way, different garments of flesh and blood woven by Hathor, goddess of love. E'Ahmose lies still as Osiris beneath me as I admire all the lovely pairs of breasts exposed to the invigoratingly cool temple air. From small and pert to full and heavy, every firm yet luscious bosom is oiled to a golden perfection shining in the light from braziers being lit around us. Naked servants whose black skins blend with the darkness make it seem as though the flames spring to life of their own volition, and they walk away so silently on their bare feet the illusion is complete.

Priestesses never bear children, so all my sisters' bellies and hips are as taut as Khnum fashioned them on his potter's wheel, and to me it is obvious his hands lingered lovingly on the round cheeks of their buttocks, but especially on the ripe bud of flesh between their legs containing all the delights of earth.

I love looking at other women's bodies that are as sensually graceful as mine, knowing they are feeling very much the same things I'm feeling. During the rite, our combined sensations will flood the space between the stone papyrus stalks in invisible yet irresistible currents of pleasure, lapping with a swiftly deepening power between our thighs. But only part of my attention is concentrated on my fellow priestesses, for most of it is devoted to the splendid sight of my priest's shaft surging straight up from the soft mound of his groin, and then to the sensation like no other of planting it inside me as I lower myself over him, my sandaled feet resting on either side of his hips. In this position, holding my back perfectly straight, I can feel the lips of my sex gaping open, and the tender petals protecting the darkly moist mouth of my flesh gladly accept the crown of his stiff penis, longer and thicker and harder than any vegetative stamen.

He does not move a muscle as I mount him, seemingly alive only in his erection, which becomes everything to me as it fills my belly. Continuing to hold my back straight with my arms crossed over my chest, I can tell from the soft cries rising around me that I am not the only one overwhelmed by the experience of slowly stabbing myself. I must sink all the day down around him, taking his hard cock so deep into my body the fulfillment is excruciating, as I crouch like a woman giving birth to the divine soul of ecstasy. We merge completely, then hold utterly still for a brief eternity.

Gasps of mingled effort and pleasure echo mine as all the other priestesses willingly impale themselves while opening their arms wide to spread the invisible wings of love over the inert men below them.

As Isis resurrected Osiris, we hold our torturously arousing positions until the temple floor seems to come to life, all the priests suddenly moving as one. There is no choreography now as every couple does as it pleases surrounded and observed by other beautiful bodies consecrated to the dark god Anubis.

The strong shoulders and chests of the other priests are all embracing me when E'Ahmose's beloved arms come around me. Yet he is mysteriously more than just one of the powerful physiques I see thrusting their erections deep into the holes of moaning priestesses. And as I watch them, the all-consuming sensation of my lover possessing me from behind jackal-style is intensified to the point where all the gasping, groaning energy in the hall feels devastatingly concentrated between my own thighs.

My mouth opens in hungry sympathy observing a rampant penis penetrate a lovely upturned face held possessively in the man's hands. Then I see a couple only a column away who seem a reflection of E'Ahmose and me, and I find it intensely exciting watching the girl's breasts bobbing swiftly back and forth just like mine are doing as our lovers ram into us.

My Priest of Anubis is feeling vicious tonight, and I love every moment of his strong body beating against mine. My sex is slick as perfumed oil and hot as the pulsing flames when he grabs me by my finely braided hair, and makes me face in a different direction so we can watch other couplings together. The blessed suffering of his cock once again spearing me is almost more than I can bear, especially combined with the vision of another rock-hard column of flesh disappearing into the soft depths between two slender legs. It is the sound of his balls slapping against her helplessly juicing sex as he pumps in and out between her widespread thighs, and the sight of her delicate breasts quivering beneath the onslaught of his selfish thrusts, that make the shadowy temple vanish in a blinding flash of joy for me as the seed of divinity bursts open in my womb and for a few timeless moments I glimpse what paradise will feel like…

I moaned in protest against the cold stone, but the living temple slipped out of my grasp as I sank down into my heavy body again, descending from the higher realm of my dream into a dark and dreamless sleep.

* * * *

The sun rose abruptly in the heart of the pyramid and momentarily blinded me with its intense beauty.

'My love.' Richard set the lamp down on its stand and approached me. He was wearing a sexy contemporary outfit now—form-fitting black jeans and a tight black short-sleeved shirt. 'Do you remember the dream we shared, Nefer-marymun?' Naked hope shone in his eyes as he awaited my response.

'Yes, my lord,' I smiled, 'I do.'

'Were we alone?' he prompted.

My smile deepened. 'Hardly. In fact, we were part of an orgy.'

With a triumphant grin, he slipped his arms beneath my body and lifted me up against his warm chest. 'It wasn't exactly an orgy.'

'No,' I agreed, 'it took place in a temple.'

'The instant after sunset, symbolically re-enacting Isis resurrecting Osiris.'

'Yes! And the amazing thing is,' I said earnestly, 'is how, how pure it felt. I mean, it didn't feel at all sinful to be making love in front of all those other people.'

'I know.'

He smiled indulgently as he kissed my lips and set me down on the floor of the burial chamber.

'It was so beautiful and exciting.'

I was reluctant to leave the world of my vividly sensual dream and re-enter the pragmatic twenty-first century.

'Yes, it was,' he agreed soberly, picking my white dress up off the floor. 'And you'd better get used to feeling that way about everything now that we're together again.'

He handed me my garment and I slipped it on in a languid daze, lifting my hair up out of the way so he could snap the halter top against the nape of my neck. It sent a delicious chill down my spine when he kissed me lightly just between my shoulder blades, and I sighed happily.

'What time is it?' I asked, and then laughed because it seemed such a silly and irrelevant question in the heart of a pyramid with a man my soul had known for centuries.

'Does it matter?'

'Not at all.'

'It's two o'clock in the morning, time to get you back to my hotel room and into a hot bath with a glass of champagne to celebrate, then we'll have a snack before we go to bed and sleep all day.'

'That sounds wonderful. But I should really let Carol know where I am.'

'My men have already informed your friend that you're with me and perfectly safe.'

'She might not believe them,' I said doubtfully. 'I should call her.'

'Of course, you can call her from the hotel.'

'But I don't know her number.'

'I can obtain it for you.' He came and stood before me so I could slip my arms around him and look up into his eyes. 'I intend to give you all you desire, Mary, and I don't just mean that in a materialistic sense.'

'I know.' I felt my heart perching on his thin mouth like a bird freed from the cage of thinking true love was only a dream.

'It's a great responsibility being wealthy, Mary, but I know that together we can make the best use of our energy and resources in this world. Perhaps we can help others to dream together as we do.'

'Yes, without letting their cynical modern brains get in the way of their passionate ancient hearts.'

'It's not that simple, but I agree with the sentiment. The scientific mind and the poetic soul have to come together again. This re-unification has already begun with individuals like us, and is symbolized by the discovery of Imhotep's mastaba at this moment in time.'

I frowned. 'Why do Simon and Steve dislike you so much, Richard? I imagine they're jealous of your money, but it doesn't explain their intense animosity.'

'Well, they'll just have to get over it since I'll be helping to finance the dig once it's made public. The Antiquities Department is more than happy to accept my generous contribution.'

I pulled away from him. 'You are trying to take their discovery away from them!' I exclaimed in despair.

'Mary, think about what you're saying. Do you really believe that about me?'

I looked at his stern, handsome face and into his eyes, unfathomably dark in the fire-lit chamber. 'No,' I said with relief, 'that was definitely not Nefer-marymun talking. I'm sorry.'

'Simon Taylor is one of the brightest, most enlightened Egyptologists out there. In exchange for my considerable financial gift, the Antiquities Department has agreed to grant my request that Simon and Steve be allowed to run the project. They'll be in charge of the find from beginning to end, which means there's no reason for them to keep the discovery secret for fear of losing it. Everyone knows about it all ready anyway. I would have told Simon straight out if I had thought he would believe me. Besides, I find the man extremely irritating and I've enjoyed watching him sweat a little. We'll never be friends, but I imagine he'll manage to be cordial to me in the future even though now he'll have two reasons for resenting me.' He pulled me back into his arms again. 'If he thought I was wealthy before, it's nothing compared to how rich I am now that I have you, Nefer-marymun.'

* * * *

After we finally got out of bed the next day, I was loath to leave my Priest of Anubis, but it was necessary for me to return to Carol's apartment, and not just to collect my belongings. I felt compelled to apologize to her for disappearing on her the night before, after we emerged from the bathroom at the club. I had essentially saddled her with the task of explaining my vanishing act to Simon (not that he had probably needed an explanation) and worse still of dealing with his reaction to it.

That Richard's politely insistent servants had left me no choice in the matter was no excuse for abandoning my friend and date the way I had. I did not in the least regret my actions, but I was so happy that for a while I even entertained the idea of seeing Simon again and personally asking him to forgive me for being so rude by vanishing like a genie from the club (after which I ended up in the very plush bottle of Richard's limo). I quickly abandoned the idea, however. I would see Simon again soon enough when he finally deigned to announce his discovery of Imhotep's mastaba, at which time he would learn that he and Steve would be in charge of the excavation of the legendary tomb because the man I had chosen over him—the rich and handsome Sir Richard Gerald Ashley, more fondly known to me as E'Ahmose, Born of the Moon—was contributing a considerable sum to the project.

I would have plenty of opportunities to make it up to Simon, for I was not returning to Boston. My head was still spinning with the realization that I would be staying in Egypt indefinitely. I could never have dreamed that my last day at the office before my long-awaited vacation to the land of the pharaohs would be my last day of work ever. Richard had made it clear, as we sipped champagne in bed, that I was free to pursue my love of Egyptology in whatever way I saw fit because money was no longer a concern for me. This last fact I couldn't quite wrap my brain around yet. I had been on a budget for as long as I could remember, but being wealthy was a challenge I was more than happy to face with Nefermun's help.

Part of me felt it was perfectly natural to drink champagne until sunrise and then sleep most of the day, even as another part of me suffered the thrill of being wickedly decadent. I could sense these two sides of me had a long way to go before they would be fully reconciled with each other, but all I had to do was look into Richard's eyes to see the beautifully centered, sensually confident and fulfilled woman I would one day be in the magical world created by the horizon of his arms and his love for me. There was no rational explanation for the chemistry that had existed between us since the moment we met, or for the passionate love deepening between us. All I knew was that even since before I could remember I had been dreaming of, and waiting for, a man like him, and now that we had finally found each other, I felt my life was really beginning as Nefer-marymun.

That evening, my trip to Carol's apartment was very different. Richard had seen me off in his limo, in which I was to return to him after I had set things straight with my friend and packed all my things.

'Not that you'll really be needing them,' he had remarked as he'd kissed my cheek outside the hotel. The car waited at the curb. 'I'll buy you everything you need and anything you want. I think Nefer-marymun will be needing two whole new wardrobes.'

'Two?' I asked giddily.

'Yes, one for public appearances and one for private parties.'

I savored the promise all the way from the Mina House to the residential area of Cairo where Carol resided.

I knew I would find her at home because I'd called before I'd left the hotel, and she greeted my quiet knock at the door with a scowl that almost managed to dispel the languid cloud of daydreams I was drifting on.

'You said you were coming back to the table last night,' she accused, making it a point to slam the door behind me.

'I fully intended to,' I defended myself wistfully, 'but…' I shrugged. 'Oh Carol.' I hugged her. 'I'm so happy!'

Her tense body resisted me for about half a second before she hugged me back fervently. 'And I'm really happy for you.'

'I know you are, you're just pretending to be mad at me.' I grasped her hand and led her towards the guest bedroom. 'Come in here with me while I pack so I can tell you all about it. I spent half the night in King Unas's pyramid lying naked on the sarcophagus!'

She snatched her hand away. 'What? Why?'

'So the skills I possessed as a wearer of the Winged Sandals would hopefully come back to me more quickly —priests and priestesses of Anubis were initiated in pyramids—and it worked! I deliberately met Richard in a dream, only he wasn't Richard, he was E'Ahmose, and—'

'Mary, stop, you're not making any sense.'

'And wait till you hear what I have to tell you about Imhotep's tomb.'

EPILOGUE

E'Ahmose the cat jumps on my back. I gasp in surprise and open my eyes because I am lying naked on the couch and his claws are sharp. But I need not have worried, for he always keeps them carefully sheathed when he is being affectionate with me, and his soft paws actually feel good as he walks down my legs to curl up in the accommodating hollow of my knees. Smiling, I close my eyes again.

'You know you can't stay there very long, you silly cat,' I murmur affectionately, and my smile deepens as the subtle vibration of his contented purr provides me with a soothing little massage.

The increasingly warm spot created by his heavy body makes me even more appreciative of the cool breeze wafting in from the garden. The sun is slowly setting and I am doing one of my favorite things—relaxing in the late afternoon twilight. Usually I am awaiting my lover, who always joins me for refreshments before dinner and our invariably stimulating nights together, but whenever possible we spend the whole day with each other, and this is one of those special times when he is already here with me, spread out on his back across his own couch reading the latest details of the tomb's progress.

I open my eyes again just for the pleasure of looking at him. His profile is beautifully stern when he's concentrating, and the sight of his soft, generous penis resting on his naked lap makes me want to take it into my mouth and hold it there contentedly, letting him rest the papers on my loving head as he continues reading.

It is not lost to me that my cat and I have much in common in that we spend most of our time sensually expressing our devotion to our master, and are both as happy with our lives as any living creatures have a right to be.

Setting his business aside abruptly, my lover remarks, 'That cat of yours is quite ingenious.'

'What do you mean?'

'He is making sure I cannot spread your legs and claim your affections for myself as he knows I love to do.'

I laugh. 'Yes, he is very possessive, isn't he?'

'I cannot possibly blame him.'

I feel E'Ahmose the cat raise his head off my calf sensing a challenge, then his hot, heavy weight is lifted off my knees when he leaps off the couch, wisely retreating as his namesake rises and approaches me. I turn languidly over onto my back, and smile up at the beautiful man who seats himself beside me.

'Do you know how much I love you?' he asks quietly.

'As much as I love you, I hope,' I reply happily.

He returns my smile as we look earnestly into each other's eyes for a few timeless moments, then he glances at the blue circle of water out in the garden. 'I believe it's time for a glass of wine and a little fun in the Jacuzzi,' he concludes. 'Then, much as I know you enjoy supervising all the chopping and stirring in the kitchen as my cooks prepare the delicious recipes you come up with, I want to take us out to dinner tonight. And after that, I feel it's time we climbed the pyramid and behaved very wickedly at the top in front of the entire city. What do you think, Nefer-marymun?'

'I think it sounds like a plan,' I sit up so I can slip my arms fervently around him, 'my lord.'

Other Magic Carpet Erotic Romances

THAT CERTAIN SOMEONE	Shauna Silverton	0-9726339-46-3
THE ESP AFFAIR	Alison Tyler	0-9726339-45-5
DREAMS AND DESIRES	Laura Weston	0–937609-35-8
BLUE VALENTINE	Alison Tyler	0-9726339-0-1
WHEN HEARTS COLLIDE	Marilyn Jay Lewis	0-9726339-1-X
THE ENGAGEMENT	Lucy Niles	0-9726339-2-8